SHEPARD'S

RISE

By

Sheryl Livingston

Library of Congress Cataloging-in-Publication Data has been applied for and in process.
FIRST EDITION

Published by Egnahb, Inc.
Contact information available at www.egnahb.com or email Egnahb@yahoo.com

Acknowledgements

There are some special people in my life that I would like to know how grateful I am for their help and support of my writing.

First of all is my husband Gary who supported my decision to return to college for a degree in English/Writing.

Second, my oldest daughter, Suzie, who at age fourteen helped me pass my college algebra class and also illustrated my book..

Then, of course I can't forget my other three children, Jason, Hilary and Kat, who have supported me all the way.

I want to thank my friend Diane for her friendship and support through the many years we have been friends. Kristan, I sincerely thank you for telling me about a place for writers that led me to meet William. William, thank you for your encouragement , friendship and in helping me find somebody who could help me publish my book. And, last but not least, I want to thank Janelle for her faith in me and my book.

Chapter 1

"Something woke me up. The room was dark, with barely any moonlight shining through the window. I could feel my skin crawling with the sensation of being watched. I could see even darker shadows as my eyes adjusted to the darkness. One such shadow detached itself from the others and moved. I realized it was my father and he was moving toward me. There was something very frightening about him. I was already frightened of him, but this evening he seemed ...evil. I was just a child and I didn't even know what evil meant, but I began to learn that night...

"I was very frightened. It was not like him to come to my room. As far as I could remember he never come to tuck me in, and this was late in the night anyway. The clouds blocking the moon parted. The moonlight shining in my window suddenly illuminated him as he stood over me. He looked even larger than he was, and he wasn't a small man to begin with. He knelt down before my bed and slowly pulled my sheet down. I lay very still... I didn't want him to know I was awake. I shut my eyes very tightly, so tightly the skin in my face hurt.

"He placed his hand on one of my legs and then started running it up my leg, touching me. I tensed up at his awful touch. He had cold moist clammy hands. I couldn't help the shudder that ran through my body. He chuckled under his breath as he kept going all the way up my leg." Kelly had to stop and gulp some air. She was sweating just from the memory of that touch. It still made her skin crawl. She wanted to take a shower for an hour and scrub her skin raw. She was shocked at how strong that memory had come back. His clammy skin tainted her soft skin. The person she was reciting the story to sat quietly and let Kelly collect her thoughts. Kelly composed herself once more and continued.

"It felt strange, weird, I was so scared. It didn't feel right. I just knew it couldn't be right. I tried to stay still, but as he continued further up my leg my body tensed up. I heard him chuckle beneath his breath at that.

4

"I said that already, didn't I?" she asked the woman who sat across from her. She paused as the psychiatrist just gave a small reassuring smile and then continued. "He seemed to delight in my being uncomfortable. It seemed my discomfort only made him keep going. He delighted in it. He lowered his other hand to my other leg and started to move it up under my night dress. I was frozen with the fear. I was sweating under my nightgown, beads of sweat running down my face, or maybe it was tears, I don't know. I couldn't move, was afraid to open my eyes even a little. I was afraid if I let him know I was awake he would be mad, would beat me."

Kelly Wells paused in her story another moment to gather her nerve before continuing the story she had so long repressed that caused her to feel those touches again, making her feel dirty. It wasn't a feeling she cared to remember. She had repressed how horrible it had felt that night. She stared at her locked hands in her lap. Her eyes traced the white lines running over her tense knuckles. She then took a deep breath and rushed back into the story.

"He was just reaching the top of my legs when there was another noise outside my door. I heard it open. My Father quickly pulled his hands away and straightened my bed sheet. He was standing up when my Mom came into the room.

'What the hell do you think you're doing in here,' she asked? Her voice was dangerously soft but I heard a new hardness in it I had never heard before. I could feel this strong anger radiating through her, a strength that surprised him as well as me. She suddenly seemed very dangerous. It even made him pause before answering. He finally said something like he had seen my bed covers were messed up and falling off the bed. He was just covering me back up. I wanted to cry out that that was a lie, but I still pretended to be asleep.

"I was afraid of being punished. I knew this had to be my fault somehow. He always told me everything was my fault, and that I deserved to be punished all the time. I must have been naughty again in his eyes and

5

this was my punishment. I peeked thru half closed lids to see Mom advance further into the room. There was this strange terrible look on her face. I had never seen such a menacing look before. I don't think he had ever seen it either because he left as fast as he could.

She stood over me for a long time, just staring at me. I didn't want to upset her any further, so I still pretended to be asleep. I scrunched my eyes shut so tight I was getting a headache. She came over and pulled my blanket up over me and ran her fingers through my hair.

She leaned over the bed and whispered to me, 'He won't do this to you again baby. I won't let him hurt you anymore.' She then turned and left, pulling the door shut tight.

I heard her voice rise in the next room as she verbally attacked my Father and then a thump. I couldn't believe that she actually threw something at him. Unfortunately she missed." Kelly paused in the telling of her story. She smiled slightly at the memory of the sound of something heavy hitting the wall. She remembered how disappointed she had been that it hadn't hit her father on the head. She would have loved to hear him yelp in pain just once.

This time she looked over at her Psychiatrist whose head was bent over her note pad. The lady looked up with one painted on eyebrow raised. Gloria Stein was a petite thing, in her mid forties, hair and face made up like a porcelain doll. Kelly's first impression was, how could a china doll understand her feelings? She nearly turned around before even talking to her, but after that first interview, she found that under that porcelain like exterior lay a warm individual with a great capacity for understanding the pain of others. She has been coming to her now for nearly a year. It had been a long year of painfully dredging deep into her very soul.

They covered many of the issues that kept Kelly from truly being free of her past and look forward to the future. Kelly always skirted the issue of her father and her late husband. Now though, Gloria had pressed that it was time to confront them. To Kelly, the timing couldn't be worse with her mother sick in the hospital, but she finally grudgingly agreed. Now, here she was digging up long repressed memories of her dreaded father.

"You ok?" Dr. Stein asked. At Kelly's nod she added encouragingly, "Do you want to continue?"

"Yes," Kelly answered, took another deep breath and went on. "The next day Mom took me shopping. She got me a couple of new pairs of pajamas. I never wore a night gown again for as long as I lived in the same house as him. She also bought a bolt lock and put it on my side of the door. I was to lock my door each night and to never open it at night to my Father."

"Then that was the end of that?"

"No, I wish it had been," Kelly answered with a sigh. She learned that with that man nothing ended easily. She closed her eyes, took another a deep breath and once again continued with the painful story.

"The next night I woke to hear him trying to open my door. He wiggled it against the lock. I heard him curse under his breath, but he didn't try to force it or anything. The next day when I came home from school and went to my room I noticed that the lock had been removed."

"How old were you when this happened?" Dr. Stein gave no emotion in her questioning. They were clinical questions meant to keep the story going, and to give Kelly a chance to breathe a second while thinking of the answer.

"I was eight or nine."

"What did you do when you discovered the lock was gone?"

"I ran to the garden where my Mom was weeding. I told her my lock was gone. She smiled at me and said not to worry, to go play on my swing set. I did as I was told, and after a while she got up and went inside. She returned in just a few minutes and went back to her weeding like nothing had happened. When I went back up to my room to do my homework after supper, there was a new lock on my door."

"Your mother was trying to protect you." It was a statement not a question. Kelly frowned at the petite female sitting in the chair across from the sofa she was occupying.

She wondered how anybody could understand how frightening living under this kind of stress was for an eight year old. Or, how could somebody understand what it took for her mother to fight her silent campaign against her father. She knew the usual questions. Why didn't her mother just leave him? Why did she put up with his abuse? Why? Why? Why? Kelly knew the questions because she had asked them in her mind many times before. The only person who had the answers was her mother and she wouldn't answer them.

"Mom didn't look strong but had this inner strength she used quietly," Kelly said calmly. "He was never allowed to go near me again or be alone with me. It was a covert campaign she waged against him. She never yelled or threatened him, at least not since that first night. Mom never said anything to his face as far as I could tell, but the threat was there in the background if he even looked my way. One good thing that did come out of this was that he never hit me or punished me in anyway again. I think mom had made it clear he was to stay away from me period."

"So, he stopped trying to get into your room after that?" she prompted.

"No," Kelly answered with a nervous laugh. "One thing I can tell you about my father is that he is either very stubborn or just plain bullheaded as hell. Now I think about it, he is just plain dumb when it comes to certain things. He never learned lessons from any of his actions.

"He came to my room again that night and you could tell he was surprised as hell that the door was once again locked. The idea my Mom would defy him had never crossed his mind. He actually ran into the door when he tried to open it, thinking it would open easily. I remember laughing out loud at the thump. He stopped and I quickly covered my mouth in case I made another noise. He tried the door several times as if by magic it would

8

suddenly open. He stood out there for an eternity. That is, to me it felt like a long time to hold my breath. I was getting dizzy when I realized I wasn't breathing. I had to force myself to slowly and quietly breathe. Then he left once again. He removed the lock again the next day."

"You found it that way when you came home from school?"

"No, actually he waited this time till just before I went to bed. I noticed it was gone when I shut the door to change into my pajamas."

"What did you do?"

"I didn't have to do anything, Mom came in to tuck me in and she saw right away the lock was missing."

"What did she do?"

"She just smiled down at me and told me to get ready for bed, she would be right back. She left, went into her bedroom and sure enough she was back before I was even finished putting my pajamas on. She must have had a stash of the locks hidden somewhere in her room.

"She came back with a new lock still in the package and a screw driver. She put up the new lock, then came over and read me a chapter from a book we were reading together. She made no fuss over it; acting like it was just a normal everyday thing to put up a lock each night. When she was done, she reminded me to lock the door, kissed my forehead and left the room. I followed her to the door and locked it immediately."

"So your Dad came again that night?"

"My father," Kelly replied back with a hiss as she changed the identity of that distasteful man forcefully, and then added sadly with a sigh. "He was never a Dad."

Kelly could remember the hurt she lived with that her father didn't consider her worthy of love. As she grew older she realized that his sort of love was something she could live without.

"I am sorry." The Doctor rephrased her question. "Your father came again that night?"

9

"Of course," Kelly chuckled derisively. She could picture the look of astonishment on his face when he walked into the door again. "I told you he was bullheaded. He came again and ran into the door when he figured it should have opened. It was so funny I had to hold my hands up to my mouth to make sure I didn't laugh out loud again." Kelly mimicked the action as she said it.

"He was not a very happy fellow, I can tell you that. He cursed some rather nasty words loud enough for me to hear. This time I heard Mom behind him saying something softly, too softly for me to understand. He cursed at her and then, all was quiet. That was the last time he tried to come into my bedroom at night, at least for a while.

"He would occasionally, over the next couple years, remove the lock and try again. Each time Mom would replace it before bedtime and each time he would walk right into the door thinking it should open. He never learned to test the door first. It was so funny by then. I would hear a thud, some cursing then all was quiet and all would be okay for a while. I never went to bed without locking that door."

"You don't know what your Mom said to him that third night?"

"I couldn't hear her. She always was soft spoken, but this time she was even more so. I think she actually threatened him, although that seems far fetched."

"Why far fetched?"

"Mom always seemed afraid of Father and his moods. She did everything she could to placate him. He could get rather violent, but when it came to me, she stood her ground."

"Your Mom sounds like a rather strong person."

"She had a quiet strength most people didn't see, specially my father. He thought she was weak, but then he doesn't have a very high opinion of women."

"How did your father treat your brothers?"

10

"Oh, they are the apples of his eyes. They looked like him, acted like him, and have grown to be little miniatures of him." Kelly had a hard time keeping the distaste from her voice. "They are a menace to women the same as my father."

"You're not very close to your brothers I take it?"

"Hell, I never had a chance. Father taught them from the very beginning to treat me like dirt. I was their whipping girl, so to speak. Even though he kept his distance from me, they were given free rein to be mean to me." Kelly put her hands to her temple and started rubbing at the beginnings of a headache. These sessions always gave her headaches. No matter how many times she talked about the past and her father's abuse, she couldn't get rid of the tenseness that followed thinking of him.

"We are almost done now." The Psychiatrist reassured her. "Next time let's talk about your husband, would that be ok?"

"Yes, I guess so, but we weren't really married very long, and he was rather a sweet man."

"Regardless, I would like to spend at least one session on him. You agree to that?"

"Yes, yes," Kelly agreed, still rubbing her temple. She suddenly had a thought. "Oh, I don't know if I'll make our next time though."

This brought a raised eyebrow. Kelly had not missed a session since they started working together about 11 months ago. "Oh?"

"My Mom is very ill," she explained. "She has cancer; it has spread throughout her body. They say it's just a matter of days. She is in the hospital now and I'm going back right after we finish."

"I'm sorry to hear that," the Doctor said as she rose from her chair. This was the sign the session was over. Dr. Stein was very punctual. Kelly rose at the same time. "You can plan on the session and if anything happens before the next time, you can call and reschedule. Does that sound acceptable?"

Kelly smiled and nodded. She liked Dr. Stein. For a psychiatrist, she was rather unassuming and ended nearly every sentence with a question.

"Yes it would," she answered, and then added, "but, there is one more thing."

The Doctor quickly glanced at her watch then gave her attention back to Kelly. "Yes?"

"After my Mom dies," she choked slightly on the word, regained her composure and continued. "I may be moving."

"Moving? Where?"

"For some reason Mom is adamant that I leave Chicago and head west. She mentioned Montana."

"Goodness, that's a rather isolated State. You have any idea why she wants you to go there?"

"I gather I may have family there but I don't know for sure. Mom never mentioned her family before. I hope she says something else today, if she feels up to talking."

"Well, keep me informed please."

"I will," Kelly answered as she walked out the door. A quick glance back through the door showed the Doctor already at her desk bent over the notes she had taken during the session. Kelly sighed and closed the door behind her. She waved at the receptionist as she passed by.

There was no need to stop to make another appointment. It was a standing appointment for 3pm every Thursday afternoon. She didn't even have to worry about paying the bill. When she went to pay it the first week, she was told that it was being taken care of. She assumed it was her late husband's insurance policy. She had given them the card the first time she came in to consult with Doctor Stein. He had had the foresight to make sure she was covered in the event of his death, which had occurred less than a year after they were married. He hadn't even known she was pregnant with their child. She had just found out herself and was waiting for the right time to tell him. That time never came. He had a heart attack just before their first year anniversary.

Chapter 2

The building that housed the Mental Health Center was three blocks from the main Hospital. The whole complex was built in a circle around a central park area. Paths wound their way through the park, breaking it up into sections. There was a playground, a picnic area, a small band shell for outdoor concerts. People either sat on benches that were spread around the edges of a nice grassy knoll or brought lawn chairs or blankets to relax on. Flowering hedges lined the walkways that crisscrossed the park.

Kelly had walked the short distance across the park to the center and decided to walk back as she needed to unwind after that grueling session. She took the main path that dissected the park through the center back to the Hospital.

She had talked about her father before but never on such an intimate scale. She avoided delving deeply because it made her feel dirty and was something she wanted to keep buried deeply. She always knew why she had the lock on her door but the actual memory had been deeply hidden away. She wasn't sure why she had suddenly dreamt about it earlier this week.

She dreamt after her mother was admitted to the hospital and all the Doctors told her she wouldn't be coming home this time. She hadn't lived in that house for over seven years now. She wondered what connection with losing her mother had to do with remembering the main time she had been there to protect her.

The path was quiet, with just a few others out this cool late afternoon. It was late fall and the trees had lost nearly all their leaves. There was a definite chill in the air. Snow would be falling soon. Kelly glanced at her watch, just past 4pm and already starting to darken. She walked at a leisurely pace but still passed the few others who were slowly strolling along with patients from the different care units that circled the park. It was a beautiful place to be alone with her thoughts. Kelly watched a couple of birds flitting around in a water fountain. The idea of them playing in the chilly water made her shiver as she pulled her jacket tighter around her. A child's laugh echoed from the other side of the low shrubbery that separated the playground area from the walkway. An old couple strolled slowly arm in arm heading toward the senior housing that was next to the building she'd just left. The complex was situated perfectly for all different needs, with everything close enough for care to be efficient and near-by.

She sighed at the perfect picture the old couple presented. They had to have been in their late seventies or more likely in their eighties. They walked slowly, more like a shuffle, side by side. The gentleman had his ladies arm cradled in his; she had her head on his shoulder. He turned his head to gaze into her eyes and whispered something that brought a quiet breathless giggle. It was a lovely sight but nothing that she could relate to.

Her father, Phil Morris, was not the cuddling, nurturing sort. The idea of him ever ambling down a peaceful path showing any love what so ever for his mate was laughable. Kelly had never seen anything remotely loving about him. He was a controlling, manipulative, abusive person. Even the sort of love he showed his sons was distorted. It consisted of bullying, manipulating, and generally teaching them that others needs never mattered over their own. He taught them to take instead of ask, to push instead of wait their turn, to use force if one didn't give into their demands immediately.

At this moment though her mind turned from her abusive father and his clone-like sons back to her mother. The lady had spent the better part of 27 years submitting to the abuse of this man, yet she never seemed to lose sight of what was important to her; protecting Kelly and showing her she could be strong, independent, kind, and giving. She taught her that a person could give without losing their identity

The trouble Kelly had though was in trying to figure out how a person so internally strong could, or would for that matter, stay with a man like Phil Morris. She wondered if she would ever figure it out.

15

As she approached the hospital's main building , Kelly's thoughts turned to her Mom's strange request that she move to Montana. In fact, it wasn't a request so much as an order. She was adamant that Kelly leave as soon as she was gone.

She hadn't said where in Montana to go or why Kelly should go there in the first place. When Kelly questioned her about this, she had said only that Kelly would find out when the time was right. Kelly knew time was running out to find the answers, and she decided she would try to question her mom more today.

As she approached the main door, an old beat-up car swerved up the circular drive and screeched to a halt in an eschewed angle. She didn't need to see the man stumbling out to know who it was. Kelly knew Morris' car by sight, sound and smell.

For as long as she remembered he had never had a decent car. Morris would wear out one junker and replace it with another, at about one a year. He didn't see spending more than a couple hundred dollars on a car. It was easier for him to just replace it than to take care of it. All the cars had rusted bodies, torn interiors, noisy mufflers and smells one didn't want to identify.

A cold spot formed in the pit of her stomach as she ran to the main door in order to intercept him before he could enter.

"Where do you think your going?"

The big man, who looked like he had spent more than one night in his dirty wrinkled clothes, blinked at the intrusion and stared at her through his alcohol hazed mind.

"I was," he paused to search for the reason he was there. His head jerked a little when his foggy mind found the answer. "I...I was going, huh, going to visit my...huh, my....my wife," he stuttered. His speech was as blurry as his eyes. Kelly wasn't surprised he was pulling this stunt. Leave it to him to decide to visit his wife for the first time three weeks after she was admitted to the Hospital and drunk as hell to boot.

16

A new noise from the car caught her attention. She glanced over Morris's shoulder to see an equally drunk woman falling out of the passenger door of the car. She dropped to her knees as she slid out of the car. She used the car door for support to pull herself up right. She leaned against the car for several seconds before becoming steady enough to push away and stagger toward Morris and Kelly. It seemed to Kelly that this was a routine the woman repeated often.

She stared at the woman as she fell against Morris' chest. He had to wrap his arms around her waist to keep her standing. The couple teetered back and forth a few times but managed to remain standing. Kelly just shook her head. She was surprised that they hadn't gone down. She watched them cling to each other for support. Actually, nothing about this man surprised her anymore.

"Ducky," Morris burped out. "I told you to stay in the car?"

"But sweet cakes," the woman answered shrilly, "I was already missing you."

Kelly rolled her eyes at this nauseating scene. 'Oh, brother,' she thought. It was enough to make her feel physically sick. Morris suddenly remembered Kelly was standing in front of him. Belatedly he tried to introduce the two women. "Huh, Ducky," he stuttered, hesitating a moment, "Huh this is... huh, this is Ke...Ke. This is my little girl."

'For heavens sake,' Kelly thought as she pressed her fingers to her forehead trying to keep that headache at bay. 'He can't even remember my name.' Aloud she said forcefully, "Go away,"

"What?" Morris looked confused. "What did you say?"

"I said," Kelly started to raise her voice but caught herself as she saw several people turned their heads in their direction. 'Great,' she thought, 'an audience.' She took a deep breath before continuing in as steady a voice as she could muster in her anger. "Go away. Mom doesn't want to see you."

"Of...of...co...course she does," he stammered. "I'm...I'm...I'm her husband, so, so step a...a...aside little girl."

17

Kelly pulled herself up to her full height, which towered over him by at least six inches. He might not be a small man but it wasn't in height. She wasn't going to get into an arguing match with this man in a public place. "I won't say it again," she rasped out harshly. "Take your whore and leave now or I'll call security if you try and see mom."

He looked at her through his red fuming eyes, trying to focus on this woman in front of him. His eyes were so hazed over she couldn't tell if he was angry at her for standing up to him, or if he even remembered why he was here. She wondered for a minute if he even realized who she was. After several long seconds he was finally able to pull up her identity from his muddled brain and exclaimed. "How dare you talk to me like that? I am your father for God's sake!"

"Not by any choice of mine," she replied quickly.

"Phil," the shrill voice set sharp electrical currents running up her already frayed nerves. "Phil, I thought you were going to see a sick friend?"

Kelly turned back to her father with a raised eyebrow, a technique she'd copied from Dr. Stein. She didn't need to say another word. He actually got the silent message and turned to the woman who was still trying to just stand up on her own. He grabbed her arm roughly and spun her back toward the car. The quick action caused her to lose her balance completely and go sprawling onto the sidewalk. "Come on," he growled under his breath, yanking her to her feet. "She seems to have enough company at the moment."

"Oh, okay," the shrill voice follow Kelly as she turned and headed inside. She did not want to see anymore of Morris' man-handling of the woman, who seemed quite oblivious to it. She stopped inside the door and watched her Father's car pull jerkily out into traffic. Satisfied he was gone, she started towards the elevators shaking her head, wondering why women let men do that to them. She stepped into the first elevator letting Morris quickly fade from her mind soon to be replaced by the questions she had for her mother.

18

Kelly never got her chance to ask them. She arrived to find the room crowded with people. They all turned in unison as she entered the room. It seemed uncharacteristically quiet. Where were the sounds of the multiple machines hooked to her mother? The reason for the silence suddenly dawned on her. She glanced from one face to the other. She knew from the looks on their faces she had missed it, her mother was gone. She went to the bed to look down at the still pale form. The noisy machines that had earlier been monitoring her condition were now silent. Kelly knew that she would never get her answers now.

Chapter 3

The outside of the crumbling old building in the distance did nothing to relieve Shel's thoughts. He had driven hundreds of miles to end up in the middle of nowhere looking for a Hospital. He had been told the Captain from his Special Forces unit was staying here. He was sure he had followed the directions to a tee, but this was the only building with-in miles of the road he was directed to. It looked like an old transplanted English Manor.

He had spent the better part of the last two hours driving up and down various cross roads, but nothing revealed itself that looked remotely like a hospital. 'Why anyone would put a hospital way out here in the first place is beyond me,' he thought. It was at least a 30 minute drive to the nearest town.

Shel finally returned to the drive of this ancient building. He looked over the directions one more time. He was wondering if this was all a prank by somebody who had learned he was looking for his military buddy. The call had come in the middle of the night and in an urgent whisper. He looked up at the mansion again and figured he had no choice but to go up to that monstrous house and ask for directions. As he put the truck into gear, Shel couldn't help but think he had become part of some cheesy vampire movie.

Shel wouldn't have gone to this trouble for just anybody, but Captain Mitchell had saved his life. They were the only two, in their unit of twelve, who had survived a deadly ambush in Afghanistan about two years before. Shel hadn't been sure if the Captain had survived. He had been out of it for weeks from injuries incurred during the attack. When he finally came to his senses, enough to inquire after the others, the news, of course, was bad.

His father had been there when he came to and had quietly and carefully answered his questions. He gave the information the officers had given him. After the ambush Mitchell had found Shel and dragged him into

20

hiding. Nobody would tell him what injuries Mitchell had sustained or where he was. He had tried to find him during the past two years, but with no luck. All his inquiries went unanswered till a couple weeks ago when a late night caller gave him directions to this place. He looked up at the run down building, he was approaching, perched by it self on top of a hill.

A faded dilapidated sign at the beginning of the decrepit drive indicated only that it was Millsburg Manor. The place had to be hundreds of years old. The old English mansion came complete with ghastly gargoyles on the ramparts. He was sure he misunderstood part of the directions. Well, if there was a Veterans Hospital anywhere near this place, perhaps the residents would know. That is, if the place was even inhabited.

Shel followed the drive over the crest of a small hill. That was when he saw the guard shack placed in the entrance of a long fence. While driving all around this place Shel hadn't noticed a fence around it and he was one to notice such things. He realized how it was cleverly hidden behind the hills that surrounded the base of the hill the mansion was sitting on. 'Well, I'll be," he thought with shock. He had been in the right place all along. Shel pulled to a stop in front of the guard's station. 'This is something you usually don't see at a Vet's Hospital,' he thought. He was very confused by the mystifying air given to the mystery of his missing Captain.

He had put in inquiries about the whereabouts and condition of his former Captain everywhere he could think of to no avail. Just when it seemed that his buddy Bryant had disappeared off the face of the earth, an anonymous phone call came late one night giving him directions to 'the Hospital' that the Captain was at. He had asked several questions of this caller but she had only repeated he could find Captain Mitchell here. The woman gave the directions in a whispered, deep sexy female voice that still sent sensations through his body.

He paused a moment to ponder that quiet sexy voice. He could almost imagine what a lovely women this lady must be. Then he laughed to himself, 'like voices couldn't be deceiving about what was really behind

21

them,' he thought. He was sure the caller would turn out to be fifty-something with the hint of a mustache. Another idea had squeezed its way into his thoughts. The thoughts of another sweet voice only it was saying good-bye for a final time. The last thing he wanted now was to meet a sexy woman. He hadn't gotten over his ex-wife yet. Her soft voice had hid a selfish personality that had revealed itself the moment he said "I do". Shel shook his head to rid himself of the thoughts. They were for another time, now was time to think of the Captain.

Shel was still at a loss as to why all leads had ended up in a dead end. Why would the Captain be hiding, and why still in a hospital? The sudden knock on his window from the uniformed guard startled Shel out of his thoughts. He rolled down his window and handed his credentials over. He had been told to make sure he brought them in order to be admitted.

"I'm here to see Captain Mitchell." He still wasn't sure he was at the right place. Then again, what else could be the reason a military guard would be protecting this old place? Still it was perplexing why there would be such security at a Vet's hospital.

The guard gave the papers a quick glance, handed them back, and without a word or a smile, waved Shel through. Well, at least he hadn't been turned away, that was a good sign. He hoped.

He pulled into a larger circular drive that took him right in front the exaggerated large gothic doors. 'Maybe this is it, but?' Shel thought as he walked up the front walk to the immense medieval door. 'How could this be a Hospital', he wondered once again if this could possibly be the right place.

The immense gothic building resembled an ancient English Manor house out of the dark ages. He looked up and counted five gargoyles standing watch along the crumbling ruins just in the front of this section of the house. Their evil grins made him shiver even though it was full sunlight and quite warm. He wondered how safe it was to be standing under one of those crumbling gigantic things.

The main or what looked like the original section was centered and recessed slightly into the two wings that rose up on either side. The dirty gray stone was slightly darker on the wings. Great steps led to a massive front door. Ornately carved pillars stood on either side. Shel noted the carvings depicting angels and demons in a great war. 'What a cheerful greeting' he thought.

Each wing was three stories with gables around the third story window guarded by more gargoyles. 'All this place needs now is a couple of towers on each side and dungeons beneath,' he thought as he looked for the knocker.

'Where the hell is the knocker on this damn thing?' he asked himself under his breath. He had spent several seconds looking over the door when he spied the modern buzzer set in the ancient door. 'Well, at least something is modern around here,' he mused as he pressed it. The heavy door immediately swung open easily and quietly causing Shel to nearly jump out of his skin. It was both the swiftness of the door opening and the quietness of the hinges that caused him to look it over again. He had been half expecting an eerie creaking sound, like in the old movies.

As he walked thru the doors he felt like he had left the twenty-first century and gone back a couple hundred years. The front foyer was decorated in antiques the likes of which were museum quality. He scanned the room slowly, doing a full circle till he came around and spied what he could only call an 'angel in uniform' standing a short distance away with a quizzical look on her face. He was unprepared for the instant heat of desire he felt at the sight of a vision of light in this dark room. Shel had the sense to redden slightly as he waved back toward the door and tried to explain.

"I was expecting it to creak and groan like in the movies," he chuckled. "I had to make sure a monster or vampire wasn't lurking in a dark corner." He watched as her eyes lit up and she actually smiled and laughed with him. He noticed her round face, big brown doe eyes, and the full lovely naturally red lips a smile was perched on, all capped with short soft brown hair that framed her face. He found an unconventional beauty about her.

"You're not the first one to expect that," she replied in a strangely familiar voice. "Hello, I'm Nurse Chapman. What can I do for you? You're?"

Shel just stared at this picture of loveliness inside this huge mausoleum of a house. She was at least 5'10", with a slender build and soft perfect curves.

Her brightness didn't fit into this cavernous foyer with the medieval furnishings. She looked like she belonged out in the sun in a very skimpy bikini. Once again he felt that heat of desire rush through him.

'Whoa, there boy,' Shel shook his head slightly to get rid of those fanciful thoughts. He noticed long legs that flowed from under her traditional nurse's uniform. He liked the nice length of leg that continued below the skirt. It had been a long time since any female aroused such a male response in him. He immediately sank those feelings as he realized she was studying him closely with a half amused smile on her face, waiting for his answer.

"I'm sorry," he coughed slightly to ease his tensions. "I am Sheldon Shepard. I'm not even sure I am in the right place. This is a Military hospital?"

"You're in the right place," she answered crisply as she turned and indicated he should follow her. The voice sounded familiar but Shel wasn't sure where he may have heard it. If he had seen this lovely vision before, he wouldn't be living the single life with his father on their ranch.

'Where did that thought come from?' he wondered. He had just returned to the single life less than a year before and now he was thinking this? She continued talking as she started toward a doorway in the back of the foyer. "It's not your normal sort of hospital though. You see, we are a rehabilitation center, but for the more seriously handicapped people. Some

24

may never leave," she added sadly. "Some never wish to. All the isolation and security is for their privacy."

She turned to look at Shel. "We saw you coming long before you arrived," she laughed. "You aren't the first person to drive by thinking they had the wrong place."

"It's not like you have it clearly marked," Shel remarked. This brought another light laugh. It wasn't a girlish giggle but a deep inner tremor. The deepness matched her voice. Shel stopped suddenly in his tracks causing Nurse Chapman to turn and look oddly at him again. He knew he had heard that deep sexy voice before. Now this definitely added to the mystery.

"Its not suppose to be clearly marked," she answered quietly. "We know we are here, its not important for anybody else to know." She turned back and continued walking through the doors.

Shel could tell she was deeply affected by the patients here just by her voice. 'Such a caring person didn't belong in a place like this,' he thought. A place like this could drain a person pretty fast. Then again, I bet the patients appreciate having her around,' he added to himself covertly studying the figure walking in front of him. Her words were a forlorn warning though about what to expect when he saw the Captain.

"I was told that Captain Bryant Mitchell was a patient here?"

Nurse Chapman frowned at the name. It wasn't a puzzled frown from not knowing the name rather it was an, 'Oh yes, he's here,' sort of frown. Shel had to laugh. The Captain had that sort of affect on people in his good moods. He could only imagine what sort of affect he was having now. Shel still wasn't even sure why the Captain was here. All he had ever been told about the Captain's injuries were that they weren't that bad, but when he tried to contact him to invite him out to the ranch for a visit, nobody could tell him where the Captain had gone. He had tried his family in Boston but they refused to even talk to him. It was like the Captain had disappeared and didn't want to be found. This place was four states away from his Massachusetts home and definitely out of the way.

"I see he's in his best behavior mode." Shel joked. Nurse Chapman threw him a dark look over her shoulder. He couldn't help it; he threw back his head and laughed. At her startled look, he quickly explained. "I'm sorry. It's just you have to know the Captain to know what I mean. He's always been a bit of the surly sort."

"Hate to tell you this," she said softly with a sad smile fluttering over her full red lips as she slowly shook her head. "He's long passed surly." By this time they had reached a door at the back of the hallway.

Chapter 4

"We don't normally allow visitors through here without prior clearance. But, I remembered him mentioning you and I have you cleared"

"He has mentioned me?"

"Oh yes," this time the Nurse blushed as she answered. She looked around the quiet room then leaned forward slightly and whispered in the same voice of the mysterious caller. "I hear you're looking for a certain Captain Mitchell."

Shel was totally astonished. No wonder that voice had seemed familiar. He shook his head, now he had just been thinking about that voice and he still almost missed it. He wasn't sure what to say, she didn't wait for a reply but continued. "He had talked about you. Mentioned the state you lived in. So, I looked up your name and took a chance I got the right Sheldon Shepard. If anybody finds out, I will be shipped out of here faster than you can say your name. They rather frown on us breaking security."

Shel looked into those deep doe-like brown eyes. He knew he was being drawn into them by the strange feeling in his stomach. He announced in his best cowboy drawl, "Well, shucks little lady, they won't find out from me." He then continued normally, "And it probably would be best if the Capt'n. thought I found him on my own." Her smile was thank-you enough as she turned and opened the door.

Shel followed her through and instantly felt transported to a new location. Gone were the dark furnishings of the Gothic era only to be replaced by a long hall with bare white walls. Nurse Chapman laughed softly at his expression. "The front keeps the curious out."

"That guard shack is sort of conspicuous."

"Could you see it from the road?"

"Now that you mention it," Shel mused, remembering the last two hours he kept driving back and forth sure this couldn't be the place he was looking for. "No, I couldn't, and you could have warned me." He was rewarded by a soft chuckle.

"Actually, few people know we are here," she started to explain as she led the way down the hall. "We look like an old decrepit English manor house. We don't advertise our presence. Everyone who works here is Military and assigned here. We live on the premises. The living quarters are in the main house you just came from."

"I thought of an old Dracula castle myself," Shel laughed as he followed. He wasn't minding the view from behind at all. "I'm sorry; I forgot your first name?"

"I didn't give it," She actually winked at him as she walked up to a window in the wall and knocked on it. It slid open and she talked to thin air. "I need the paper work for Sergeant Sheldon Shepard." The window slid shut and she turned back to Shel. "As I said before, I took the liberty of starting the paperwork so you wouldn't have to wait to see your friend. I hope you don't mind?"

"You were that sure I would come?" Shel carefully watched her expressions as she answered him back.

"When I called, you remember what I said?" she asked.

"I believe it was 'I heard you were looking for Captain Mitchell?'"

"I wanted to gauge how much the captain meant to you," she said carefully. "I wanted to know if he was as important to you as you seemed to be to him. So I phrased the statement as if I thought you were looking for him."

"You didn't know I was looking for him?" Shel asked with surprise.

"No," she answered with a smile while still studying him closely. "If you had said no, you weren't looking for him; I would have hung up and let the matter drop."

"But I did say yes," Shel said as he looked her in the eye.

"That's right and when you answered with such deep concern in your voice, 'Of course I am do you know where he is?' I just knew that you would come."

"You really didn't know I was looking for Captain Mitchell?" Shel was having a hard time getting past this. He had looked so long and left so many inquiries that the fact she had found him on chance was just too much.

"It was more a guess," she replied with her hesitant smile. "I was hoping there was somebody in this world who gave a damn about him."

Now Shel was really perplexed. What had happened to the Captain to have him stuck here, alone? Where was his family, his fiancée? Why did the nurse act like what affected the Captain was more mental then physical? At least that was the impression Shel had gotten from Nurse Chapman's voice, and he was good at deciphering thoughts and intentions from people's voices. It had come in handy on the battle fields of Afghanistan.

The window slid open again and the papers spontaneously appeared. Shel tried to look closer to see if there was a person behind there but the window snapped shut. Nurse Chapman laughed at that. "Yes, there is a person back there."

"That's good to know," he laughed, "After going through that other part of the building, floating objects would be a bit over the top." He was happy she laughed with him. She had a nice laugh; it went along with her compellingly deep soft voice and dazzling smile.

"Captain Mitchell's room is this way." She turned and started to head down a nearby corridor. At this point there were several corridors leading away from the window. Each one had doors lining the walls. It was very quiet in this place, almost didn't seem like there was another living soul around. He could hear faint murmuring from people talking or television sets behind some of the closed doors.

"The patients here want their privacy," she said, watching Shel's curiosity cross his face. "There are other places in the institute that are more cheerful, but along here are those who just wish to stay to themselves." She turned to lead him up one of the halls.

The walls were plain white, no pictures to break the monotonous affect. They passed a few nurses along the way. Shel would give a quick smile but they just walked by basically ignoring his presence. They finally turned down yet another hallway and that's when Shel knew for sure he was in the right place.

The sound of something crashing to the floor followed by, "Nurse? Nurse?" as Bryant Mitchell bellowed. "Nurse?"

Nurse Chapman gave Shel a, 'see what we put up with,' look, and then went at a swift walk to the door where all the commotion was coming from. Shel followed at a short distance. He didn't want to give his presence away just yet.

Nurse Chapman turned and whispered to him, "You can enter, he won't see you." She then turned into the door and entered.

"I see we didn't like our lunch again Captain," she replied with artificial cheerfulness, bending to pick up the food tray. "And what was wrong with it this time, undercooked or overcooked?"

"Its hard to tell what is wrong with it when there is absolutely no flavor to it in the first place," he growled.

Shel picked his way silently into the room, around the spilt food to stand up against the side wall just inside the doorway. He watched the Captain carefully throughout his exchange with Nurse Chapman. He took in the deep scar across the sunken cheek, the burn scars along the right side of his face and neck, the overall skinniness of the once robust frame.

He also noticed that the impeccable cleanliness that had been the Captain's trademark was missing. He was wearing a dressing gown that long needed washing and grubby slippers. He had been adamant about his physical health and now before him was a man who was emaciated beyond belief and it was obvious he hadn't exercised in months. In short, where a

31

once proud, strong, independent man had been there was now a lost, broken person taking his place. What the hell happened to him?

Shel's heart fell to the pit of his stomach. He suddenly realized that Bryant was staring sightlessly ahead of him. Of course, he couldn't see him. He was blind. This was all because of him. He knew the Captain wouldn't be here, in this condition if it hadn't been for him. This had happened when the Captain was attempting to carry Shel out of the bomb littered field when another shell dropped behind them. The blast had knocked Shel out and when he had come to, he was on a hospital ship. They told him the Captain had been sent on to the hospital in Germany. They said his injuries weren't critical but they wouldn't give Shel details. Shel had no idea how bad until now. He looked over to the Nurse who had risked her career to let him know. She must be a special lady indeed.

He couldn't help but wonder why she had done this violation of policy. Could she have feelings for the Captain? It wouldn't be the first time a lady had fallen for him. Sure he had been ruggedly good looking but there was more to him that attracted the ladies. Shel had watched him with the women when they were on leave.

The Captain had a commanding presence to him in the first place. You couldn't ignore he was there even if you were on another side of the room. He treated each lady as if she was special. He always said all women were ladies in their own way. The Captain always treated a woman with absolute courtesy and charm. Even though he wasn't looking like his old self, perhaps his old charm was still there.

"You could try ringing the bell and asking for something else to eat then," Nurse Chapman gently admonished.

"The fact that I am here and the bell is over there," Bryant waved his hand in the general direction to the front of him, "is only part of the problem."

"And the other part is," asked the nurse sweetly? She shot Shel a look that told him she already knew the answer.

32

Bryant also knew she knew, "You know why," he grumbled.

Shel couldn't take this any longer. This was not the man who had led his men into battle time and time again. This was not the self assured leader who made no promises and lived with no regrets. That man was long gone. Now all that was left was just an empty shell. There was nothing even remotely like the old Bryant living inside. He knew he had to do something to try and resurrect the old Bryant. He knew he couldn't go in softly, or pussyfoot around the issue. He had seen how Bryant would treat an injured soldier to keep his mind off his injuries and on just surviving. He forced a man to fight for his life. He decided it was time to use the same tact. He stepped away from the wall into the center of the room.

"I'm sorry to have bothered you Nurse," Shel said in an abrupt tone as he stepped away from the wall. "This isn't my old friend. There is nothing remotely familiar about this man."

"Shel," Bryant's voice was just a whisper as if it seemed to fail him. "You're here?"

Shel watched as emotions flicked across Bryant's face. He wasn't sure if it was happiness or dismay. He watched the other man struggle to compose himself. He glanced at the Nurse only to see complete surprise on her face. She had never seen him having difficulty articulating anything. Maybe there was hope for him yet. Maybe she had done the right thing after all. She looked back toward Shel and gestured for him to continue.

Shel squared his shoulders and attacked with full force. He walked up to the Captains chair and leaned in close. "Yah, I am here," he said harshly, "Too bad you aren't." The Nurse nearly choked on that statement, but she maintained her silence. Kindness hadn't put a dent in the wall Captain Mitchell had erected so maybe this new strategy would work. She had never thought of tough love before but then again, maybe some love was needed in the first place.

She could see that the bond of brotherly love was tight between these two. She had suspected it in the things Bryant had said and knew it in Shel's face as he had asked questions. If she had had any doubts about breaking policy before, they evaporated now. She knew Captain Mitchell had family and had wondered why they had abandoned him here in the place the staff all called 'Last Chance Hotel'.

She stood waiting for Shel's response. For some reason she didn't think of him as Sergeant Shepard but the more intimate first name Shel. That was how Bryant had referred to him, always as Shel, not Sergeant Shepard.

She prided herself in not getting emotionally involved with patients. That would burn one out fast, but she still tried to be compassionate to the needs of her patients. She had come to the conclusion that Captain Mitchell had needed his friend Shel. She was glad she had acted on that assumption.

As she studied Shel standing before his former Captain she knew he was definitely not one of her patients. A sudden desire she had thought she had buried deep rose to fill her. That scared her more than any rampaging patient. She didn't need to deal with feelings she no longer wanted.

Nurse Chapman realized her thoughts were wandering in the wrong direction about this friend of Captain Mitchell's and struggled to pull herself back into the situation at hand. She needed to keep a watchful eye in case she needed to jump in. The patient was her first concern.

Shel was hoping Bryant would rise to the bait, but instead the other man slumped into his chair, a look of utter defeat on his sightless face. "You don't understand," he muttered.

Shel was quiet a moment, trying to figure out if this was the right approach to take. He cast around in his mind for what to say next. He was the quiet one. He wasn't use to being the aggressor. "Ah, Hell," he muttered under his breath, in for a dime in for a dollar and lashed into the Captain ruthlessly.

"I don't understand?" he asked harshly. "I understand more than you think. I understand you were injured. I understand it was while trying to haul my sorry ass out of Hell. I understand that you and I are alive while the rest of the men are not. I understand you are in pain."

34

He paused a moment, realizing he had gotten right down into the Captains face and was nearly shouting his ear off like a boot camp drill instructor. This was a reversal of roles and for a moment he wasn't sure he could continue the assault.

He glanced over to Nurse Chapman. She was staring back at him with enlarged eyes. He thought for a moment she was going to say something to him, but instead she gave a small smile of encouragement and waved him on with her hand. Shel took a deep breath and turned his attention back to the Captain.

He hadn't moved or tried to say a thing. Shel was beginning to think he wasn't getting through till he noticed a slight pulsing tick in a vain in Bryant's neck. It was beating fast, a sign of Bryant's anger beginning to grow. Shel smiled and jumped into the situation head first.

"Well," he shouted in his best boot camp drill instructor's voice! "You think you were the only man wounded seriously? You think you're the only man who has come home from war with something missing or not working? You think you got it so bad?"

Shel straightened up and stepped back a pace, looked down at Bryant. The tick in his neck was really pulsating now, but he didn't speak. Shel hid a smile and continued but dangerously softer this time. "Like I said before, where is the man I knew back in the force? You're not him. He wouldn't be sitting here wallowing in self pity. He wouldn't let one little thing like blindness keep him down."

This was the last straw for Bryant. He leapt to his feet and stood before Shel with clutched fists at his side. The anger was raging in his face. "Maybe you should stop talking before I put a fist in your face," he shouted! "You don't know anything about what is going on with me!"

Shel held his ground. "I don't care what's going on with you," he shouted back! "Its obvious your legs work, your arms work, and your mind works! So tell me what makes being blind so fucking special? You think that's the worse that could have happened to you?"

35

Bryant seemed to run out of steam all of a sudden. "Julian is gone." He whispered harshly as he dropped back into his chair.

Shel stared at him for a moment, waiting for Bryant to continue on his own. One thing he knew about the Captain was, if he was going to give an explanation you had to wait for him to decide when he was going to give it. Just as Shel was beginning to think Bryant wasn't going to continue he began to speak.

His voice held all the bitterness he felt for being abandoned by everyone he had thought was dear to him. Julian was only the last straw in the haystack of family and so-called friends who had promised to stand by him and failed to do so.

"She didn't even know about the blindness at the time she heard of my injuries," he choked out the explanation. He was not a man who did the heart to heart thing very well. Shel knew this was difficult and let him continue at his own pace. Bryant laughed harshly and went on. "They told me that when she was notified I had been injured, the first thing she asked was if my face had been scarred. When they said yes I had been burned on one side from a bomb explosion, she..." he paused again, took several ragged breaths before going on.

Shel and Nurse Chapman just stood there. She had never seen the Captain open up and say anything personal about himself since he arrived. He had been totally enclosed in a monstrous wall of his own building. The only thing he ever talked about from the past was his friend Sheldon Shepard. He had wondered out loud a few times if he had recovered from the injuries he had received in the same battle the Captain had received his injuries. Since this was the only thing that he seemed interested in the real world, she had taken it upon herself to find Sergeant Shepard. She was very glad she did. This was the most "alive" she had seen the Captain since his arrival.

Shel glanced over at the Nurse. He saw she was deep in thought and wondered if she was thinking of calling security on him for upsetting her patient. She looked back at him and mouthed something. He wasn't sure he understood it right, but he thought it looked like, "good job, keep it up." He wasn't sure if she was being sarcastic or not. He was going to say something to her when Bryant started talking again.

"She said, 'oh I am sorry to hear that. Please give him my regards and that I hope he recovers soon.' She shut the door. She shut the damn door in their faces. That was it. She never tried to contact me. I heard 3 months later she married some rich banker from New York, forty some years her senior." He sat with his head down breathing deeply.

Shel knew by instinct that he was finished. The Captain had never been one for long explanations and this one had been long for him. He was also not surprised he hadn't mentioned his own family not being around. He already knew the story of Bryant's expulsion from the family when he decided to join the Military rather than follow his Father's footsteps.

He knew now was the turning point, either he jolted the Captain out of his lethargic mood or he let him stay here drowning in his self pity. Shel had a thing against self pity so he squared his shoulders and forced himself to act totally out of character.

"I see," he said with all the disgust he could muster. "You're letting her stupidity and shallowness ruin the rest of your life?"

Bryant slowly lifted his head to stare sightlessly in Shel's direction. The pup had grown teeth. He knew things had to be rough for him also. Though he wasn't sure of the extent of Shel's injuries he knew that his leg had been damaged pretty badly even before that last bomb had hit so near.

He also knew Shel had a family to go home to. He had a wife and father and a ranch and everything Bryant had envied each time he had heard Shel speak of home. "You're out of your league puppy dog. Go teethe on another specimen for a while. In fact why don't you just go home to your wife and leave me alone."

This was it. This was what Shel was waiting for. He knew the Captain would bite back and choose family as the subject. He thought Shel had everything he could ask for. He didn't know that Shel had lost a lot also.

37

Shel now had ammunition Bryant wouldn't be expecting. He had waited for the Captain to finally have enough of Shel's sharp tongue and say just what Shel needed to give the Captain something to think about.

"Well, Captain," he drawled in his slow heavily accented Montana voice. "I would be glad to do that but you see you're not the only one to lose a woman to this conflict." He paused to let it sink in but continued when he saw the Captain getting ready to retort an answer back. He had to finish this before letting the Captain talk. "You see, she couldn't handle being with a scarred up old soldier any more than your lady could. She lasted 2 months but then one morning I woke up and she was gone. She packed up a few things and scooted away during the night, not even a goodbye. All she left was a note saying she was sorry."

Bryant just sat there trying to think of what to say. This cut through his self pity like a knife. Shel had adored and worshiped his wife. He had bored Bryant and the rest of the team endlessly with the plans he had for when he returned home to her. Secretly Bryant had relished the times Shel talked of home, but he couldn't let him know that.

Shel had come from a loving home. He had been raised by his father alone for his mother had left when he was just six. His father had not let his bitterness spoil Shel's love of life or love for a woman.

Bryant had been immensely intrigued by the older Shepard the one time he had met him. He hadn't been impressed by Shel's wife but he didn't let Shel see that. Now, it seemed Shel was experiencing the same thing his Dad had years before. What a hell of a thing to have in common with your parent. Still, Bryant almost felt envious of that. He had nothing what so ever in common with his father.

He wasn't surprised to hear of her running away; she made him think of his ex-fiancée. He couldn't understand why a city girl would marry a country boy in the first place. He had wondered what Shel had seen in her but had been too much a friend to ask.

He didn't know what to say, so he didn't say anything at this time. His hand went to the scars that traced their way over his neck and up his left chin. He could feel the roughness and imagine the hideousness of them. Shel had been such a good looking young man. Bryant had teased him about being a pretty boy. The teasing was for a reason. It caused Shel to get his hackles up and learn to fight. Being from Montana and living on a ranch all his life, he wasn't just a pretty face; he knew how to survive in rough situations. He knew what hardships were, but one thing he wasn't use to, was being around people.

Bryant's means to toughen him up for the rigors of living with a dozen or so hardened soldiers was the only way he knew how to do it. At the same time he was trying to toughen Shel up, he also became the younger man's best friend. If you were going to survive in bad situations, you had to know who was watching your back. Bryant trusted his life to Shel and Shel trusted his life to Bryant. That terrible night when the world was exploding around them, they both knew that they needed each other to make it through alive. They nearly didn't, but one thing Bryant was sure of, if they hadn't done it together, they definitely wouldn't have made it.

Shel watched Bryant's hand as it moved over the scars on his face. He knew he was getting to him. He couldn't quit now, he had to break the wall that Bryant had built around him and he had to do it now. He wouldn't get a second chance. Now he had a crack in the armor he had to hammer away at it relentlessly.

He backed up away from Bryant and motioned for the Nurse to step to the door. She did as he indicated and waited for the next step. She had a feeling this was the make or break moment, the moment of truth. She wasn't sure what he was going to do but she was glad she was a safe distance away. There was a good likelihood of an explosion.

Shel reached the side of the bed and leaned against the foot of it. He reached down just below his knee and literally unsnapped his leg. The click of the sound reverberated in the now silent room.

He leaned forward and in a quieter but unyielding voice said. "I looked up to you Captain. You were the shoulder to lean on, the strength to make it through anything, and the leg to stand on when we thought all was lost. Well, Sir, I guess maybe you need this more than I do. Now you can have an extra leg to stand on."

Shel leaned forward and tossed his leg into the Captains lap. Bryant instinctively caught the object that landed in his lap and instantly realized what it was, a prosthetic leg. It was Shel's prosthetic leg. He had lost his leg!

The implications hit instantly. Shel was a cowboy. His livelihood depended on his strength and endurance, his ability to ride a horse, to stand tough against the elements. To still be able to do this with a fake leg meant a lot of hard work, an inner strength to endure the endless pain and rehabilitation, and Bryant was letting the loss of his sight and a woman who wasn't worth the time to think of her keep him down.

He burst up out of his chair once more, but this time he wasn't clutching his fists or ready to fight. Actually, he was ready to fight now but not with Shel. He was ready to fight for his own life, ready to get his soul back.

He stood there facing where he had last heard Shel. He held out the leg and quietly, but in a tone more like his old self, said, "I think you need this more than I do. Put it back on and get me the hell out of here."

Chapter 5

Kelly leaned her heated forehead against the cool window pane. The rain that had been threatening all morning finally let go and was pounding at the window. She stared out at what once had been her mother's bright colorful garden. Now all that remained was a brown patch of soggy weeds. She closed her eyes and wished she could morph through the glass into the past where colors had once abound. That little garden was the one place in this world her mother had had control.

In years past there had been spring flowers followed by the summer varieties and finally the fall colors would pop up. In the corner was the spot where her Mother had planted vegetables. They would have fresh beans, peas, carrots, radishes, cucumbers, and finally nearly every variety of squash imaginable. Kelly wished she could walk through the narrow paths one more time. She wanted to see her mother kneeling down before the rose bushes pruning the old buds off to make room for new blooms, one more time.

Kelly often wondered how her mother had managed to produce so much from such a small plot of ground. Then again, perhaps it wasn't such a big secret. It was where her mother spent most her time. It kept her out of Morris' way. It rewarded the love she lavished on it with plenty of vegetables and flowers.

Now, due to her mother's illness, there had been no garden this last summer, no colors brightening the dreary backyard, no fresh vegetables for her to bring over to Kelly's house. The little plot looked forlorn and lost in the absence of its mistress. In her absence weeds had sprung up to cover everything. They emphasized the cheerlessness of the place. Of course, Morris had no time or ambition to clear it away.

A hard and cold rain was falling, hitting the window pane with a tat-a-tat that was somehow fitting. It seemed the little garden was weeping for

41

the lost of its keeper the same as she was weeping for the loss of her mother. It knew somehow that it would never see its mistress again.

Morris was standing behind her talking but she had long ago stopped listening to his monolog. The phrase, "you're not my daughter," still rang in her ears. She didn't know if she should rejoice that his blood didn't run through her or be angry that her mother had not told her. The emotions that raged through her went from one spectrum to another. Questions to which she could find no answers assaulted her brain. Questions! Questions! Lately there seem to be nothing but questions. She raised her eyes to the ceiling and implored silently, 'Why Mom, why didn't you tell me?'

Kelly felt Morris come up behind her. He leaned close breathing his hot smelly breath on her neck. He was within her comfort zone. She could smell the booze and stale cigars on him. All she wanted to do was get away from him. Her skin was already beginning to crawl. He reached out and ran his hands up and down her arms in what she could only believe he thought was a caressing manner. His touch was enough to make her feel ill. It was the same feeling she had described to her physiatrist just days ago. It felt like ants running up and down her skin.

She twisted out of his arms and retreated to the far side of the room. If he thought he was going to continue what he had tried when she was a child he had another thing coming. She had taken self defense classes after her husband died. She would truly enjoy running a knee into his fat groin. "Don't you ever, ever touch me again," she hissed.

"Aw, sweet cakes," he murmured softly. He thought it was a seductive sound, she found it scratchy and grating to her tattered nerves. "You know you always wanted it. Those looks you use to throw at me were pure invite."

"Invite?"

"I tried to come to you when we could be alone." He continued not realizing how nauseated this made Kelly to hear it, to even think it. "You never said no when I came to your room. If that bitch of a mother of yours hadn't of interfered, we would have had a lovely relationship."

"I don't think raping your daughter can be called a lovely relationship," she hissed

"You asked for it."

"Asked for it?" she ground in ragged breaths.

"I could tell by the way you would look at me," he crooned. "All those looks you'd cast my way."

"Those looks were looks of fear and hate," Kelly rasped out from clutched teeth. She was glad she hadn't eaten anything. She was sure she'd throw up any minute now. "How could you consider forcing yourself on a child? How could you do that to your own daughter!"

"I just told you," he shrugged, "that you are not my daughter, so that didn't matter."

Kelly shivered at the harshness that had suddenly come into his voice, but she was bound to see this through and find out all the facts she could.

They were in his den. It was his private domain. Nobody was ever allowed in here, not even her brothers. It was as dark as his heart. Heavy musty drapes kept the sun out. Bookcases lined the walls but instead of books lining them they were covered in fishing equipment and magazines. Stuff was stashed in piles and heaps all over the shelves and floor. He never had to worry about her trespassing into this dirty dingy place; it was the last place she ever wanted to play. It surprised her when he had brought her up here today. They had just buried her mom and the reception was going on at this very moment downstairs. He pulled her aside saying he had something important to tell her. He wasn't kidding about that. He barely shut the door when he bluntly told her she was not his child.

"Aw, come on sweetie," Morris whined trying a new tactic to break through her defenses. "Why do you keep your distance from me? It's not like we are breaking any them stupid so called morals."

Kelly stared at him with a sick feeling in her stomach rising up into her throat. 'So-called morals, that's what he called it?' To the eight year old child who didn't know he was not her father, those so-called morals were to her, the lifelines of trust a child should have in her parent. It was a trust he had never cultivated. He couldn't really think she would have anything to do with him? To even think he would suggest anything so vulgar with her mother just hours buried was totally disgusting. The fact that he did suggest such a thing really didn't come as any surprise to her either. She took a deep breath; she had to remain calm so she can get some answers.

"You're saying Mom had an affair?"

Morris' harsh laugh filled the room. "Oh yes, she had an affair all right, but not against me." He crossed over to his chair behind a big oak desk that was his pride and joy. Kelly was relieved to have the distance between them once again. The desk was the one thing he kept spotless and in mint condition. He took out a cigar from a built in humidor, cut the end and leaned back while he lit it. He stared at her a long moment while puffing heavily to get it going, a ring of smoke circling his head. She stood with her back against a bookcase, arms hanging tensely down the sides of her slender body.

She really wasn't his type. He liked the voluptuous type with big breasts and asses. Still, he recalled the times he had attempted to have it on with her as a small child. That bitch of a wife kept spoiling his fun. He had had to raise the bastard kid, so why shouldn't he get something for it? He had a right to something for his troubles taking care of somebody else's brat, specially that jackass Shepard's. He was going to enjoy telling this stuck up bitch the whole sordid story.

"I was the one she was having the affair with."

Kelly didn't say a word as her thoughts raced. She had asked herself this same question a million times. 'What did her mom see in this man to put up with all he had done to her?' She couldn't see how a woman would leave anybody for this slob of a being. 'Did that mean her real father was actually

44

worse?' 'Oh God,' she groaned inwardly, glad of the solid bookcase behind her. She couldn't even imagine worse. That was too much a stretch of the imagination for her, but still, why would her mother leave her real father for Morris?

Even though on the inside her emotions were making mush of her organs, on the outside her expression never changed. It remained rock hard and expressionless. She knew a person couldn't show any weakness to Morris as he would attack with a vengeance. She had seen him do it so many times in her life. That's the way he lived, looking for others weaknesses and exploiting them. 'What had her Mother's weakness been?' When she didn't react to his last statement, Morris continued.

"You see," he said between puffs. "Your mother was married before she met me. The guy was some big-ass rancher who expected her to live in isolation on his big spread. He was too busy spending time with his horses to care how she felt. He didn't care that she was starving for attention and being around other people besides the farm hands. He never wanted to go into town, so she started finding reasons to go in herself. On one of those trips, she found me. Your mother was a lovely one in those days. She shouldn't have been hidden away in the middle of nowhere. I showed her there was a whole lot more to life than cooking and keeping house for a stuck-up man and a kid."

Kelly's eyes enlarged at what she just heard. "Kid?"

Morris laughed wickedly. He was delighted to see he finally got a reaction. "Oh yes, she had a brat boy about six years old. Three guesses what his name was."

Kelly was lost for a moment. What was he talking about? How could she know what this child's name was? Then, it dawned on her, 'Oh God!' Her eyes opened wide as she realized what he meant. His harsh laugh echoed affirmation through the room to her sudden thought. Her mother's words echoed through her head. 'I always liked Sheldon for a boy's name.

45

Please name your son that.' She had been so insistent about it that Kelly had finally given in. She had to admit the name sort of grew on her.

"You got it sweet cakes," he laughed out then turned serious. "Not only did I have to live with the fact that you weren't my child but now I had to put up with that brat's name attached to your son." He was deriving a wicked sense of pleasure in telling her all this. When Kelly didn't respond any further Morris continued with his story. "Anyway, she told me she hadn't had any type of a relationship with her husband in months. I finally convinced her to leave the asshole and go to Chicago with me. We set up house and got married."

"You mean after she got divorced from her husband?" she asked.

"Now, why would I want to go to the expense of a divorce?" he answered with a question. Kelly was horrified as she realized what this meant. Her mother hadn't even been legally married to Morris. She stared at the man as if he was the devil himself. This didn't discourage him at all from finishing his story. The more distressed she looked the more joy he derived from this.

"I realized the moment I set eyes on you that no way could you be my child. You looked just like your father. You had his eyes, his chin, and his hair. That meant she had been sleeping with both him and me. She had lied to me the whole time."

Kelly couldn't remain silent any longer. This pompous asshole had the audacity to look as if he was the one injured here.

"Excuse me," she interrupted his tirade. "You stole a woman from another man. You convinced her to run away with you. You married her illegally. You treated her child as if it was poison its whole life, and you are upset that she lied to you?" She realized she was speaking of herself as more like an object than the lonely child she had been. Then again that was all she had been to him, and she had been raised to think of herself as no more than an object that should have been taken to the dump.

"She said the child was mine," he explained nastily. He leaned forward pumping his cigar in the air for punctuation. "I would never have ran away with her had I known otherwise. Why would I want to raise somebody else's brat? How can anybody expect somebody else to love a child that's not his own? That's asking too much of a man."

Kelly could only stare at him. His warped sense of reasoning shouldn't surprise her but it always did. Just when she thought she couldn't hate this man more, he opened his mouth and she found new reasons for hating him. She clamped down on her raising anger and carefully asked the most important question.

"What's his name?"

Morris had sat back totally enjoying her discomfort during the story telling. Though, there did seem to be some disappointment in his voice that he hadn't been able to rattle her more. He seemed slightly confused by her question. "Who's name?"

"My real Father's," she answered slowly and determinately. "You said he was a rancher, who is he and where does he live?"

Morris suddenly lumbered to his feet and leaned over his desk. "That sweet cheeks, is my secret. Your Mother was the only other person who knew and she took it to her grave."

"You refuse to tell me?" Kelly asked angrily as she moved defiantly toward the desk, stopping in front of it. Morris tipped back his head and laughed mirthlessly. He leaned over the desk, his fat hands bracing him up, his jaw working the cigar in his pudgy soft lips. Kelly had thought him an ugly little man before, but now, she could see that the ugliness was more than skin deep. It penetrated to his very soul. As unlikable as he had ever been to her now he was just being cruel for the sheer joy it gave him.

"I could, perhaps, be persuaded to change my mind," he answered seductively, or rather, his version of being seductive.

Kelly could have gladly punched him in that horrid alcoholic enlarged nose of his. Instead she leaned forward with a slight smile on her

47

face. She placed her hands on either side of his and forced herself to go nose to nose with him. Then very slowly and softly replied, "I wouldn't consider what you had in mind in my worse nightmare. You can just go screw yourself."

She reached up as she spoke and plucked the cigar from his lips and rubbed it out on his expensive oak desk. Then she turned and walked slowly to the door. Once in the hall she fled to the relatively safeness of the crowded room below. People turned to look at her curiously wondering why she was so red faced and breathless. She pasted a smile on her face as she looked around for her brothers. She spied one and went toward him. She quietly told him she had to leave now. Sheldon would be waiting for her. It was a lie. She had left her son with a playmate for the night, but her brother didn't know that. She left the house as fast as she could without looking too conspicuous.

All Kelly wanted was to get home to some peace and quiet. She had a lot to think about. She could already feel a headache coming on. She was glad Sheldon wouldn't be home for the night. The last thing she needed now was a rambunctious six year old chasing around the house. Morris had said that her brother was six when her mother had ran off with him. She wondered if Sheldon looked anything like his mysterious uncle.

How could a mother leave behind a child? Her best guess was that Morris had refused to take the boy with them. The boy, she realized she couldn't refer to him as that; he would be older than her by about 7 years. His name was also Sheldon. She smiled remembering how much her mother had pushed that name. Kelly couldn't understand the persistence at the time. When she asked her mother about it all she said was that it was a name she had always liked.

Kelly let herself into the apartment and headed straight for the medicine cabinet. She had to try and catch this before it became a full-blown migraine. She needed time to think. The questions crowded her brain incessantly, one after another. 'Who was her Father?' 'Where did he live?'

"Wait a second," she spoke out loud startling herself. "Montana?" 'Could that be why her mother wanted her to move to Montana?'

Chapter 6

This situation was too much and Kelly knew she needed somebody to talk to. She made a phone call and the next day she was in Gloria's office. This was the one place she had always found it safe to just talk. The older lady was sitting back in her chair watching Kelly carefully as she was trying to figure out where to start. She never started the session with questions. She let Kelly talk about what was on her mind first then gently led the rest of the session into deeper feelings and memories.

This time Kelly related the funeral and what then occurred in Morris' office. Dr. Stein raised her eyebrow when Kelly referred to her father as Morris. Kelly saw this and explained. "He isn't even my father now!"

"He is still the one who raised you."

"You call what he did raising me," Kelly bit out harshly.

"You are what you are because of him."

Kelly stared at the Doctor for a few seconds wondering what she meant by that. She knew she was what she was because of her mothers protecting love. "What do you mean by that?"

"You are still very much under his influence," she explained. "Everything you have done up to now has been because of him."

"I have done everything I could to not be like him," Kelly harshly replied!

'Yes," the Doctor gently continued, "and that's why you have made the life choices you have. You were always very afraid that you would turn out to be like your father. Now you find out he isn't your father, so we know that biologically you are different but mentally, he is still every bit the 'Father' who raised you to be what you are now." Kelly couldn't argue with that.

"You even married a much older man just to get away from that house, right?"

"I married Mark because he was a good and kind man," Kelly quickly defended herself!

"He was the opposite of your Father."

"Morris isn't my father," Kelly yelled, jumping up and pacing. "I wish you would stop referring to him as such."

"Does this new fact make you happy or sad?

"Why would it make me sad?" Kelly looked confused. "He wasn't ever really a father anyway. I should be jumping for joy to find out that he wasn't."

"But you're not." This wasn't a question but a statement of fact.

Kelly felt deflated as she sank back onto the sofa. Dr. Stein had just hit the nail on the head. She looked up with such sadness in her eyes. "Why?"

Dr. Stein leaned forward slightly. "You tell me?"

Kelly sank back even further into the soft sofa. She welcomed the soft comfort it seemed to bring. Her head was spinning with all of the 'whys' going through her head. She knew the first question was the hardest to face. Kelly looked at Dr. Stein and asked it.

"Why did she let it happen if she knew I wasn't his child?"

"She is the only one who could answer that question," she replied softly. "You need to let go of that and face the other questions in your life that you can answer."

"Such as," Kelly asked?

"Why did you seek out and marry a much older man?"

"Why do you keep going back to this," Kelly asked frustrated. "My mother just died. I just found out my Father isn't my Father, and you keep harping on my marrying an older man. Many people marry older men, it's not a crime!"

"You can't move on to the future," Dr. Stein continued softly, "till you figure out why you did the things you did in your past."

"Mark was a good man," Kelly stated firmly. "He always treated me kindly."

"Like an adult?"

"Now what do you mean by that?" Kelly was getting frustrated again.

"Did he let you think for yourself?"

Kelly was speechless. She thought back to her brief relationship with her husband Mark Wells. She had met him when she went to work for him at his diner. He had taken her under his wing teaching her all she needed to be a good employee. She had started as a waitress, and then worked the cash register and finally graduated to doing the books.

He started showing an interest in her personally. They started to see each other and he had naturally taken the lead in everything they did. He chose where they went, what they did and even what she ate. He taught her how to be a good companion. She in turn did all she could to please him.

When they married, all the decisions were his to make. He took care of all finances, all home matters even down to what they ate each day. He even chose what kinds of clothes she wore.

Kelly began to see what Dr. Stein was getting at. The marriage had been one sided. Mark had been just another 'Father' figure to her. She had followed it because he was the opposite of Morris and she found safety in that. He had treated her with kindness and generosity, but he didn't treat her like an adult or an equal. He gave her anything she wanted but even that was what he chose for her. She had given him all authority in their relationship.

Even now after nearly seven years his influence was still there. The apartment was exactly as he had left it. She hadn't changed a thing. She had even reflected on that the night before as she was waiting for her pain pills to take affect. She had looked over the living room and realized she hadn't changed anything in the seven years since his death. She hadn't even considered changing anything to something she might like better.

The one time she had thought about redecorating, she remembered looking at things with him in mind. With each thing she had looked at she would think, 'would he approve of this' or 'he would never like that.' She had finally given up and left everything the same. Her clothes still reflected how he had thought she should dress. It was always stylish but conservative. He had influence over her as much now as when he was alive.

"You're right, he was just another Father," she stated sadly. "All I did was trade one father figure for another."

"Good, now we got that out of the way," Replied Dr. Stein, "we can now start your healing."

"What do you mean?" Kelly asked looking very confused at the moment?

"I mean," answered the Doctor, as she looked over some notes in her lap. "This is what we have been aiming for from day one."

"I don't understand?"

"Your mother thought she was raising you to be independent, continued Dr. Stein, "but she wasn't." She looked up at Kelly and smiled softly.

"You see," Dr, Stein softened her voice to soften the blow she was giving, "you saw how your mother acted to make sure things ran smoothly. So you learned that to have a quiet house you needed to placate the one deemed as the head of the house. You then, as such, were being trained to please the man rather than be an equal to him."

"Trained?" Kelly looked shocked to the core. She thought she had been careful to not fall into the same trap her mother had. Now it seemed she had headed right for it.

"You met a man who seemed safe because of his gentleness," she paused a second to let Kelly take this all in. "Then you thought you loved him because he was the opposite of what you were raised with, when in fact Mark was just the flip side of the same coin. He was just as controlling as

54

your father but in a much different way. He had learned to control with finesse as opposed to brute strength."

"Wait," Kelly cried out as she jumped to her feet again pacing back and forth in front of the sofa. "You're saying that instead of finding somebody different than my fa…, Morris, I actually found somebody just like him?"

Dr. Stein nodded. "He just did it in a different way."

Kelly sank back onto the sofa and dropped her head to her hands. She sat that way for the longest time. Dr. Stein let her be, allowing her time to absorb all the information. She knew Kelly had to go over the facts in her own way to realize the truth.

Kelly looked up with such sadness that even Dr. Stein was touched. This was too much pain for anybody to bear, to learn that you were just going in circles and didn't even know it. Kelly had traded one type of abuse for another. She didn't recognize the second form because of how subtle it was. Control of one person over another was wrong no matter how it was applied. Kelly was a strong person though and in the last seven years has learned to stand on her own two feet. Yet, because of her conditioning as a child it was easy for her to fall into the same behavior since she wasn't aware of it in the first place.

"Kelly," the Dr. leaned forward and made eye contact, "This is what we were aiming for all this time. You have made a tremendous amount of growth. Now, you recognize the behavior, you will not fall back into it very easily."

"But, how will I know if I meet somebody," she asked desperately, "that he's not the same sort of man?"

"Believe me," the Dr. assured her, "you will recognize the signs. You know them now. Just one thing though, don't be afraid to love somebody when the right man comes around. They aren't all like the men you know now and you do deserve a good man to love."

"What do I look for then?" Kelly asked. She thought back to the few men she knew in her life. Not one of them stood out as anything she would want for a husband or even a friend for that matter.

"I can't tell you that," Gloria answered. "I can tell you that real strength doesn't come from some outside force but from inside. A strong man knows he doesn't need to boss but to let others around him see their strengths."

"I haven't met anybody who would fit that criteria as of yet," Kelly laughed sadly.

Chapter 7

The once cool night air was now on fire. Explosions lit up the previously placid sky. Bryant was crouched down behind what was left of his armored personal carrier. One moment he was a passenger in the lead truck, the next he had found himself on the ground. He had been thrown from the vehicle when a shell landed in front of it. He found the driver, who hadn't been so lucky. He searched the rubble for any signs of movement. It wasn't the enemy he was looking for but his men. "Charro, Maloney, Shepard," he yelled out over the noise. There was no answer.

He flattened out on the ground and crawled to the next big object he could see. This was once a jeep. He found the driver on the ground. Bryant felt for a pulse and found nothing. He looked at the man's dog tags for identity. It was Kilburn, a lad of 19 from Philly. Bryant worked his way down the line trucks and carriers looking for survivors.

The ambush has taken them totally by surprise and had been fierce. Multiple mortars had hit them at once. It had been done with precision and Bryant was sure it wasn't just a chance attack, but he wasn't thinking of that as he crawled from one man to the other looking for survivors.

Bryant crawled around flaming debris. Machine gun fire erupted from the hills around them. All the vehicles were hit. His hands and legs were cut and bleeding. He didn't care. He had to find out if any of his men had made it out of their trucks. So far he had found every man dead.

Where was Shepard? Bryant finally made it to the forth and last transport amid more explosions. Fires burned everywhere. All the vehicles had been hit. The enemy had been ready for them. Bryant wondered if they had been set up. Looking around at the destruction of his unit Bryant knew this was not just a random attack. The assailants were too well fortified. This ambush had been well planned and that meant the insurgents had known they were coming.

The mission into this particular grid had been top secret. Only a handful of people knew it was even taking place. Somebody had leaked the information. If Bryant succeeded in surviving, heads were going to roll.

Right now, there was one thing on his mind. He had to find Shepard. There were no survivors so far, but he wasn't going to give up till he accounted for every man. Bryant didn't have time to contemplate why he was still alive. He was praying that Shepard hadn't met with the same fate as the others. He searched around the final transport and found the driver on the ground. He then went from one body to the next looking at each tag. Shepard wasn't among them.

Bryant rose up as far as he dared and cast his eyes over the area. He couldn't see anymore bodies lying around. He had counted as he found each man; all were accounted for except for Shepard. He had to be nearby.

"Shepard," Bryant bellowed out over the noise of more explosions. "Shepard you asshole, answer me!"

"Pssssssssst, hey Capt'n," a weak voice called from beneath a pile of debris a few yards away. Bryant rushed over to it and jerked a large piece of twisted metal away. He found a bloody but very much alive face staring out at him. "Hey, you looking for anybody in particular Capt'n?"

"Shepard, how badly are you hurt?" Bryant asked ignoring the impertinent question. Shepard had a way of using humor for any situation. Bryant didn't mind as long as he kept talking. That way he knew he was hanging in there.

"Bloody hell, Capt'n," the man answered in forced cheerfulness to hide the pain he was in, "I have been mauled worse by bulls in the rodeo."

"You been hanging around those British troops too much I see," Bryant tried to force the same cheerfulness into his voice, he failed completely. "You're starting to sound like one." The face in the rubble smiled back at him.

"Anything to ruffle your feathers Capt'n," was his cocky answer. "Now, do you think maybe you could help me out of here?"

In answer Bryant grabbed another piece of hot metal and jerked hard as he could. He was rewarded by the piece giving way and flying to the side. He then kneeled down next the younger man. "Where do you hurt the worse?"

"You pick a spot Sir," returned the cocky voice. Leave it to Shepard to try and keep up beat even at this time. He was always the one to keep troop moral up. In any of the missions they had ever been on it had always been the young man from Montana to get them rallied up to press forward.

Bryant started at the top of his body and worked down feeling the limbs for fractures and other injuries. When he got to Shepard's left leg, the young man let out a yowl to waken the dead. "I think you found it, Sir."

Bryant cast around for cover. He had to get them both off the road before the insurgents came looking through the wreckage. The sound of advancing gun fire told him they were getting closer. They would be dead for sure if they were found. Bryant searched the side of the hills closest to them for any break in feature. He finally spotted a dark spot in the flaming light deep in the face of the hill, on the other side of the road. He hoped that indicated a small cave they could possibly take cover in. These mountains were riddled with caves. That was what made finding the insurgents so hard.

He pointed out the spot to Shepard. "You think you can make it up there?"

"I can sure give it a try Capt'n," was the reply as Shepard pulled himself up to his knees. Pain coursed through him as he tried to put weight on the injured leg. "I think I could use a hand though if you don't mind?"

Bryant was already pulling the other man's arm over his shoulder and pulling him up. They struggled to the other side of the road picking their way through the debris and up the hill. The cave could be seen clearly now but was a bit further up the hillside than Bryant had anticipated. He tightened his grip on Shel and they slowly crawled and scratched their way to the entrance. Bryant kept looking behind him for any signs of insurgents but so far none had appeared. They seemed satisfied to keep dropping mortars and spray machine gun bullets.

It took what seemed an eternity to make it to the face of the cave. Exhausted, Bryant pushed Shepard into the front of the cave, and then turned to look for something to cover the entrance. An exploding bomb less then ten feet from the entrance threw him back against Shepard and everything went black.

Chapter 8

Shel watched his former commander as he slept fitfully. It had taken a day to get the necessary paper work done to release Captain Mitchell into his care. That vision of a nurse, Nurse Chapman, had helped expedite the matter. Once Bryant got some fire into him he was not staying any longer than he had to in that place. They had taken off at first light this morning.

The only thing Shel regretted was not seeing Nurse Chapman again before they left. He still hadn't gotten her first name and was hoping to get that and a number to reach her before they left. But that was not to be, she wasn't on duty this morning and the nurse helping them gather the Capt's things wouldn't give out any information on her. He settled with giving a note to the nurse who promised to give it to Nurse Chapman. He asked her to call him sometime and left his number again in case she hadn't saved the one she had before.

Another moan from the Capt'n had Shel wondering if he should wake him. He knew where Bryant was in his dream and the power of those dreams. They were so real they sucked you back to that horrid place that smelled of sand and death. Shel had awakened in the night many of times covered in sweat. He had shouted loud enough a few times to wake his father.

The first time that happened was a few days after returning home from the rehabilitation center. Megan had already left by that time, not being able to handle a husband with missing body parts. Weldon came to his son's bedside and just sat there silently until the shakes had subsided and his son was breathing easy again. Words weren't needed, just his presence. A presence that was strong and positive, one that said its ok, you're home now, and you won't be left alone.

Shel couldn't understand a father like Bryant's that abandoned his son because he didn't become a clone of him. How can a parent turn his back on his son when he was down and injured? How could he not be proud of the sacrifice his son had made for his country? How could he be so selfish as to ignore the ordeal his son was going through now?

Shel couldn't understand it because his father had been beside him every step of the way, but he hadn't coddled Shel either. That first day back he had Shel in a saddle and herding cattle to pasture. It was tiring but satisfying work. It didn't take long for Shel to get back into shape and do everything almost as easily as before. He was forever thankful for his father's tough love and undying support.

He was going to do the same for Bryant. He was going to let the man learn to be whole again on his own while Shel provided as much help and support as he needed.

Bryant woke with a garbled yelp. The young man at the steering wheel beside him reached out and put a comforting hand on his former Captain's shoulder. He didn't say a word; just let the other man get his bearings.

"Where are we?"

"Just outside of Bozeman," Shel answered cheerfully, and then sobered up. "You're having those flashbacks also, I see." It wasn't a question just statement of fact. He figured no sense in pussyfooting around the fact but to get it out in the open.

"Yes," Bryant replied warily. He was silent a moment, weighing his next statement carefully, he wasn't sure just how much Shel knew or wanted to talk about that night. "They never told me what happened after the mortar hit the hill by us."

"Well Sir," Shel started only to be cut off by the other man.

"I'm no longer your commanding officer Shel," he replied bitterly. "So call me Bryant now, Okay?"

"Yes Sir," Shel started then amended, "I mean Bryant," Shel drawled out slowly. The familiar cockiness of the younger man was like balm on Bryant's tattered nerves.

"Nice to know you haven't changed any."

There was a short pause then a quiet, "We all have changed some Sir."

After another awkward pause Bryant asked again, "You going to tell me what happened?"

"Like I started to say before," Shel tossed back at the other man. "When the shell hit, you were thrown into the cave. Right on top of me, I might add," Shel added in his cockiest cowboy manner.

"I might also add that hurt like hell," he laughed. "You are not a small man."

Bryant actually smiled slightly, "Sorry about that."

"Anyway," Shel continued, "The entrance was partially blocked from the explosion and when the enemy came at dawn to inspect their work, they overlooked the cave entrance and moved on down the road.

A few hours later our forces arrived. When they came to check out the crater in the side of the hill, I was able to get somebody's attention. You were alive; I was happy to know but you never came to. I had pushed you off me best I could but the space was small so we were rather close for a while, Sir." Bryant couldn't miss the teasing quality in Shel's voice.

"Long as it doesn't happen again," he retorted back in the best officer's voice he could muster.

He could imagine Shel's grin busting from ear to ear. That was another enduring quality of the young man's. He was always smiling that cocky smile, swaggering around acting a fool. He could lighten anybody's mood anytime, but if there was business to be done, Shel was all business and didn't take crap from anybody. Bryant knew he could depend on the younger man when he needed something done and done right. He figured that was why the young man had come to mean so much to him.

Bryant had promised himself that no matter what, he was going to make sure this young man made it home to his Father and wife. That reminded him, he hadn't asked about either one of those people who had meant so much to Shel. Shel had already mentioned his wife had left, but he had to ask.

"So, how is your father?"

"Dad's as ornery as ever," He replied cheerfully. "He is looking forward to your coming."

"I bet," Bryant laughed, "like a headache."

"He likes you," Shel laughed with him. "He insisted you come. You see, you couldn't have turned us down if you had wanted to."

Bryant was silent for a minute. He wasn't sure how to put his thoughts into words without sounding sappy. "I want to thank you both for welcoming me into your home."

"No problem," Shel blew it off but Bryant wasn't going to let him.

"I want to tell you…" Bryant floundered.

"You're family now," Shel broke in cheerfully. "Dad said you are family and we don't leave family behind."

"Thanks."

"Your welcome."

Silence followed for a short time before Bryant got up enough courage to ask Shel about his wife.

"You want to tell me about her?"

There was another short pause. Bryant knew that this was another one of Shel's qualities. He paused whenever he had to say something not so pleasant. He was very careful to pick his words. "Megan left about two months after I got back stateside. She couldn't handle the isolation of the ranch anymore or other things."

Bryant didn't say anything to that. He knew more than anybody that it wasn't the isolation that she probably couldn't handle. He thought of the robust young man, as he had looked before that night. Shel was tall, wildly handsome with strawberry hair that tended to curl if it got more than an inch long. He was forever taking cuff from the men for this 'girlish' attribute. He took it as good naturedly as he took everything else. He had a square jaw

64

that tended to set firm when he was serious about something. He had full lips that were perpetually in a grin. Bryant couldn't imagine what Shel looked like now. It seemed the younger man read his thoughts.

"Actually," he answered the unasked question. "I haven't changed all that much physically." When Bryant didn't say anything he continued. "They couldn't save the leg. It had been too long after the injury before they got to us. Infection had already set in. The amputation is below the knee which made it much easier to get use to."

He told his story easily. Bryant could tell by his voice that it wasn't something he dwelled on. He reflected on how easily Shel has said, 'the amputation.' He remained quiet letting the young man continue on his own.

He realized that he was taking some strength from Shel's easy, 'that's life' attitude. He wondered if he would ever reach that point where he could take life with the injuries he had. His hand went up to his temple of its own volition it seemed. He quickly lowered it wondering if Shel had noticed. The other man gave no indication that he had.

Shel was watching Bryant out of the side of his eye as he drove down the road. He noticed every nuance of movement the man made as Shel related his side of the story. He noticed the hand going to the temple and just as quickly dropping. He made no comment but continued his story.

Nurse Chapman had quietly filled him in on the condition of Captain Mitchell as they got his things together. It seemed that the Doctors thought Bryant's blindness might be more psychological than physical and he could get it back eventually.

"Anyway, you already know," he continued quietly, "we were the only ones to survive."

"I knew that much," Bryant answered. "What they wouldn't tell me is how did the insurgents know we were coming?" He waited for an answer but none came. He felt Shel tense at the question.

"You know who the mole was, don't you?"

"The official story is that it was somebody working inside the Afghanistan government." Shel related what he had been told. But Bryant heard the hint of disbelief in the voice.

He didn't comment on it for a moment. He had his own suspicions as to who had given their mission away. He had an idea Shel also had the same suspicions. They both knew that very few people if any in the Afghan government knew of the mission. It wasn't the Military's habit to inform them of top secret missions.

"By the way," Bryant asked carefully, "How's Darby doing these days?"

Shel's snort told Bryant they did both have the same suspicions.

Darby had been a fairly recent addition to their unit. He hadn't blended in very well. The group was a close-knit one; most of the men had been together a long time. It always took a new comer a while to adjust but in Darby's case, he never did quite fit. He never tried. There was always something unsettling about him. Bryant hadn't trusted him as far as he could throw him. Then again, Bryant was an expert in hand to hand combat and could toss a man quite a long distance, but still he didn't trust him.

Bryant silently chuckled at the image of him tossing Darby; it was an image that had kept him going since the disastrous mission. Darby had mysteriously and suddenly gotten ill just the day before the mission and was the only man from the unit who wasn't on it. When Bryant had made inquiries about him after the fact, he couldn't get any information. It was like the guy never existed.

"Darby disappeared shortly after we left for the mission," Shel spit out in disgust. "He was gone when we returned. He was missing for months after that."

"Was?" Bryant's interest was suddenly peeked.

"A friend of mine who stayed in touch told me," Shel couldn't keep the sound of glee quite out of his voice while giving this info. "His body was found a couple months ago,"

"Where," Bryant asked?

"Somewhere in the mountains," Shel continued at Bryant's prompting. "A unit was descending on a group of insurgents in the north. They resisted and after a short battle our men were able to move in. He was found dead inside a cave. They shot him in the head. Seems his new friends had turned on him. Maybe they figured he had given their position away. Turn a bout's fair play in my book." Bryant silently agreed with that.

"First he was listed as AWOL," Shel continued. "Then it was changed to missing in action. His death was then listed as died in the line of duty. I protested that to General Overton but he said let it drop. I got the feeling he knew something he couldn't share. Out of respect for him, I let it go."

He let the subject drop and they remained silent for a long time as they continued down the road. Shel finally broke the silence trying for easy conversation. Bryant, relieved at the change in atmosphere, went along with it.

"I called Dad and told him we would make it by supper."

"I hope he doesn't mind my coming with such short notice," Bryant suddenly felt uncomfortable over the circumstances.

He hated relying on people. Those he had thought he could rely on had let him down and he wasn't about to let friends take care of him, but somehow this felt different. Somehow he knew he could rely on Shel's help without the other man making him feel like an invalid. A bond had forged between the two men during their work together in the Special Forces unit they were in. Bryant felt like Shel was the younger brother he never had, but always had wished for as a child.

"Shoot, Dad said exactly what I knew he would say," Shel commented easily. "You are welcome for as long as you want to stay." He didn't say needed to or had to or any of the other words that could have replaced wanted.

"Hey, this isn't a free ride, buddy."

This new tone caught Bryant off guard. "What do you mean?"

67

"You're expected to work for you dinner," Shel continued in his half serious tone. Bryant wasn't sure how serious he was about this. "I figured you can help out in the stables."

"Doing what?"

"Mucking out stalls comes to mind," Shel answered trying to suppress the chuckle he felt in his throat. He knew Bryant couldn't see the smile on his face as he was talking. He was having difficulty staying serious. But he also knew the best thing for Bryant's recovery was to make him feel like he was capable of taking care of himself.

Shel remembered the feeling he had right after he found out he had lost his leg. He had wanted to curl up and die. He thought that all the things he loved like hiking, horse riding, and working on the ranch were now long beyond him.

His father wouldn't let him feel sorry for himself and when he returned home with his new prosthetic leg, he had Shel's favorite horse already saddled and waiting. He wouldn't take no for an answer and had Shel up and riding before the young man could protest. That act let Shel know that as far as his father was concerned, he was still as whole to him as before. Shel couldn't imagine a father not standing behind his son in a time like that. He thought back once again to Bryant's father. He just couldn't understand Bryant's father at all. How did a man reject his son when he needed a father the most? He was ever so grateful for his father's hard love. It was what had made him the man he was before he joined the military and what fixed him when he had come home broken.

"Mucking out stalls?" was Bryant's immediately shocked response.

"It's a ranch Bryant," Shel continued in a nonchalant tone, biting his tongue to keep from laughing out loud at the look on Bryant's face. "There is a lot of shit to be tossed everyday."

"And you trust me to toss it in the right direction?" The lightheartedness in Shel's tone was catching on. Bryant could almost see himself shoveling horse shit from a stall and tossing it into somebody's face if they should pass by at the wrong time.

"Don't worry, I'll aim you in the right direction," this time the laughter was obviously evident in the man's voice. "And, I'll warn the rest of the hands to stay their distance from you when you're armed with a shovel." Now both men were actually laughing at the picture conjured up. Bryant felt the car turn onto a gravel road. He knew they were almost there. He wanted to say something but wasn't quite sure how. Being emotional and even thankful to another person was a foreign thing to Bryant. Shel seemed to know what the other man was thinking once again.

"Lets not get emotional here, Capt'n," he said quietly as he drove up the long drive to the ranch house. "We wouldn't want anybody to know you got feelings. It'll hurt your rep." The jaunty way Shel said it made Bryant feel welcome.

Chapter 9

Bryant felt the car slow before the turn into the main driveway, so Shel's "here we are" was unnecessary. He had his door open soon as he felt the stop and was out stretching his stiff limbs. He took a deep breath and marveled at the fresh air that filled his lungs. He had half expected a different aroma, the idea conjured up from the mucking talk he and Shel had earlier. He stood still and listened to the sounds. This was a new sensation for him, trying to get his bearings from the sounds around him.

He could feel, as well as hear the breeze; it had a slight chill to it as it was fall. He wondered how cold it got here on the edge of the mountains. He heard the dried leaves rustling from beneath a nearby tree. A cat meowed from his left and a dog barked in the distance. He sniffed the wind and caught a faint whiff of that aroma he had expected before. He realized then what direction the barns were. He turned slightly so his ear was facing that direction and could hear faint whiney of horses and the low mooing of cattle. He heard a light tinkling sound and turned toward it. He pointed toward it and asked. "Wind chimes? That's the house?"

"Yes," answered Shel from behind the truck. Bryant turned toward him. He followed the muffled voice and made his way along the truck to the back. The soft gravel beneath his shoes crunched. He liked the sound of that.

In the hospital everything was muffled, distant, and he was never clear from what direction people were coming. The front door opened and hit the edge of the wind chime. Bryant turned toward that sound and listened to heavy feet coming down the steps and across the walk to the drive. He had never realized how much noise a person made just walking. Not a loud noise but a distinct one when listened for carefully. He knew when the man left the cement walk from the crunch of the gravel drive. He also knew instinctively that it was Weldon Shepard, Shel's father. He knew he was right as he felt strong hands take his hand in a hearty shake.

71

"Bryant, I am so happy to see you again," the strong hearty voice of the old rancher greeted him. Bryant couldn't help but smile in return. He would never have trouble hearing this man.

"Nice to meet you again, Sir," Bryant answered the handshake back. "I appreciate you letting me come stay a while."

"Now, I don't want to hear all this Sir business," the older man replied as he clapped Bryant on the shoulder hard enough to make him stumble slightly. He heard Shel chuckling from the back of the car.

"Dad," Shel spoke to Weldon, "if you knock Bryant's shoulder out he won't be able to do any chores."

"Oh, yah," chuckled the older man, "sorry, I forget my own strength sometimes. Come on, let's go on in. Rosa's got a wonderful supper waiting for us. Shel will warn you of the consequences of letting it grow cold."

Bryant found himself being practically manhandled into the house. He knew it was easier to just let the old man drag him along. He heard Shel bringing up the rear, chuckling the whole time. One thing Bryant already knew, he wouldn't be coddled in this house hold.

Next thing he felt was the warmth of the kitchen with all its cooking odors that hit his nostrils and he realized how much he missed real food. The hospital stuff had been devoid of flavor no matter what you did to it. He felt a chair being placed behind him and he automatically sat down. He also heard Shel whispering to his father, something about treating Bryant normally and trying not to do anything more for him than needed.

Bryant smiled slightly and pretended he didn't hear a thing. He was also thinking it might not be such a good thing he could hear so well. Could that mean his other senses were increasing because he will never get his sight back?

Bryant found himself standing outside on the balcony after dinner. The evening air was cool but not uncomfortable. He heard Shel come through the sliding door.

"You've got a good cook," Bryant mentioned.

72

"Glad you enjoyed the meal," Shel replied lazily. "Maybe Rosa can fatten you up a bit."

Bryant laughed and made his way to a chair. He already knew where they were lined up along the back wall. He had explored the small balcony earlier when he first came out. Shel joined him and silently put something in his hands.

Bryant knew what it was instantly. He had always abhorred the cane but realized he would need it here if he didn't want to walk into something. He murmured his thanks and set it down. Weldon joined them and set a tray down on a table nearby.

"What'll be your poison?" he asked good-naturedly.

"Poison?" Bryant asked back.

"A drink," Weldon laughed.

"Oh, yah," Bryant laughed with him. "I'll have anything, thank-you."

"That's a dangerous thing to say around here," Weldon laughed as he pressed a glass into Bryant's hand. "I'll start you out with a beer. The table is to your right."

"Thanks," Bryant added as he took a deep swig. That did taste good. He couldn't remember the last time he had a beer. "Man, I missed that."

He leaned back and closed his eyes listening to the sounds around him. He was surprised at how relaxing the evening noises were. He heard the rustling of the dying leaves still in the trees in the light breeze. Also, some sort of animal was rustling in the dried leaves on the ground. A sudden loud barking identified that animal as one of the several dogs on the ranch.

He heard low mooing and whinnies from the barn area. Shel had told him they had a sizable heard of cattle in the lower pasture for winter. These pastures started at the barns and stretched out over several miles. He had not realized how big a spread Shel's father had.

The paddocks, he was told, housed over a hundred head of horses. Some were the ones trained for riding, others were for breeding, and some were the off-spring waiting for market. The whole idea of living out here away from the city was still new to him. He smiled slightly when he heard as well as felt the house cat at his feet.

He had never listened to the sounds before. Even right after he had returned to the states he hadn't bothered. He was sure he would get his sight back. Why concentrate on something he didn't need worry about? The Doctors said he would regain his sight, but over the last year nothing had changed. Things had gone from bad to worse.

First he had called his parents to let them know he was alive and wished to return home to recuperate. He hoped his father had forgiven him for not following him in the family business. It wasn't as if he planned to stay there forever. He knew he wouldn't be able to stay in the same house with his father for too long. The man was immoveable when he wanted things his way. Bryant soon found out how immoveable. He was told by the butler no less, that his father didn't feel his coming home would be the right thing.

He called his fiancée to test the waters there. He already knew of her reaction, or lack there of to the news of his injuries. He found she had left the country for a European vacation, her honeymoon no less. She had moved the day after she found out he had been injured.

Oh, she had left a message. He remembered it word for word. Her mother had given it to him over the phone. It was something he wished he could forget. She had said that she couldn't face life being a nurse maid to an invalid. She called him an invalid, even before she knew the full extent of his injuries. She had labeled him based on superficial injuries. She didn't even know about his blindness yet. He wondered if she ever found out. The main thing that mattered was she couldn't even face him to tell him herself.

He found out two months later she had met an older banker and married him within weeks of that meeting. He knew then that it wasn't him she had loved. It was the position he could have occupied in the family business she loved. It was the wealth that he rejected that she loved. Well, at least now he knew for sure why she had postponed the wedding several times. Of course he had suspected it. He just ignored the suspicions.

She had been waiting to see if he would make amends with his father and go home to the family business. How had she put it? "Darling, when are you going to stop this foolish macho thing of being a mere soldier, and go home to where you belong?"

Where he belonged? He had known since he was a child that sitting all day in an office dressed in a stuffy three-piece suit wasn't where he belonged. He had always loved the outdoors. He played football and baseball in school. Where most parents pushed their kids into such things, his father thought of it only as a waste of time. His Dad hadn't gone to any of his games. He didn't have praise for wins or sympathy for losses.

He loved hiking and camping. Now he realized as he took a deep breath, how much the sounds and smells had been part of what he had loved seeing. He had just never realized it before.

As a commander in the Military he knew how to use his other senses to be prepared for whatever could be out there waiting for him and his men. But it had always been a matter of unconscious use and not something he had to think about.. He suddenly realized he had been ignoring his two hosts. It seemed they had gone silent while he had been day dreaming.

"Shel," Bryant spoke into the silence?

"I'm, right here Bryant," Shel answered lazily. "Dad went to answer the phone. You looked like you were resting. I didn't want to bother you."

"Sorry," Bryant apologized, "I was just listening to the sounds and smelling the air. It sure is fresh out here." He heard Shel laugh.

"What," Bryant asked puzzled by the laugh?

"Wait till the wind shifts," was all Shel would say.

Bryant heard the old mans footsteps coming back down the hall. Something seemed different in them, slower not so strong and steady. He wondered what that phone call could have been about. Shel greeted his father as he reemerged from the door.

75

"Shel," Weldon said slowly, hesitant. He paused a minute and Bryant could hear him pulling out his chair. He heard the man taking a deep drink from his beer. Suddenly he felt he was intruding. He stood up to leave the patio.

"Well, this has been some strange day," he started. "I am drained, so I think I'll call it a night."

Bryant couldn't see the look on Weldon's face as he crossed the patio. Shel saw it. It was the stricken look of loss. He recognized it. He had seen that stricken look on his father's face just once in his life. It had been the day he had come home from school to find his mother had left.

Just the thought of it brought back all the deep pain and anger he had buried all those years before when, as a six year old, he had found out his mother hadn't loved him enough to stay with him or his Dad. He had come home to that same look on his father's face. He barely heard Bryant talking till he got to the 'call it a night' part. He forced himself to acknowledge his friend.

"Oh, yah," he stammered. "I'll show you to your room."

"That's ok," Bryant swiftly replied. "I think I can remember how to get there."

"I'm sorry," Shel was still looking at his father as he talked to Bryant. "I didn't mean to…" Bryant cut him off.

"I know," he waved in the direction he had heard Weldon sit down. "You take care of …" He wasn't sure what to say so he dropped it.

"Wake me in the morning so you can give me that grand tour you promised."

"Yah, I will," Shel answered. "See you at daylight."

Bryant turned from the doorway at that. "And what time is daylight?"

"About 5am."

"Oh," he replied and tried to force some levity into his voice. "And I thought the Army was bad for getting up at the crack of dawn."

76

"Welcome to the country old boy," Shel shot back, a hint of his old self in his voice. "See yah in the morn,"

After Bryant had gone thru the door Shel turned back to his father. Bryant was still in the hall and could hear their voices drifting in through the open door.

"Dad?"

Weldon didn't reply right away and Bryant was wondering if the older man was all right? He finally heard the older man's voice drift through the door. He should have kept going but something made him hang back to hear the conversation.

"I have had a private investigator keeping tabs on your mother." He heard Weldon say.

Shel's mother? Bryant knew that she had abandoned Shel and his father when he was just a boy. It was one of the few things Shel was reticent about talking about. He only revealed what happened one night in Afghanistan when they had been pinned down by enemy fire for a while. They talked about family, or the lack there of for each man as a way to get through the wait.

"Why?"

"I just needed to know," the older man answered.

"What was that call about?"

"Your mother…"

Shel cut him off. "I don't have a mother!"

Weldon waited a moment and started again. "Your mother passed away a few days ago." Silence followed those words and after a moment Bryant turned back towards the stairs and made his way to his room.

Chapter 10

Kelly sat on the sofa sipping coffee looking around the sparsely decorated room. She removed Charles pictures from the walls and the few figurines he had thought tasteful that had graced the shelves. She gave them all away. She had packed away all the books Charles had bought for her to read, which she'd never gotten around to reading anyway, and gave them to a used bookstore.

She recovered the sofa and chairs with brightly colored flowered sheets that she found brightening. She was surprised how much that had lightened up the room. The place looked empty now but she hesitated to start redecorating. She still wasn't sure if she was going to stay in Chicago or not. She no longer had any ties here.

She hadn't spoken to Morris since the day of the funeral. She hadn't heard from her brothers either. She didn't miss their company anyway. The only time they had ever visited her was when they were hiding out from Morris' wrath. She had finally put an end to that. They would come over and eat her food, watch her TV and bad mouth her the whole time. No, she didn't miss them at all.

Kelly felt bad about her brothers though. They didn't have it easy with Morris. He manipulated them for his own needs. She wished she could help them but knew that as long as Morris had any grip on them she was powerless. She had to think of herself and her son. She wasn't going to let them teach him any of their bad habits. She had to cut the ties to them.

It had been a month since Kelly's mom had passed away. Kelly had to pick up her life and decide where to go from here. Her mother had been trying to persuade her to move away from Chicago from the day she had found out she was sick and didn't have much time left. Kelly's job wasn't so important that she felt bad about leaving it, but to move to Montana?

Kelly wished she had been able to find out why her mother wanted her to move there. She also needed to know where in Montana she had wanted her to move to. After all it was a rather large state. She figured it had something to do with her real father. He must be from there or still lived there, Morris did say he had a ranch, but she had no idea where or how to begin a search. She didn't even know his name.

She knew that her son had the same name as her brother. Sheldon, it had a nice ring to it. She had liked it when her mother suggested it, almost insisted on it. But, having the first name did no good without a last name. Kelly thought hard. Had her mother ever mentioned anybody's name? No amount of racking her brain brought an answer.

Kelly's grandmother had also lived in Montana if she remembered right. Her mom had talked to her on phone her once or twice. Kelly had heard her mom talking to her. It seemed more like she was pleading with her. She hung up though when she saw Kelly standing in the doorway. Grandma had never come to visit nor had Kelly ever talked to her on the phone.

Another memory made itself known; grandma had died a couple years back. Kelly remembered that now. She had gone over to see her mom and was coming down the hallway when the phone rang. She heard her mom answer it, murmur something too quietly for Kelly to hear, and then hang up the phone. She had then sat down and cried. Kelly had come up to her and wrapped her arms around her. Her mom told her that her mother had died. Kelly felt bad for her mother and remembered feeling bad for never having met her grandma. They never mentioned her again after that.

The ringing of the phone brought Kelly back from her thoughts. She reached over and absentmindedly answered it.

"Hello?"

"Mrs. Wells?" a soft deeply refined voice replied.

"Yes?"

"I am George Gregory," the soft voice continued, "of Gregory Associates."

"A lawyer?"

"Yes Ma'am," the deep voice replied seemingly unaware what it was doing to Kelly's senses. 'Man,' she thought, 'I wonder if he is even aware how he sounds?' She laughed silently to herself as she also thought, 'I know it's been a long time since I have been with a man but I shouldn't melt at the sound of stranger's voice.'

"What can I do for you Mr. Gregory?"

"Actually, it's what I can do for you Mrs. Wells," The lawyer continued in his soft yet matter of fact manner.

"And just what can you do for me Mr. Gregory?" Kelly asked. Sexy voice or not warning bells were going off. What would a lawyer want with her?

"I'm sorry Mrs. Wells, I didn't mean to alarm you," the voice softened even more. "I was your mother's lawyer."

"My mother didn't have a lawyer."

"Actually, she did, but it seems she never told anybody about it," The amused voice replied. Kelly got the distinct feeling that Mr. Gregory was enjoying this little game they seemed to be playing. She didn't feel like playing at this moment.

"I am sure Mr. Gregory that you must have the wrong person," Kelly answered him. "There are more than one Kelly Wells in the area."

"Yes, I know there are," he replied, " but I know I have the right Mrs. Wells. Your mother, Kate Morris, gave me your number to contact you after her death."

Kelly wasn't sure how to answer this. Why would her mother hire a lawyer secretly? "Okay Mr. Gregory, I'll bite. What do you want?"

She was sure she heard a distinct laugh this time. "Mr. Gregory, are you making fun of me?"

80

"I am sorry Ma'am," the voice was once again all business. "This is a very different type of business than I am use to conducting."

"I am afraid you have lost me once again Mr. Gregory," Kelly replied. This was getting more and more puzzling by the second. "Just what sort of business did you have with my mother?"

"Your Mother came to me to keep some things for her."

"What sort of things?" Kelly asked. This new mystery was starting to intrigue her. Her Mother had actually gone behind Morris' back. This was a side of her mom she hadn't realized existed. Kelly thought he mom must have been weak to stay with a man like that. But, every time she turned around she was finding a new strength to her mom. It seemed that she didn't really know her very well at all.

"Well, I would rather not get into it over the phone Mrs. Wells," the lawyer replied. "If you could make time to come to my office, I would be happy to explain every thing to you."

Kelly thought that maybe this was a trick but then again, what could be the purpose behind it? It wasn't as if she had anything that was worth scamming.. She knew she had to meet this guy. He had certainly peaked her interest and curiosity.

"When would be a good time to come to your office Mr. Gregory?"

"Would 10AM tomorrow be good with you?"

"Tomorrow?"

"Yes Ma'am," was his simple reply. "I waited this last month to give you time to get over your Mother's death but now is the time to get things in order."

"Things?"

"Your Mothers affairs," he continued in his soft but firm manner. "She left some property for you and a few papers. Basically, she had a Will and it's my duty to dispense it."

"A Will," Kelly asked shocked. "She can do that without her husband's knowledge?"

"Since they weren't legally married Mrs. Wells," he answered, "She could leave you anything she wished without Mr. Morris' knowledge."

"You know about the marriage being void?"

"Of course Ma'am," the lawyer seemed surprised at her shock of this. "I would not have taken Mrs. Morris as a client for this matter if I thought there was any way it could be illegal. I assure you I checked out the legalities immensely."

"I am sorry Mr. Gregory," Kelly quickly tried to sooth him, "I was not questioning your ethics. I am just surprised my mother has done something like this behind my fa..., behind Mr. Morris' back."

"Aw yes," Mr. Gregory was back to his firm business voice. "I can understand your shock Ma'am. Can you make it tomorrow morning? I will then be happy to explain the whole situation to you."

"Yes, I can make it" Kelly answered as she jotted down the time and address of the lawyer. "Thank-you Mr. Gregory for your call and I'll see you in the morning."

Kelly ended the call, thinking as she hung up the phone that her life was suddenly going to take another sharp turn. She wondered if this time it was going to be a turn for the better. She could use some good news for once. She also wondered if this could be the opportunity to find out why her mother had been so adamant about her moving.

Would this also answer the question of who her real father was? Was she finally going to get some truth? She had to stop thinking about all this for a while. She was beginning to get another headache.

She turned her thoughts to that voice. It should be illegal for a man to have such a sexy voice, especially when he seems totally unaware of it. Kelly had to laugh at herself. She would be willing to bet that when she finally met this man he would be in his fifties, balding, married and with a half dozen kids.

Chapter 11

The next morning at 10AM sharp Kelly found herself sitting across the cluttered desk of a nice looking man in his fifties, slightly balding and the picture on his desk showed a nice looking older lady and six girls. Do I know how to call it or what, Kelly laughed at herself.

Mr. Gregory might be soft spoken but his demeanor was that of a strong willed self-confident man. He looked up from the papers he was shuffling through and smiled. Kelly found an instant affinity for this man and felt she could trust him. His smile had gone clear to his eyes. It wasn't a forced formal one.

He stood up and held out his hand. As Kelly shook it, she also noted a firm but not an over clenching grip. This man didn't get his way with force, but he had a more subtle way of making his mark, Kelly surmised. Kelly smiled inwardly. She had found that since her conversations with Gloria about her late husband and the subtleties of men and force, she was watching everyone she met now and taking stock of how they acted towards others.

"Hello, Mrs. Wells," he spoke softly and indicated she should sit back down, "thank-you for coming today."

"How could I not," she replied back. "You definitely got my curiosity peaked. Going behind Morris back and getting her own lawyer just doesn't seem like my mother."

"Since you referred to your father as Morris yesterday and now, I'll assume you know he is not your real father," he commented. It wasn't a question, just an observation.

"Yes," she answered anyway. "He took great pleasure in telling me that fact the day of her funeral."

"I can believe that," he said back as he watched Kelly's reactions. "From what your Mother told me about him, I am surprised he waited that long." Kelly couldn't help thinking that he was very much like her psychiatrist. Maybe it took somebody who could read people to make a good lawyer. She looked around the cluttered room. Obviously Mr. Gregory was a hard worker though he didn't seem to be aiming for fame and riches in his clientele base.

"So," Kelly leaned forward asking, "you going to tell me what is going on?"

Mr. Gregory sat back in his chair and gave Kelly a long searching look. "Your mother was very fearful of your reaction to finding out about Mr. Morris not being your father."

"Relief was the first thing I felt Mr. Gregory," Kelly answered him honestly. "Then puzzlement over why Mom would keep such a thing from me."

"And have you thought about that question these last few weeks?"

Kelly had to smile. "You know you remind me so much of my psychiatrist. You sure your not related to her?"

"I doubt that," he smiled back. "I come from a family of all boys."

Kelly glanced to the picture again. "Looks like you made up for it."

"Oh, yes," he laughed as he took the picture tenderly in his hand. "Alma always wanted a boy, but alas, after 6 girls she finally gave up on the idea. I myself enjoy having daughters."

Kelly believed him as she watched him gaze at the picture, his eyes full of love. Now, that's the kind of love she wished she could find someday. He put the photo carefully back in its place and when he looked at Kelly he was all business once again. But, Kelly could see the tenderness just didn't quite leave his eyes. Such soft brown eyes they were. Kelly envied Alma this love she had from him.

"You managed to not answer my last question," he said as he looked back at Kelly.

"Of course I thought about it," Kelly spit out vehemently. "How could I not think about such a thing? My whole life has been a lie."

84

She looked at the man sitting across the desk from her. The last time she had been across a desk from a man had been when Morris had told her about her not being his child. She remembered his sneer, his cocky 'I don't give a damn' attitude. She had never hated anybody with her whole being before like she did Morris that day.

That day she was filled with questions about what the truth really was. Morris wouldn't help but maybe now things were going to change. This time a totally different man sat across the desk. Here was a man who had ethics, a man who cared about people, and a man who had answers and seemed willing to share them.

"Now," Mr. Gregory placed his hands on his desk and stood up once again. He reached for a small package sitting on top of a stack of papers. "Your mother made this video for you. She felt it was better than you reading the information you are going to receive or hearing it from another person. She just couldn't bring herself to tell you face to face." He handed Kelly a package with the tape in it.

"I have a TV set up in the next room where you can watch this then we will talk some more. I have more things to give you, but she will tell you what they are herself." He led Kelly to another door and escorted her into another room. It had a sofa and chair placed in front of a TV. She had a feeling that many people had gathered here to watch a pre-taped Will reading. He took the tape back from her and set it up in the VCR. Kelly sat down on the sofa waiting for him to turn it on.

"I'll be in the next room if you should need me," he said as he turned back to her before hitting the power button. "Can I get you anything to drink while you watch this?"

"No thank-you." He hit the play button and left the room, softly closing the door behind him. Kelly was alone now, half dreading what was on this tape, half holding her breath having trouble calmly waiting for it to start.

85

"My dear sweet daughter," Kate Morris' face came on the screen. The tape must have been made at least a year or more earlier for there was no sign of the ravages of the cancer that had worn away at her over the last year. She looked younger, more vital. It seemed that telling this story was something that lightened her heart. Kelly sat back to watch and hear what her mother had to tell her.

An hour later, Kelly was once again facing Mr. Gregory across his cluttered desk. He had had the foresight to have some hot coffee ready. She sipped it letting the warmth seep through her cold body. She was still trying to assimilate the information she had just gotten from the tape. Watching her mother talking on the tape, on the very sofa Kelly was sitting on watching it, was almost too much for her. She looked up with sorrowful eyes.

"Why did my Mother rob me of the chance to have a real loving father and brother? Why, if she knew Morris' wasn't my father, didn't she give me to the man who was? If this man, Weldon Shepard, is so great why did she leave him in the first place?" Kelly was asking these questions out loud though she didn't expect Mr. Gregory to answer them.

He didn't. He just let her ask them and think of the answers herself. Kelly had watched the video through and had listened to her mother's explanations to these questions. But, she still couldn't absorb it all. She knew she would have to watch the video many times before she could get a grip on her feelings. Maybe she would never understand all these feelings she was now going through.

Kelly had listened to her mother talk about a life that had happened before she was born. She had talked about a world that should have made anybody happy but for some reason had left her mother wishing for more. Or was it not so much her mother had wanted more but wanted different things than she had.

It seemed she had never wanted for anything with this man Weldon, but the life they led isolated on a Montana ranch was too much for her mother who craved for excitement. She had grown up on a ranch and now lived with

86

a husband on a ranch. She wanted to experience more than that. She had wanted to live in the city for a while, experience the night life.

Her mother had described how Morris had come into her life when she was feeling especially lonely and had offered her a life that seemed exciting. He had offered all she had yearned for, travel, city life, and parties. That wasn't what he gave her. Instead he gave her a life of pain, worry, and frustration.

One question Kelly had was, 'why did her mother stay with Morris after she found out what he really was?' Her mother had answered it.

Her mother was filled with shame first of all. This shame was strong enough to keep her from going back to her real husband, from asking him for forgiveness. Self-hatred was another thing. She had left behind a child she had deeply loved. She had thought at first she would be able to change Morris' mind about not raising another man's child. After Kelly was born and her mother realized he knew Kelly wasn't his and saw the way he treated her, she knew she would never see her boy again. She felt she deserved what she had gotten. It was punishment for the pain she had caused others.

The next question was, 'why didn't she give the new baby to her real father to raise her?' Kelly had wondered if maybe her mother had been afraid her father wouldn't accept the child, but after seeing this tape, she was sure it was another reason.

Though her mother never came right out with it, Kelly felt that if her mother had given Kelly up to her real father, she would have died right then. Her mother talked about how having Kelly with her all those years had been the only reason she had had for living. She had given up one child. She wasn't selfless enough to give up the other. She had done all she could to protect her child, though she knew she was failing at it. In the tape Kelly could see in her mother's eyes as she talked that she had been fully aware of the scars Kelly was going to have to live with.

"Mrs. Wells?" Mr. Gregory broke into her thoughts.

"I am so sorry Mr. Gregory," Kelly started to apologize but her cut her off.

"Nothing to apologize for," he assured her. "I was wondering if you wanted me to call your Doctor."

"My Doctor?" Kelly asked puzzled. "I don't need anything from him."

"I didn't mean your medical Doctor Mrs. Wells," he softly answered.

"Oh," Kelly replied. "I did mention I had a shrink didn't I?" She laughed softly and this brought a smile to Mr. Gregory's face. "I have her number on speed dial if I need it, thank-you."

"I am glad to see you are able to take this in as well as you have," he said softly. "I know it won't be easy processing all this new information?"

"I assure you Mr. Gregory," Kelly tried to explain how she was feeling. "I may look calm on outside but inside I am all jumbled up. I am not sure how I am feeling at this time."

"Anger towards your mother?" he asked carefully, watching how she reacted to this forward question.

Kelly sat quietly for a minute thinking about how she felt toward her mother. She had felt sadness for her, pity for her, but was there any anger? She dug down in her heart trying to picture her feeling anger toward the woman who had done so much to make a mess of her life, but ended up messing up the lives of so many other people. She knew there was anger, but was it directed at her mother?

She was angry at Morris, that was a given. The man had no idea what he did to other people, nor did he care. He was a man who cared only for his own comforts and desires. She knew her anger for him would never go away. She also knew that she had to let it go though, or it would eat her up, the same way her mother had been eaten up by her remorse for the bad choices she had made.

"I am angry," Kelly began carefully. "I am angry that she made the choices she did. I am angry that she was so selfish as to rob me of a chance at a real father who might have loved me. I am angry that, even though she knew her choices were the wrong ones, she kept making them. I am angry that she felt she had no choices left. I am angry with what she squandered. But, I am not angry at her. I pity her." Kelly looked up at Mr. Gregory who had sat silently through her little tirade. "I think that may be even worse."

Silence filled the room for a few minutes while the lawyer let Kelly compose herself. She was thankful that her mother had found such a nice and gentle man to do this for her. She suddenly wondered how her mother had found him, but decided now wasn't the time to ask. She knew that she had taken up a large amount of his day so far and he must be a busy man.

"You said you had some things Mom had left for me?"

"Yes," he answered quietly as he let Kelly shift things back to business. Kelly noticed how relieved he looked at this switch back to business. "She should have mentioned the items in the tape."

"Yes." Kelly tried to remember all the things her mother had mentioned. She had been surprised at the amount of things her mother had hid from Morris through the years. "I believe she had some jewelry, and she mentioned a bank account?"

"Yes," he answered simply as he pulled a bank passbook from the pile and handed it Kelly. Kelly looked at the amount logged in it and gasped. Her head spun at the size of the amount of money in the account.

"There must be some sort of a mistake here," she gasped! "There is no way my mother could have this much money!"

"Well she did and now it's yours," he asserted softly but firmly.

"But where did it come from," Kelly asked?

"When her mother died," Mr. Gregory explained. "She left this money and some property in Montana to your mother. That was about two years ago. That's when your mother came to me. She told me her whole story and that she didn't want her husband to know about the inheritance. Since they weren't legally married, she could do just that, keep it a secret. He has no claim on the money or the property. I helped your mother set up the account and put the property into your name."

"My name," Kelly looked up startled?

"Yes, by transferring everything into your name," he continued his explanation, "she was able to avoid you having to pay a substantial death tax."

"But, how did she do that?"

"Do you remember about two years ago when your mother had some papers for you to sign?"

Kelly tried to remember back that far. There was a time her mother had come to her and said she was setting up a small bank account for her son. She had needed Kelly's signature to set it up. Kelly had wondered why there had been so many papers for just a small account. When she asked to see the papers, her mother had grabbed them and said to not worry about anything she would make sure it was all set up. Kelly had let her do it since it seemed so important to her and had forgotten about it. There was an account for her son. She already had the passbook for that. He mother had brought it over shortly after she signed the papers.

"You mean the ones for Sheldon's bank account she wanted to set up?"

"That's how she got you to sign without asking questions," the lawyer chuckled. "Your mother was a resourceful person I might add."

"Yes," Kelly agreed with him. "Apparently she was."

Kelly looked at the large balance once again. She could quit her job and make the move to Montana at anytime and not worry about finances. She looked up at the lawyer who was waiting patiently for her to drink it all in.

"You said property?"

"Yes, it's a small house on the edge of Bozeman," he answered as he rummaged through the stack of papers. "Here it is." He handed over a

90

picture of a nice modest house set on a fairly large yard. It looked in remarkable shape. This must be an old photo.

"When was this taken," she asked?

"That was taken just this last summer," he answered. When Kelly looked up from the photo with a puzzled look, he continued. "Your mother made sure the house was well taken care of. There were tenants living there till this summer. She asked them to move so the place could be made ready for you and your son. I went out a couple of times to make sure all renovations and updates to the house were going along as planned."

This was really blowing Kelly's mind. So, this was where her mother had wanted her to move. Another thought entered her head. "How close is this to my father?"

"About a mile from his main house," Mr. Gregory replied. "The property is adjacent to his. It once was a nice sized ranch also, but your grandmother sold off most the property to Mr. Shepard many years ago. She had kept the house and 5 acres for herself.

I think she had always hoped her daughter would return and wanted her to have a place to stay if she did. When she passed, she left everything she had, which as you can see was quite significant, to her only child. The only stipulation was that it could not fall into the hands of her daughter's illegal husband. Your mother agreed with that and that's when we set everything up to make sure it was yours without any claims from Mr. Morris."

"You're sure he can't claim this?"

"To do so would mean producing a valid marriage certificate to Kate," Mr. Gregory said as he pulled yet another piece of paper from the pile. He handed it to Kelly. It was her Mothers marriage certificate to Weldon Shepard. "He would also have to produce a divorce decree. And since there never was one, he can't lay claim to anything your mother inherited from her mother. In fact, he would open himself up to the legal issues."

91

"I would like to see him try," Kelly smiled bitterly. She thought of something else. "Does my real father know about this house and who it went to?"

"I can't say," was the lawyer's evasive answer, and Kelly had the feeling he knew a lot about the matter he wasn't telling her.

Chapter 12

Spring was in the air. Bryant stood outside the horse barn leaning against the corral fence soaking up the yet weak sun. The last six months had changed Bryant drastically. First, his weakened and underweight frame had filled out and strengthened from the good food made by the housekeeper Rosa. He learned fast Rosa was a force to be reckoned with. You ate what she put in front of you or she took it as a personal insult. Eating her food wasn't a problem. Her cooking was superb and brought back the hearty appetite he once had.

Second, he gained not only weight but renewed muscle tone from the hard work Shel pushed on him. From day one Shel had not let him feel pity for himself nor did he give any mercy. He pulled Bryant out of bed the morning after they arrived at 5:15AM. He tossed him some old clothes he had dug out of a box and dragged Bryant's ass down to the kitchen table.

Weldon was already attacking a large stack of pancakes and sausage. He could hear the fork hitting the plate as Weldon shoveled in each mouthful. Bryant's nose was assailed with the smells of pancakes, sausage, bacon, and eggs. He found his chair and before he was seated Rosa had placed a heaping platter before him. He forgot how he had lost his appetite while in the hospital and went about attacking his plate in a similar manner as Weldon's. He could hear Rosa murmuring her appreciation of his hearty appetite as she went back to her stove. He would learn soon that she was happiest when she was sure the guys were getting their fill and enjoying her cooking.

Third, Bryant's attitude had done a complete 360 degree turn. He had to in order to survive. It was obvious from that first day the Shepard's weren't going to wait on him or let him slide. He was going to earn his keep or die trying. And that was exactly how Bryant had felt that first night after Shel had put him to work in the barn. His muscles ached from head to toe, and he felt dying would be a better solution. He took a hot shower instead

93

and let deep sleep take him for the night. The next day seemed just a fraction easier.

Most horses were kept outside, except the main riding stock. They were kept stalled, brushed daily, and basically spoiled. Bryant's first lesson was how to muck a stall. He learned it by having Shel place a pitch fork in his hand and aiming him at a pile of dirty straw in a stall.

Each morning the horses were let out in the paddock to get exercise and that was when the men cleaned the stalls. Bryant had never held a pitchfork in his hand before and had no idea how to actually use one. And not being able to see Shel or the other men doing it, he was totally in the dark as to what to do. Fortunately Shel had enough mercy to talk him through the procedure of forking the dirty straw and depositing it in the wheelbarrow that was at the entrance of the stall.

After a few attempts, most of them missing the wheelbarrow, Bryant finally found his farm legs, so to speak, and was actually making good time. He had some trouble getting use to the smells of the barn though. First there was the smell of the horses themselves. It was rather strong and musky. Then there was the scent of the fresh straw which was kept in bundles to one end of the enormous barn. As he passed the feed bunker he could smell the grains and hay used for the horses. Last, but definitely not least, was the sour odor of the horse dung in the dirty straw. That was one scent he could have done without. How could anybody spend their whole life smelling this stuff? The second day, Bryant found that the dung smell didn't hit his senses so hard. It got easier to stand the smell as each new day passed. Like everything else they became part of the surroundings around him.

By the end of that first day Bryant was so exhausted he didn't think he would make it past supper. When he went to his room to get showered up he was very tempted to go straight to bed afterwards rather than make his way back downstairs to supper. As he was finishing up his shower though, the smells of Rosa's cooking wound their way up the stairs and through his door. The mouth watering scents of roasted beef, potatoes and some other foods he couldn't identify wrapped themselves around him and pulled him down the steps. After many slices of roast beef, southwestern beans and cornbread, Bryant was beginning to feel more like his old self.

He went back to the barn the second day thinking things would go smoothly not realizing the playfulness of the cowhands. Seems there was an initiation he would have to go through to be accepted as one of them.

Bryant had wondered what they thought about having a blind guy come in amongst them. The first day not one person approached him to say hi or anything else. He could hear their whisperings around the place as he went back and forth to the dung heap with his wheelbarrow. He just ignored them and concentrated on not missing the barrow when he flung the dung, and in not going the wrong way when he had to unload it in the pile outside.

One thing about Bryant was his sense of direction. It didn't take him long to get his marks down and know exactly where he was by either counting steps or the sounds and smells in the area he was standing.

The second day Bryant learned what it meant to be one of the gang. He was wheeling his fully loaded barrow toward the far door to dump it when he hit something and it flung over dumping the contents to the floor. Grumbling beneath his breath Bryant righted the wheelbarrow and started scooping up the spilt dung and straw.

He took the first hit of horse droppings to the head. It was followed by several others coming from multiple directions. Bryant dived behind his barrow positioning it the best to reflect the most flung dung and started heaving any dung balls he could find with-in his reach. A self satisfying reaction went through him when he heard a sharp yelp by one man when one his dung balls hit their mark.

He honed in on the sound and pelted more that way. Systematically, by using his ears for any sounds coming from the direction of the dung balls, Bryant found his marks and soundly got them back.

He heard roaring laughter coming from the men as they played out their small battle with Bryant in the center. By the time it was over Bryant and all the rest of the cowboys were covered in dung. He could hear them coming his way and readied himself for another battle. Instead, he found them clapping him on the back and congratulating him on surviving the dung war.

A throat clearing loudly behind them stopped the noisy cowboys in mid shout. Bryant knew instinctively it was Weldon himself. He knew it wasn't Shel because he had figured out during the dung fight that Shel was one of the assailants. He had recognized the yelp when he hit him with a good throw. He could hear the men shuffling around him, trying to look innocent he was certain, but the ravages of their little war were very evident.

"I hope you fellas had a good time here," Weldon drawled out slowly in his even tone. Bryant couldn't tell if he was angry or not. Apparently the guys weren't too certain either, since from the murmuring around him, he could hear a few, 'we gonna catch it now,' floating around him.

"Dad," Shel stepped forward, "I'm the one to blame here. I let them, ah… well we were just, ah…" Bryant almost burst at laughing at Shel's stumbling.

"Yes," Weldon's voice had a definite tone of mirth in it as he struggled to sound stern, as if lecturing a group of school boys on their arrant ways. "I do hold you totally responsible. You're supposed to be the boss and you're the worst one in the bunch. Now, you all better get this mess cleaned up." Weldon started to turn to leave but stopped.

"By the way boys," he added with jest, "good thing none of you boys were using real ammo. Bryant would have had all your asses in slings." He turned away shoulders shaking with suppressed laughter. From that day on, Bryant was one of the 'boys' and each man took it upon himself to show him the ropes. He wasn't treated like a blind man, just an inexperienced bloke who needed guidance.

Now, standing here six months later Bryant had trouble believing how well he had taken to the rancher's life. He liked the active life and roughing it was part of Military life, but to move to such an isolated area so far from the city's night life? Bryant had thought the night life meant too much to him. When he lived in the city with his fiancée they went out every night. The exotic food, the dancing, the noise, he had loved the crowds. He also liked the times spent with his men on a mission. The camaraderie with them was different than he had ever had with other male friends.

Once he had proven himself to the cowboys there was once again that sort of camaraderie. He enjoyed their company, their jokes, but he thought he would also miss the company of his old friends and women. He didn't. Well, he had to admit the company of a woman would be nice once in a while, but he had no plans to give his heart again.

As he leaned against the paddock fence he wondered if he had even given his heart in the first place. After the initial shock of Julian's abrupt betrayal, Bryant realized he was relieved she was gone. He was starting to realize that she wouldn't be happy being a soldier's wife. For that matter the only type of wife she would be happy being was a rich one. He knew that his status as the potential heir to a vast family fortune was what drew her to him, but for the life of him he couldn't remember what drew him to her.

He threw his head back and laughed. He wished he could see her face when she found out he traded his fatigues for cowboy boots and jeans. That would be precious. He was proud of what he had learned here.

He could now muck stalls with the best of them, if anybody laid claim to being the best stall mucker that is. He could ride any horse they gave him, and in their jesting ways, he had been given some pretty green horses. It had become a game to see if he could stay on any horse. One thing this did was make Bryant a good bronco rider. His determination to stay on a horse was greater then their determination to see him thrown to the ground.

He also learned to read the small nuances of how a horse sounded and felt beneath him at different gaits or in different moods. He could now read a horse's mood and if it was in good condition or if something was wrong with it.

97

Right now he was relaxing and waiting for Shel. The two of them were riding up into the mountains to a cabin the Shepard's had up there. Bryant was looking forward to a few days of just rest and relaxation. He'd also noticed that Shel and his father had been on edge for a few weeks. He had no idea what it was about, but could feel a strain between them.

Chapter 13

Bryant heard voices coming from around the corner of the barn. Shel and his father were having some words. Bryant didn't hear them arguing very often and was uneasy when it happened around him. He hoped they would finish whatever it was before they reached him and realized he could hear them.

"And you have no idea who it could be." Shel's angry voice floated around the corner. Fortunately they had stopped on the other side. "Why didn't you buy the place after granny died?"

"I couldn't buy it," Weldon answered in his usual reserved voice. Bryant was amazed at how much it took to light his torch and get him mad. He wished he had Weldon's patience and self control. Weldon would have made a good field captain.

"And, why not," came Shel's heated response. Bryant couldn't figure out what they could be talking about. Far as he knew, Weldon owned everything for miles around.

"Your granny left it to somebody," Weldon answered.

"Her?" Shel asked heatedly. "But she is dead, gone. And why would Granny leave it to her? She wouldn't have the nerve to come back here! She didn't have the nerve to come back here!"

"No," Weldon answered again in his quiet way. "It wasn't left to your mother from what I understand."

"Then who was it and why didn't they come back here sooner?" Shel was really steaming now. Bryant could just picture him getting red faced and beads of sweat breaking out on his forehead. Shel had always had a bit of a temper. Bryant had worked hard to teach him some temperance of it when they were training together.

Weldon must have finally reached his breaking point. His voice raised just a touch as he answered his frustrated son. "Why do you think I have all the answers," he barked out like a staff sergeant with new recruits. "I really didn't have that close of a relationship with your Granny. She didn't confide in me as to whom she left her inheritance to, and frankly I really didn't care."

"As long as it wasn't to Mom," Shel's voice cracked at the word that should have been easy for any son to say. There were a few moments of silence before Weldon answered.

"Actually son," he said so softly Bryant barely heard it, "I almost wished it had been her. We need to close this whole deal." Bryant could hear the crunch of the older mans footsteps as he turned and walked the other direction. They seemed slower, more dragging than usual. His heart went out to the older man. It must have been hell having your wife leave and then to raise a son alone, not knowing the answers to his questions.

Bryant heard Shel resume in his direction so turned back toward the paddock trying to act like he hadn't heard a word. He put all his concentration on the horse and cowboy working in the paddock. The young man came up beside him and leaned against the railing with a sigh.

"Bryant?"

"Yes?"

"What's worse," Shel asked slowly, "Not knowing your parent because they left or knowing them and having them turn their back on you?"

Bryant knew what Shel was referring to. Just as Bryant knew the bare details to Shel's mother's abandonment, Shel knew the bare facts to Bryant's father disowning his son for not following in the family business. He didn't take offense to the question either.

"I have no idea," he answered carefully. "I have the feeling neither is any better than the other." They both stood there silently for a while.

Bryant was listening to the horse being worked out on a tether line. "Shel, which horse is out there?"

"That's Posse," he answered. "Why?"

"You better have his left forelock checked." Shel was silent for a moment. Bryant felt him turn toward the center of the paddock where the

100

horse and trainer were. Shel watched the horse do a couple rotations around the paddock and giving an exclamation jumped the fence. Bryant could hear him yelling at the cowboy to hold up the horse.

"Hey, spuds," he yelled, "hold that horse."

"What's up Boss," asked the startled man as he stopped the horse and took a hold of the harness. Shel came up beside the horse; gently murmuring to it laid his hand on its shoulder, and stroking its neck to calm it down. He leaned over and gently lifted the left leg up. He examined the leg and hoof carefully before letting it down gently, all the time softly talking to the horse and stroking its neck. Bryant could hear the murmurs and as always was amazed at how good Shel was with animals, especially the horses. He had a soft touch that made even the most anxious horse settled under his touch and soft voice.

"Take Posse into her stall and call the doc," he instructed Spuds, giving him a hard look. "Looks like a pulled a muscle. You should have seen her favoring that leg. Hell, Bryant somehow noticed something was amiss." He turned his back to the astonished cowhand and headed back to Bryant.

"Jeeze, Bryant," Shel exclaimed as he got closer, "how did you even know she was hurting? I could barely see her favoring that leg. Thanks to you, it seems we caught it early."

"I'm not sure," he admitted. "Just, she didn't seem to be moving in a very smooth way. I could hear it."

"You're getting good," Shel added. He didn't realize he was pointing out what Bryant feared the most. Did the improving of his other senses mean his sight loss was permanent?

"Yah," Bryant replied bitterly, "isn't that just wonderful." He turned and headed for the barn. He just wanted to get going and try not to think of what life held in store for him if his sight never returned. After all, he couldn't hide out here for ever. Shel caught up to him and they saddled their horses silently.

101

"Shel," Bryant asked after they had been riding the trail for what seemed like hours? "You're not just leading me up into these mountains to lose me or something?"

"If it were that easy to lose you," Shel laughed, "I'd have done it sooner."

"You wouldn't want to be around when I found my way back," Bryant responded good-naturedly. "So, how far is this cabin?"

"I'd say about another half hours ride," he answered. "In all, it's about a little more than a 3 hrs ride. Not that far as the crow flies but riding distance it is."

"So," Bryant continued, "It's pretty isolated?"

"Yes," Shel answered. The questions were bringing him out of the shell he had wrapped around himself since his argument with his father. "The only way in or out is by horse. Not even a motorbike could make these trails."

"It so fresh up here," Bryant observed. "The smells are so different than lower down before we entered the trees."

"I never noticed."

"I never did either," Bryant remarked. They both ignored the meaning of 'before' that they both thought of. "I knew when we were approaching the stream long before we reached it. I could smell a difference in the air. I could smell the water, so to say."

"Really?"

"Then I could hear it," Bryant continued with his description. "The murmuring of it flowing over the rocks started out soft then got louder as we approached. I suppose I had always heard these things but never paid attention to them."

"Neither have I," Shel answered back. There seemed to be some awe in his voice. Listening to Bryant describe the area through his senses made Shel experience it all anew.

"Why didn't we go over the bridge rather than thru the water?"

Shel nearly fell off his horse when he jerked around to stare at his friend. "How did you know there was a bridge over the stream? We were at least a quarter of a mile from it."

"It was downstream from where we splashed across," Bryant explained. "I could hear a difference in the water pitch as it hit it and the change in speed after."

"Well, I'll be damned," Shell replied with a laugh.

"So," Bryant asked again, "You going to answer my question?"

"What was the question again," Shel asked.

"You know, Shel," Bryant answered in a mock menacing voice, "I can still whip your ass on your best day."

"Yah, only in your dreams, Capt'n," Shel laughed out loud. "Anyway, in answer to your very serious question, we were heading in a different direction and would have had to go out of our way to cross at the bridge. I might also add that it is rather little more than a foot bridge and not designed for horses to tramp over. What's the beef anyway; you afraid to get a little wet Capt'n?"

"There was that so hard," Bryant added in an even tone that belied his mirth at Shel's reply. "You know, someday somebody is going to wipe that smirk off your face."

At that Shel burst out laughing. That was Bryant's intent to begin with. It was all they needed to have Shel encased in his own inner world for the whole week they were planning on being here.

"So, tell me Capt'n," Shel continued, not even realizing he had fallen into the familiar address to his former Captain, "What else you notice along the trail?"

"It got definitely cooler the minute we went from grassland to forest."

"That's a given," Shel laughed. "The fact the trees filter out the sun is something we learned in our youth. Of course, having grown up a city slicker, you might not have noticed something like it before." Bryant leaned

103

over and broke a small branch off a limb overhanging the trail and tossed it at Shel, hitting him squarely on the head. "Ow, hey Capt'n!"

"That serves you right for being insolent," Bryant said through his laughter. He added more seriously, "It's another thing you're aware of and I know it."

"I know Capt'n," Shel answered back, still laughing at himself, "but you expected me to be insolent. I couldn't disappoint you."

"Don't worry," Bryant replied, "You didn't." They both had a good laugh again before they resumed their quiet ride, but now it was less strained.

Bryant rained in his horse, "Shel," he called in a stage whisper. "Shel!" He called again when Shel failed to stop. Shel pulled up and looked back. Bryant was pointing into the trees. Shel inched his mount backwards to get closer to Bryant and to get at the right angle to see what he was pointing to.

"Oh my," he breathed softly.

"A large buck," Bryant whispered. "I would say at least a 10 pointer."

"Now how the hell..." Shel shook his head in wonder. "He is a big one, that's for sure."

"I have been listening to smaller animals scurrying through the brush all morning," Bryant explained. "I could tell how small by the noise they made. Well, I have to admit that this baby when he was moving made a lot of noise."

"I didn't hear a thing," Shel admitted. "I would have missed him all together, and he's not 20 feet away."

"Maybe this higher sense of hearing isn't such a bad thing," Bryant commented quietly, "I am beginning to see more this way."

Indeed, Bryant realized that he was appreciating the scents and sounds of life around him more. He found if he opened his mind to what he smelled and heard he could picture what was making them. So far on this trip he had opened himself to all his senses and it was almost like he could see where they were. He knew when they were approaching the stream, when they passed a lake. They had both had a heavier feel in the air because of the extra moisture in it.

He felt the breeze on his face lessen as they got closer to the trees, then the shade of the leaves and the cooler air let him know when they had actually entered the tree line and had climbed higher.

Small rodents scurried from under leaves on the trail as they approached, squeaking as they went. He knew when it was a mouse or a rabbit. He knew once it was something larger like a fox maybe. He wasn't sure what sort of animals called this place home to be sure. He also knew when they passed through a clearing because he could feel the sun on his face.

He smelled the Buck before he heard him. It had a much stronger musky scent than the horse he was riding. He then heard it walking through the brush just off the trail. He stopped as the horses came near. Bryant heard it snort as it froze. He could just see it in his mind's eye, standing there head up, nostrils flared as he sniffed the air to see if what was approaching could be determined a danger.

He heard it paw the ground but not move to run off just yet. He could just see the three of them standing staring at each other, the two men and the buck. Shel's horse was the one to break the spell that had fallen on all of them. A small rodent running out of the brush and past its hoof made the horse snort and start. Shel gave a startled yelp as he pulled the horse to a standstill. This was the catalyst to move the Buck. He snorted again rather loudly, turned tail and crashed through the underbrush up the mountain side.

"Man, Bryant," Shel whispered before catching himself and speaking normally. "That was a beautiful sight."

"Yes it was," Bryant agreed before turning his horse back toward the trail. "Yes it was." They resumed the ride and went the rest of the way in silence. Bryant smiled, trying to picture Shel riding with his eyes half closed trying to see what Bryant was experiencing.

"We're there," Shel announced unnecessarily. Bryant could tell by the eagerness of the horses. They had suddenly picked up their pace about a mile back. He could hear and smell the mountain stream that was less then a quarter mile from the cabin.

"You know something Shel?"

"What?"

"If I never get my sight back," Bryant hesitated, and then finished his thought, "I know it's not the end of my life."

"About damn time you figured that out," Shel replied back curtly as he dismounted his horse and started leading her to the stalls behind the cabin. Bryant followed suit and was following behind when his horse, Peachy, suddenly reared back pulling Bryant with her. He stumbled over an exposed tree root and let go of the reins as he fell.

"Bryant," Shel called out!

Peachy continued to back up till she came in contact with an exposed root also and went down. Bryant jumped up feeling the pain in his ankle but ignoring it as he rushed to his horse. Shel was by his side instantly. They got the startled horse quieted before she did herself more harm, and then urged her to her feet. Bryant held the halter while Shel ran his hands down her legs.

"Well?"

"She's scraped up some," Shel murmured as he worked his hands over her hind legs. "She is favoring her left hind leg, doesn't look or feel broke. I'd say a nasty sprain."

He looked over toward Bryant. "I'd say she isn't hurt as bad as you."

"I'm not hurt," Bryant snorted.

"Yah right," Shel threw back at him, "you always stand on one foot."

Bryant looked down and realized he was favoring his right foot. "I don't think it's broken," he said as he gingerly tried to put weight on it. The

106

pain went shooting through him like hot lead. "But I suspect it's sprained somewhat."

Bryant cast Shel a sardonic look. "I've had worse."

"Somewhat," it was Shel's turn to snort! "I'll get you to the cabin and the horses to the stalls. You can remove your boots so I can get a good look at your foot.

Bryant handed Shel the halter, but turned toward the cabin on his own. "You think I'm going to let you get your cold hands on my feet," he managed to get out in a rather strained voice, "you better think again. Go tend to the horses. I'll get myself inside."

"You're a stubborn man Capt'n," Shel called out as he led peachy over to where his horse was waiting. He got a hold of the reins with his free hand and started leading both horses around toward the back of the cabin.

"You best not be forgetting that lieutenant," he heard Bryant yell after him. He just shook his head. At least now the man was acting like his old stubborn self.

Bryant made it to the sofa and removed his boots. He did a self examine and was leaning back trying to will the pain away when Shel came inside. He looked up, "Is Peachy ok?"

"She's comfortable," he replied as he walked past Bryant into the cooking area. This part of the cabin was one big room with the kitchenette to the left of the front door and the living area to the right. Two sofas were placed either side a large stone fireplace. Shel had come in through the side door that was back by the wall that separated the sleeping rooms. There were two rooms with bunks in them, a shared bath between them. He heard Shel banging some pots around.

"What are you doing?"

"I am getting you some warm water to soak your foot in," Shel answered. I got the generator running while I was out back. We should have hot water shortly. How's your foot feel?"

107

"I'll live," Bryant answered gruffly. He had had worse scrapes while in the Special Forces. "One thing about these cowboy boots, they sure protect the ankle."

"And people thought cowboys were dumb," Shel laughed as he brought over the large pan full of water and Epson salts. "Here, soak in this for about 20 minutes and we'll see how it looks."

"So," Bryant leaned back as his foot soaked, "what's the plan now?"

"It's too late to do anything tonight," Shel answered as he started piling logs in the fireplace. "Tomorrow, I got to figure how to get you and Peachy back down the mountain. She didn't break anything but she can't carry any weight."

"I'll stay here while you go down," Bryant was quick to say, "It's as simple as that."

"You think so," Shel glanced over at his now confident looking former commander?

"Yes," he replied lightly, "I think I am a big enough boy now to handle being alone for a day or two."

Bryant couldn't see Shel looking at him thoughtfully. He figured the delay was from him mulling over the idea. Perhaps counting in his mind how many ways Bryant could get himself hurt being alone up here. He waited for an argument over the subject preparing himself for a battle. Shel surprised him with his simple answer, "Ok."

Chapter 14

"Mommy," Kelly heard the wail from the back seat! "I got to go pee!"

"Ok, sweetie," she answered back softly. He had been so good during the long drive down. She knew he was getting restless. Riding in a car from Chicago to Montana was relentless enough for an adult, for a six year old it was torture. She had filled the back seat with his favorite books, comics, toys, and his blanket and pillow.

She made it a three day trip. Whenever she saw something that might interest a six year old she stopped for a while to let Sheldon roam and stretch his legs. It also made the drive easier on her. Watching Shel explore new places gave her a chance to not think about who was at the end of the road, but she was now ready to get there.

It was a good thing they were almost to their new home. She spied a sign for a truck stop just outside Bozeman and pulled in. It was nearly lunchtime so they could kill two birds with one stone. "Would you like some lunch while we're here?"

"Yes, yes, yes," he eagerly shouted back! Kelly just grinned and shook her head. If only she could bottle that energy.

Kelly found an empty parking spot in the busy place and led Sheldon to the restrooms. She couldn't help but notice as she waited for him to come out that nearly everybody who passed her in the hallway did a double take. Most were polite, said a quick hi, or tipped their hat as they hurried on by. 'Polite folks around here she thought.'

There were a few who down right stared at her though as they went by, but none stopped to talk to her. Kelly was wondering what was up as she noticed people watching her and Sheldon walk to a booth in the back corner. She could hear the murmured whisperings and had the feeling it was about her.

The waitress came over with menus and water. "Hello dear," she addressed Kelly in a brisk friendly way, though Kelly could see that she too was studying her closely.

This was a busy place just off a main highway. It couldn't be a stranger was rare here. The waitress had soft kind eyes and her warm smile could be seen in them. Kelly couldn't help but warm up to the older lady right away. The waitress continued after Kelly smiled back at her. "Hey, there sweetie," she said to Sheldon, "ain't you just a little cutie?"

"I want to see a cowboy," was all he said as he stood on the seat to look out the window! "I don't see any horsies!"

"Oh, they don't ride horses this way anymore," the waitress laughed, "You will have to go to a ranch to see one."

"We're going to a ranch," Sheldon excitedly told the lady, "we're going to live way out in the country. Isn't that great?"

"That sounds wonderful," the lady laughed again before turning to Kelly. "Nice boy you got there."

"Thank-you," Kelly murmured back. She saw the lady's name tag. "You're Mavis? I thought waitresses named Mavis only existed in commercials." Kelly laughed. Mavis smiled broadly back at her.

"Well," she laughed as she answered back, "It beats being called Vera."

"I'll leave you to look the menu over," she continued. "I'll be back in a moment."

Mavis scurried away and Kelly watched her disappear through the kitchen door. 'At least there is one friendly person here,' she thought as she checked out the menu. Sheldon's order was easy, he was on a grilled cheese and French fries kick.

Mavis disappeared into the kitchen and headed straight for the phone. She shook her head as she dialed a very familiar number. She knew Weldon would be interested in this. When he answered on the other end,

Mavis didn't waste time with niceties. "Listen Sugar," she said to the man on the other line. "You need get yourself out here to the stop."

"Don't argue with me," she spit out excitedly, "just get over here now!" She hung up.

She realized the grizzled old cook was staring at her. She pointed for him to look out over the counter. He did. "Holy shit!" He turned back to Mavis. "Does Weldon know?"

"He will when he gets here," she answered. "I better get out there. We don't want her getting suspicious. Mavis adjusted her cap on her head and went back towards Kelly and Sheldon.

Weldon hung up the phone and turned just as his son walked in the door.

"What are you doing here?"

"Hello to you too," Shel replied as he sat down. "Bryant's horse got skittish and hurt her hind leg. I had to bring her down for the vet to look over."

"Serious," asked Weldon as he pulled up a chair? He glanced at the phone as he sat down. Shel could see he seemed distracted.

"No, I think just a bad sprain. I wrapped it before leading her back home," he answered, then added, "Who was that on the phone?"

"Mavis," Weldon answered abstractedly. "She wants me to come down to the stop right away."

"Why?"

"I have no idea," Weldon answered, "but she sounded funny."

"Well, go on down," Shel got up from the table. "I am going to shower and change then go see what the vet had to say."

"Where's Bryant," Weldon suddenly realized Shel was alone.

"He's still at the cabin," Shel answered as he headed toward the back stairs.

"You left him up there alone?"

111

"He's a big boy Dad," Shel laughed to hide his own discomfort. "He can take care of himself. Anyway I left him a cell so he can call if he needs anything." He started for the door again but stopped before heading up. He had a strange feeling he couldn't identify in the pit of his stomach. He just felt that things were going to change around here drastically, though he had no idea how or why.

"Dad," he said. "You go see your girl and find out what's got into her bonnet and call me if you need me."

"Why would I need you," asked Weldon gruffly?

"Stranger things have happened," Shel laughed as he disappeared up the stairs.

Weldon hesitated a moment. He looked at the calendar. Today was the day the new owner was supposed to move into his late Mother-in-law's house. An unsettled feeling grew in the pit of his stomach.

He knew who had inherited it, but had not said anything to Sheldon. He didn't want to till he had met the girl. He knew once they met he would know upon looking at her if she was his or Morris'. Nobody knew she was coming so if that was the girl that got Mavis so wound up there was only one way she could know. She must resemble him or Shel. He grabbed his hat and charged out the door.

Shel stood by his window and watched his father drive off toward town and the truck stop. He knew his father had been seeing Mavis the last few months. It had started shortly after they had found out his Mother had died.

Weldon had not dated or gone out with anybody after she had abandoned them. He had spent all those years loyal to a paper that his mother had not seen fit to honor. But when he had heard the news, he knew he was free to pursue the one lady in the area he had always liked. Sheldon was happy that she had liked him back. Weldon had waited a month then out of the blue started going to the stop nearly everyday. Then he had asked Mavis to a movie and it continued from there.

112

Shel was happy for his father. He deserved to be happy. He couldn't help but wonder why Mavis would call and tell him to rush down there like that. Oh, well, guess he would find out soon enough. He tossed off his dusty clothes and entered the shower, letting the hot water rinse his cares away for a while.

Chapter 15

"I want to see a cowboy," the young boy demanded!

Mavis came up with their order as he said this and laughed. "Don't you worry your lil' head about that young man," she told him cheerfully. "There are plenty of cowboys around here. You won't have to wait long to see one." She placed the grilled cheese and fries in front of the boy and the grilled chicken salad in front of his mother.

"Your new to these parts I take it," she tried to ease into a conversation with the lady.

"Yes, we just arrived," Kelly answered. "We are moving here as Sheldon said before."

Mavis was without words for a minute. She just stared at the girl before finding her voice. "You said Sheldon?"

"Yes," Kelly answered. She looked up at the friendly waitress and saw a strange look in her eyes? She wasn't sure what to make of it. Maybe this lady knew her brother, but she didn't ask.

"May I ask where about you're moving to," Mavis pressed again. "I know this whole area quite well."

"To Millie Malone's old place," Kelly answered watching the older lady's face carefully. She saw the strange look deepen the woman's eyes but it didn't seem to be surprise.

"Yes, I know it," Mavis answered. "You're renting?" This girl's answer would confirm everything. She had to be Kate Well's daughter. This was a close knit area and everybody knew about how Kate had run off with a stranger from back east. She, had been Kate's best friend, but she hadn't had any idea that Kate was pregnant when she left. Kate must not have known either or she wouldn't have done such a thing. At least Mavis hoped she wouldn't have.

"No," Kelly answered carefully. She knew she was being pumped for answers. This lady seemed friendly so she didn't feel threatened by it and decided to answer her questions. Seems she would know soon enough anyway. Kelly would bet the house gossip ran faster than water in these parts. "I inherited it from my mother, who inherited it from Millie."

Mavis opened her mouth to say something but before she could a voice behind her interrupted her. "Mavis dear," the older man asked quietly, "would you please get me a cup of coffee?"

"Yes, of course Weldon," the flustered woman replied as she hurried away, looking back as she went. "Well, I'll be," she said under her breath. She had been right in her assumptions.

Weldon and Kelly stared at each other for a moment until Sheldon burst out. "Are you a cowboy?"

That broke the ice and both Weldon and Kelly laughed nervously. Weldon pointed to the seat next to the boy and she nodded. "Yes, son," he answered the boy as he sat next to him. "I sure am a cowboy."

"I'm Weldon Shepard," he introduced himself to Kelly

"I thought as much," Kelly answered. "I'm Kelly Wells and this is my son Sheldon." Weldon stared at the boy for a long moment.

"Hi there Sheldon," he said to the boy. "So you want to see some cowboys?"

"Do you have a horsy," the boy asked excitedly?

"Of course," the older man answered him patiently. Kelly could see he was good with kids. "What good cowboy doesn't have a horsy?"

"Can I see it," the boy asked even more excited?

Weldon looked at Kelly who was quietly watching the two of them interact. "I think that can be arranged," he answered the boy, "but only if you finish your sandwich and fries." As the child dug into his food, Weldon turned his attention to Kelly.

She looked so much like her mother and her brother. He could see why Mavis called him like she did. It must have been a shock for her to see

116

this girl walk in. He looked around and realized that most of the patrons were watching them. He suddenly felt like he was in a fishbowl for all to observe. He turned back to the girl trying to ignore all the eyes on them.

"I take it the house is finished?" he asked unnecessarily. He had been watching the remodeling progress impatiently. He had to admit to himself he half feared the time it would be ready and half agonized over how long it was taking. The time for them to finally meet each other took too long in coming but came too soon. He didn't feel ready, though he had tried to prepare himself for this. He had missed twenty-seven years and he knew he would never get any of that back.

He hadn't been fully sure if she was his child or not. He hadn't even been aware there was a child in the first place until a Mr. Gregory approached him after Millie had passed on. It seems she had hired him to keep an eye on her daughter and to aid her if and when she needed it. He had learned sometime after Kate had run that there was a daughter and there was a good chance she was his, but she had chosen to not tell him.

He had been very angry with Millie when he had found out but by then she was gone and there was nothing he could do about his anger. It also seemed that it was too late to have a relationship with his daughter. He knew that Millie had left the bulk of her money and other property to Kate. He didn't care. Millie had already sold most of the property to him rather cheaply with the expressed promise it would be for Shel. Shel didn't know it yet but Weldon had already put all the property he had received from Millie in his name.

All she had kept was five acres and her house which he also knew she had left to Kate. He had wondered at that time if Kate would return but when the place was rented out, he got his answer. He hadn't told Shel who had gotten the house, though he could guess Shel suspected. After all, who else could it have been? Kate was Millie's only child. With the news of Kate's passing he knew from Mr. Gregory that the girl, Kelly, had inherited all her grandmother's properties and money and would be moving to the house.

117

One thing Mr. Gregory wouldn't or couldn't tell him was if Kelly was his or Morris's. Well, it had only taken one look to know.

"Yes," Kelly answered softly. She had been watching the emotions flitting across Weldon's face since he had arrived. She could see the uncertainty that was in his eyes though his voice was still solid. It had faltered just once when he had first addressed Sheldon. She figured hearing that name had shook him some. He couldn't have known that he had a grandson; much less that he was named after his son.

"Is it furnished?" he asked. He was trying to keep the conversation normal for the sake of the boy sitting her next to him. That was another thing Mr. Gregory had failed to tell him. He had had no idea that he was a grandfather. He could see both Shel and Kelly in the boy. His heart swelled with pride, he was a grandpa.

"Yes, everything was supposed to have arrived last week," she answered. "Mr. Gregory told me it was all set." Weldon looked surprised at that name.

"Mr. Gregory?"

"Yes," she replied. "He was Mom's solicitor. You know him?"

"Yes," he answered thoughtfully, "He was also your grandmother's solicitor."

"Oh," she answered quietly, "I guess I shouldn't be surprised. He seemed to know much more than he was actually saying."

This time Weldon did laugh. He explained his mirth when he saw the surprise on Kelly's face. "I got that same feeling the few times I talked with the man myself." Kelly chuckled in agreement with her newly found father.

Sheldon had been patiently sitting and eating his sandwich half listening to the two adults talk, but a child's patience can last only so long. He finished his last fry, and he let them know he was ready to leave. "I want to see a horsy now," he exclaimed!

Weldon threw back his head and laughed. He ruffled the boy's already messed hair. "You ask your mother if it's ok for you to ride with me and I'll lead you both to your new home, then I'll take you both to my house and show you a horsy."

Sheldon eagerly looked toward his mommy. "Can I? Can I?" he asked eagerly.

Kelly just raised a single eyebrow but didn't say anything. Weldon watched fascinated over the ritual they seemed to be going through. The boy just stared at his mother for a second before giving in and asking properly. "Mommy, may I please ride with." He stopped dead and looked puzzled. Weldon and Kelly realized at the same time that Sheldon had no idea who Weldon was. Kelly leaned forward. "Honey, you remember why I told you we were moving here?"

"Yeah," he answered slowly, scrunching his face trying very hard to remember. "Oh, yeah! It was to meet my real Grandpa!" Sheldon turned back to Weldon eagerly. "Are you my Grandpa?"

"Yes, I am," Weldon answered softly.

"Oh, goody," he squealed as he launched himself into the older man's arms. Weldon hung on tightly to the boy. Kelly wanted to cry and noticed that Weldon's eyes were moist also. She looked up and noticed they were the center of attention. Mavis was standing not too far away dabbing her eyes also. Kelly knew there had to be something between the two of them. She had a feeling Weldon had held back far too long before taking the step to see another woman again. She leaned forward and placed a hand over her Father's arm.

"I think we should go now," she urged softly nodding toward the people watching them. Weldon looked around.

"It's alright," he assured her. "They all know the story and I think they have pieced the rest of it all together." He pried himself from the boy looking down on him.

"You ready to see that horsy partner?"

119

"Yes," the boy excitedly agreed jumping up and down, "Yes, yes, yes!"

Weldon stood up and held his hand to Sheldon who trustingly put his little hand into the bigger worn one. Weldon led the way to the counter where he dropped some bills. "This should cover their lunch Mavis. I'll call you later." He winked at the lady and led Sheldon and Kelly outside.

Kelly was relieved to be out of there. She never did feel comfortable being the center of attention. She helped strap an excited Sheldon into Weldon's pick-up. She then followed the two down the road to her new home. It was a ways from town and totally isolated. She wasn't use to having space around her home. The house she grew up in had just a tiny back yard and most of that was devoted to her mother's garden. She could only stare as she got out of the car.

The mountains in the distance framed her view of gently rolling pastures. The house was a single story ranch style, painted a light tan with dark brown sills. Normally this would seem drab to Kelly, but here it fit into the natural elements of the countryside. Vines wove their way up the side of the eastern wall. A fence ran around a nicely trimmed yard. Trees bordered the north and west sides of the fencing. To the east was a fenced in pasture with a small barn. It was just the right size for a pony and a horse. An irrational fear rose in her chest, and she wondered if she would be able to get on a horse. She saw another gravel road leading to the west through a gate in the fence and past the trees. She was wondering where that led when Weldon and Sheldon joined her.

"That road leads to my ranch house," he answered her unspoken question. "It's less than a mile up the road."

"Oh, good," she replied relieved that they weren't so totally alone. She was rewarded with a smile. She looked up at the older man standing next to her. "I'm not sure what to call you?"

"You can start with Weldon," he answered carefully. "If you ever feel comfortable calling me something else, then go for it." His smile was reassuring and Kelly felt more relief.

She hadn't realized how nervous she had been over this moment. She hadn't let herself think about what it would be like. If she had, she was sure it wouldn't have been like this in her thoughts. She was mildly surprised with how easy she and Weldon seemed to bond. She had been afraid he wouldn't accept her for who she was. Maybe he might even think she was here just for what she could get from him. She had to make sure he never thought that's why she had come. Still there was her brother to meet yet. Kelly wondered how he would take seeing his long lost sister. Did he even know about her existence?

She wondered what her brother would be like. She hoped he was a lot like his father. Did she look at all like him? What would he think of her? Would he accept her? She shook her head in pondering these questions. 'I guess there is only one way to find out.'

Kelly smiled at her father when he called her to follow them inside to put her things away. It took only a short while since most the things she kept had been sent on separately and she only had a few clothes for her and Sheldon to use during the trip.

She had taken advantage of the remodeling of the house to make her own furnishing choices. She had chosen cheery light colors for the walls of the kitchen, living and dining rooms. Sheldon's room was done in various shades of blues and greens. Hers was a subtle cranberry. The walls had just a tint of it, but the spreads and carpet were darker. The walls looked like they reflected colors off the carpets and spreads.

She had chosen furniture she had always liked with regard to both usability and style giving an overall homey and comfortable look. Yes, it was her style not Marks that greeted her as she walked in the door. It left her feeling satisfied and happy. It didn't hurt to hear Weldon's murmured approval of the decor.

121

Less than a half hour after they arrived at the house Weldon was driving her and an eager Sheldon to his barn.

Chapter 16

Shel was walking back up to the house after looking in on Peachy. The vet said she was going to be all right. This was pleasing because she had just completed special training to become Bryant's horse. She was trained to return to home base at just a word. This way Bryant could be anywhere on his own and know that the horse can always find her way home. That sort of training cost a lot but that wasn't the only reason he was worried for her. Shel hated to see any horse injured. He had an affinity for the creatures. They were smart, strong, and loyal.

He was amused at how easily Bryant had taken to the ranch life. He was a natural with horses. Who would have believed he was city born and raised? He used that same commanding presence he used with his men in the Military. The fact that it was tempered with patience made the horses trust him.

Shel would watch Bryant work with them and swore that Bryant could see. It was like it was an unconscious sight that even Bryant wasn't aware he had. Shel hoped this meant that Bryant's blindness was psychological as the Doctors had said and would eventually return. He wondered if it would take another shock as bad as what caused it in the first place. No man would want that kind of shock twice in his life.

Weldon's pickup coming up the drive from the direction of granny Millie's house brought Shel back to the present. Now, why would he be coming from there? As the car got closer Shel got his answer. He could see that Weldon wasn't alone. He turned back to the barns when he realized Weldon was headed that way. He was just catching up to them when the passenger side door opened and a young woman stepped out. He stopped and watched as she helped a small boy out before turning to him. When she did he was rendered speechless. Odd feelings surfaced at a face so much like his own approached him.

Kelly saw the man walking toward the large ranch house, stop, turn and follow them back to the barn. She knew who it was instinctively before seeing him up close. She glanced over towards Weldon and he smiled at her.

"Does he have any idea about me?"

"No," Weldon answered. "I didn't want to say anything till I knew for sure."

Kelly bit her lip, wondering how this man would react. She watched him walking toward them as Weldon brought the truck to a stop in front of a great barn. Kelly never noticed the barn in her observations of her brother. She realized he had a limp. She wondered if he had injured it on a horse. This sent a shiver through her.

Weldon stayed silent beside her, letting her quietly get up the nerve to face her new found brother. He was hoping Shel would be civil at the very least, but knowing the anger he still harbored for his mother, Weldon knew he could react in any which way. Weldon got out of his side of the truck at the same time Kelly got out of hers but stayed back and let Shel realize who he was looking at.

Shel was frozen to his spot. He couldn't move, breath or even think straight for a long moment. He watched as the young woman neared him. It was like he was looking in a mirror only at a younger feminine version of himself. The hair, eyes, nose, and even the proud way she held her head were the same. He looked down at the boy standing in front of her. His smile, eyes and unruly hair were straight from a picture of himself as a small child. This had to be a dream.

Who could this person be? He knew the answer of course but, it took a moment for the truth to sink in. He still wasn't sure it could be true. What was he thinking? Was it possible for his mother to have been pregnant when she ran off? Was he really looking at his sister?

This last bit of thought triggered something else, his extreme hatred for the woman who had abandoned him boiled over. He felt the heat of it boiling through his blood. Outwardly his face reddened and fists clenched.

124

He was about to say something to her, but then the boy looked up at him with a big grin.

The child seemed so innocent, so unaware of the tensions going on between the adults. He looked up at the woman again. She also seemed so innocent. That couldn't be possible, if she was so innocent then why was she just turning up now?

'What was she after,' he thought? 'After all this time it couldn't be she wanted to meet her father and brother? Then she must be that other man's daughter and she was trying to take advantage of how much she took after her mother to cash in on the wealth of Weldon.'

Shel took one look at his father and knew she had already worked her magic on him. Even though he was carefully watching his son, Shel knew he believed her. Why else would he have brought her here?

Shel searched the woman's face for any sign of deceit. He couldn't find it. She smiled tentatively at him. He recalled suddenly that he looked like his father more than his mother. So that meant that if she looked so much like him, she had to take after her father. That would make Weldon her father not that other guy. The thoughts just kept going back and forth, was she or wasn't she. He didn't want to accept she was. He didn't want to face her. He didn't want a long lost sister.

Then the question, 'why did she wait so long to come forward,' was still valid. That questioned burned in him for more reasons than he was able to acknowledge at this time.

Weldon was watching his son very carefully. He knew this was going to be a shock but the pure hatred he read in the younger man's eyes surprised him immensely. He had done all he could to take some of the blame for Kate's leaving on himself. He never spoke against her in the boy's earshot. The truth was he did blame himself for her running off with another man.

He had been complacent in his comfort here at the Ranch. It had been his father's and then his. His goal was to make it larger and better. He

125

worked long hours and consequently that meant Kate spent long hours on her own. She had also been born and raised here. Her family's ranch was right next door. They had grown-up together and were sweethearts in school. They married right after school. In all that time Weldon never imagined she wanted more; he had never imagined that she wanted something different in her life.

He never asked her if there were other dreams she might have had. He had always assumed her dreams were the same as his. He had been totally wrong and found out the night she left. She had left a long letter to him explaining all the pain and loneliness she felt. She had gone deeply into her dreams of living where there was some excitement. She desired to see a big city, to live its night life, to feel more on her face than a dusty hot Montana wind.

He had never shown Sheldon the letter, though he still had it. He had never told the boy how he felt he had caused his mother to run away because of his lack of time with her. He had been ashamed that his self-centeredness had caused the woman he loved to run away. He admitted now he had never stopped loving her even though the pain she had brought both of them had been hard to handle at times.

He watched his son's face now seeing the hatred and mistrust coming to the surface and realized he should have talked to him before bringing the girl and her son here. It was too late now to change that so he had to find a way to reach his son, to let him know it wasn't this girl's fault what happened in the past, but before he could speak young Sheldon got tired of just standing there and made the first move.

He stepped forward up to Shel and spoke loudly, breaking the silence that had surrounded all of them. "Are you a cowboy?"

"What," asked a confused Shel?

"Grandpa said I would see a cowboy and some horsies," the boy continued. "Are you a cowboy and where are the horsies?"

Shel looked totally lost for a second. This was not what he was expecting. He was lost as to where to go from here. He glanced at his father and saw an inquisitive look in the raise of his eyebrow.

He knew Weldon was wondering if he was going to be able to handle this. He glanced back at the girl, and he knew she was his sister. He knew his father was not one to have the wool easily pulled over his eyes. He knew that the questions he had would be answered in due time.

He knelt down and faced the boy eye to eye. "What's your name son?"

"Sheldon," the boy answered totally oblivious of what that answer did to the man in front of him. How could she have known his name, except that her mother had told her? That meant she knew she had another family but waited so many years to show up. She did have something up her sleeve and Shel was going to find out what it was, but for now, he would play along.

"Sheldon," he echoed totally shocked. He looked up into the eyes of the boy's mother. They were his eyes, the eyes of his father. The rest of his doubt faded as he gazed into them. They were softer than his father's and his with a hint of worry in the lines around them.

He didn't know what that man, who his mother ran off with looked like, but he knew what his mother looked like. He had spent many a night as a child looking at her picture wishing her home. He knew he took after his father in many ways. It was his hair color, eyes and chin Shel had inherited. It was his father he took after in the way he held his chin up. The boy standing before him had the same features.

If that man had been their father and grandfather there was no way they could look so much like him. This woman couldn't be anything other than his full blooded sister. He now had a new reason to hate his mother even more. She had robbed him of the sibling he had always missed having. And he wondered if he could even trust her.

As if reading his thoughts the woman stepped forward and laid a hand on his shoulder. "Please don't hate her," she whispered. "She suffered a lot for what she did."

Shel wanted to reply something back in answer to what she just said, but he looked at the boy standing patiently, if not a little puzzled as to why the adults were acting so funny in front of him, and knew he had to keep his silence, at least for now. He instead, held out his hand to the boy and said to him. "How do you do Sheldon? That also happens to be my name." The boy split a grin from ear to ear.

"Then you're my new uncle," he shouted for joy and launched into Shel's arms. Shel found himself holding the boy tightly. Just the feel of the young boy in his arms melted some of the coldness around his heart. He had a lot of questions to ask this woman but now was not the moment, he figured. He looked up into those soft eyes of his new found sister and found his voice.

"You have a name?" he asked in a voice that sounded strange even to him. He stood up to look her in the eyes. She smiled back, the warmth reaching those sky blue eyes of hers.

"Hi," she replied back softly, emotion also making her voice crack. "I'm Kelly." Anything more to be said was impossible at that time for young Sheldon loudly demanded to see a horsy. Shel leaned over to muss the boy's hair and laughed. He gazed into eyes so like his he couldn't pull away. The jerking on his shirt hem brought him back to the moment as he looked down at the young man standing next to him,

"Where's the horsy?"

"I see you inherited the Shepard persistence," he laughed nervously down at the boy. "Follow me. I think I got a horsy just your size." He held out his hand and the boy trustingly put his little one into Shel's big one and followed his new uncle. Shel looked back at Kelly and Weldon. "Are you two going to stand there all day or come with us?"

128

.

Kelly and Weldon looked at each other, both confused at how fast Shel had seemed to acknowledge her, even without asking the burning questions. Weldon looked at Kelly and laughed to himself. Kelly raised an eyebrow in question to his reaction. She didn't realize it was just the same as he and Shel did when they were questioning something silently. He acknowledged once again after seeing the two together how much they looked alike. He reasoned that Shel had figured it out that she couldn't resemble them so much if she had been the daughter of the other man. He knew Shel still had many questions and that the situation was far from resolved, but for now, a small child had managed to soften some of the stress. They followed the other two into the barn.

Shel led Sheldon to a stall at the far end of the barn. Inside was a small pony quietly chewing his feed. He looked up from his trough and nickered softly and ambled over to the stable door, stretching his neck to sniff the hand Shel extended over the half door. He lifted Sheldon up so he could see over it.

"Wow, "he exclaimed! "He is just my size!"

"He sure is," Shel replied with a chuckle. "And he has been waiting for somebody to give him exercise. You think you're up to it?" He thought how nice this was, enjoying the surprise of a child. He had always kept a pony on the ranch for the children of visitors. It will be fun, Shel suddenly thought, to teach his new nephew how to ride.

"Yes," Sheldon shouted! "Yes, yes!"

"Hang on then," Shel said as he lifted the boy onto the pony's back and led it out of the stall.

"Look at me Mommy." Sheldon called out to Kelly. "I'm riding a horsy."

"I see that," Kelly called back laughingly. It looked so good to see the pair going around in circles.

As he lead the child and pony in circles around the center of the barn Shel watched Kelly talking to Weldon. 'Could it be there was no ulterior motive? Could she just be another innocent harmed by the actions of his mother? Was the reason she showed up now tied to the death of their mother?' He knew he had to find out. He also knew that much of the anger was melting and he no longer directed it toward Kelly or his new nephew.

That night after dinner Shel was standing out on the patio watching the sun go down behind the mountains. The fiery reds danced upon the scattered clouds. There would be rain tonight or in the early morning he mused.

He hoped Bryant would be okay up at the cabin alone. He had hated leaving his friend behind but there had been no choice. Peachy wouldn't have been able to support his weight down that trail on her injured leg. Besides, Bryant seemed to relish the idea of being alone for a while. Come to think of it, that was a rare thing since he had arrived last fall. Shel realized now that in a subconscious way he had been keeping a close watch on his friend and either he or somebody else had been with him whenever he was out in the barn or paddocks.

Shel had to admit he had to let his friend regain his independence. Where once he needed the support of his friends, he was now coming into himself nicely. Bryant had gained a great deal self-esteem since he had arrived. His self confidence had grown with each new task he had learned or relearned.

Shel was glad his friend was finding himself despite his on-going blindness. He still was confused as to what was causing it though. The last check-up he had taken Bryant to had confirmed to the Doctors that Bryant's eyes were healed and he should see. They told Shel that hopefully with time whatever was causing Bryant to mentally block his vision would fade and his sight would return, but for now the best thing that could be done for him was to treat his as normal as possible. To Shel that meant letting Bryant be alone up at the cabin for the few days it would take for Peachy to heal.

131

"Penny for your thoughts?"

Shel turned at the soft voice behind him. It was so strange having Kelly here. It wasn't that he wasn't happy to find her; it was just that the conflicting emotions she brought with her confused him.

"I am afraid," he answered her with a laugh, "that they are not worth that."

"What were they about?"

"A good friend of mine, who's staying up at our cabin in the mountains."

"Your right, thoughts about friends aren't worth two cents," She said softly. At the hitch of his eyebrow, she added, "They're priceless."

Kelly stood at his side and silently gazed with him at the unfolding sunset. Once the reds had faded and the darkness had begun to creep in she turned to him. "That was beautiful."

"I suppose you didn't see sunsets like that in the city?"

"You're right there," she answered. "The suburbs where I lived didn't have the high skyline to block the sunset but the horizon was still filled with houses and trees and other obstacles to block a clear view."

"You think you'll miss the city?" Shel had good reason for asking that question?

"I never cared for the city," she answered. "Though it's all I have ever known, I've always longed for quiet nights, trees, and an open skyline."

"I think I would choke in the city," Shel acknowledged. "Is it ever quiet?"

Kelly thought for a moment before answering. "There is a time in the very early morning just before dawn when it seems even the city itself is asleep. It gets very quiet and you can hear the crickets and locust, the wind in the trees. That was the time when I would sit at my window with it open and listen. I would close my eyes and pretend I was in the country."

"Didn't you ever get to go to the country," he asked? "You weren't that far from it you couldn't drive there?"

"Of course we would take drives to the surrounding countryside," she laughed. "But it wasn't like here. There are people everywhere you turn, even in the country. On the week-ends everybody tries to escape the city. They go to the beaches and the area parks. Here, it's naturally quiet. There are no people everywhere you turn. You don't have to wait till the dead of night to hear nature. You don't have to close your eyes to imagine you're alone with just your soul."

Shel watched her as she talked. His insides twisted as she described being alone with your soul. That, he knew could be a double edged sword. He wondered how long it would take before those city lights and sounds would call to her again? As if reading his mind, Kelly turned to Shel and replied to the question in his head with another question.

"Don't you think that the country can be something born in a person?"

"I don't follow," Shel answered confused.

"I'll try to explain," Kelly laughed. "You were born here and it's always felt right, right?"

"Yes," he answered simply.

"Mom was born here but she never felt happy, right," she pressed?

"I guess so," he answered, puzzled at her line of questions.

"I know of some people born in the city," she continued, "and would never consider leaving it. I on the other hand always thought about living somewhere else."

"Really?" Shel was startled by this revelation.

"Yes," she replied and had to laugh at the look on his face. She continued, "I loved the excursions into the country. I dreamed of owning a little house with a white picket fence and a small field with horses. I yearned for a view of the mountains. I would dream I could look out my window and catch a light breeze on my face, smell the freshness, hear the birds and sounds of small animals, and see the outline of the mountains on the horizon. I

133

would then look out my window and smell the smog, hear the traffic on the road, and see nothing but more buildings blocking the horizon."

"I can't even imagine living in a crowded city," Shel said softly as he watched the darkening horizon. He couldn't imagine breathing air smelling of exhaust fumes and garbage. He inhaled unconsciously and smelled the horses, cattle, the grasses and the faint scent of the trees born on the wind. He didn't realize Kelly was watching his every move. She stopped talking and also watched the darkening hills. They watched the last of the light fade from the sky and darkness fall silently around them.

She could hear the faint lowing of the cattle in the fields, a whinny from a horse in the paddock. Somewhere a dog barked at a shadow and a cat meowed for its nightly milk at the back door. She smelled the odors from the barn and paddocks but to her it wasn't a stink but a fragrance of nature.

Granted, she didn't want only that smell day in and day out, but since it was weak and mingled with the other odors of nature, she could handle it. The scent of flowers from Rosa's garden was in the air now. She smiled softly as it brought back memories of her mother's garden hidden behind the fence of the small back yard. She realized that the garden was her mother's way of keeping a little bit of the country she had given up with her.

"Did she ever indicate she regretted leaving," he asked slowly, nearly chocking on the words. He had vowed not to ask about her but curiosity was killing him inside. His guts twisted with each word, but he waited holding his breath for the answer.

"She never talked about her life before marrying Morris," Kelly slowly answered, searching for the right words. "I didn't know about it before she died, but now that I look back, I know she did."

"How can you know this?" Shel asked harshly. He felt immediately sorry since, after all, it wasn't Kelly's fault for what 'she' had done. "I'm sorry. It's just... I just could never understand..." He stopped talking and just stood there.

"She never seemed happy," Kelly continued after a short pause. She knew he needed to hear this even as he fought against asking about it or hearing the answer. "I thought it was just because of how bad a husband Morris was. Now I know differently."

"How do you know?"

"Well," Kelly searched for the right words, "she had a garden wherever we lived."

"What's that got to do with it?" he asked angrily.

"You don't see how that was her way of keeping some of the memories of the country," she asked softly. While they were talking neither of them saw Weldon standing in the doorway. He had come to tell Kelly that Sheldon had fallen asleep on the sofa. He couldn't interrupt them though. He needed to hear the answers as much as Shel.

"How can a dinky garden do that," Shel responded mockingly.

Kelly kept her patience with the anger he had. She understood it all so well. She didn't know how to explain she had felt the same way for a short time after finding out the truth. Her main question had been, 'Why did she keep it a secret for so long?' One thing Kelly had in her favor was that she had known her mother. She had seen some of the signs her mother gave over the years that hadn't made sense then.

"I guess you'd have to see the love she poured into it," Kelly replied. Her eyes got dreamy as she tried to remember her mother on her knees nursing a plant along. "She crowded many different varieties of flowers of all colors in it. There was never a day in summer that you couldn't smell the scent of flowers in the air. She had a patch of veggies in the corners. If you had seen what she managed to grow in that little space you wouldn't question she was trying to recreate something. She spent all the time she could out there. Sometimes I would see her just sitting there on her knees staring out into space. "

"Maybe she was watching a neighbor or something," Shel scoffed.

"We always had a high fence around the house," Kelly answered. "It was something she insisted on. It got so Morris would take down the fence at one house and put it back up at another to save money."

She heard Shel snort at that. Suddenly she thought of something significant that could help Shel find some peace.

"Your birthday is June 17th?"

"Why yes," he replied, flabbergasted. "How did you know? Oh, I suppose she told you." Kelly shook her head.

"Every year," Kelly paused to gather her thoughts. "Every year till she died, she would make a cake on the 17th of June. When we asked her what it was for, she always replied it was for somebody special who couldn't be with us."

"She remembered?" Shel whispered hoarsely.

"Yes," Kelly added, "and she was always very sad on that day. She never ate any the cake, just would take a piece and sit with it all alone in her room."

They stood quietly after this revelation. Shel didn't know how to respond to this. He still had to soak it all up. He had always believed that she had just left and forgot about him. Now, he finds out that she never forgot, she even thought about him on the day he had always made a wish that she was with him when he blew out the candles. He tried to picture her in a dark room with a piece of cake wishing the same thing.

Weldon thought this was a good time to break in so he turned around, went back up the hall a few paces then came walking out the door as if he had just arrived.

"There you two are," he called out. "Hey Kelly, that young one is passed right out on the sofa. You think we should be getting him to a bed?"

"Oh goodness," Kelly spun around, "I plum forgot about the time! It has been a long day. Could you take us home?"

"Why don't you two stay here tonight?" Weldon asked. "We have plenty of room."

"Thanks," Kelly answered. She nearly said Dad at the end of the word but caught herself. She wasn't quite ready yet and wasn't sure if he was either. "But I think we need to get use to our own beds in the new house."

"You haven't even had a chance to get supplies in," Weldon pressed. "You won't have anything for breakfast."

Shel saw the look of indecision on Kelly's face. He realized she didn't want to hurt her father's feeling but also wanted to get settled in her new home.

"I could run in the morning and pick them up in time for breakfast," he broke in. He ignored the dirty look Weldon threw his way and continued. "You think you can be ready about 8am?"

"Isn't that a bit late for breakfast around here?"

"Usually, but tomorrow is Saturday," he added, "and I think we can all use an extra hour of sleep." He sent a look to his father trying to convey to the man to take it easy and not push. Weldon seemed to get the messages and relaxed some.

"Yes,' he replied. "I'll leave a note for Rosa to have breakfast at 8am and to make sure she makes some of her famous flapjacks."

"Okay," Kelly agreed. "I am sure Sheldon will love having breakfast with his Grandpa and Uncle."

"Then I can take him for his first real ride," Sheldon added.

"He'll definitely love it," Kelly said happily. She felt so at home.

"What about Bryant," Weldon asked Shel?

"Huh?"

"You remember Bryant?" Weldon continued with a smirk. "Your friend you left stranded in the mountains?"

"You left somebody stranded in the mountains?" Kelly picked up on the humor over the situation but had to mock him. It seemed natural.

"I did not," he threw back at them. "Bryant's that friend I mentioned in a nice warm cabin."

"Well, I guess that's good as opposed to a cold cabin," she laughed.

Shel realized she was teasing. "His horse stumbled and pulled up lame," he explained quickly. "I brought her down to get fixed up and he decided to stay a few days alone." He felt that's all he needed say at this point. He threw his father a warning glance.

Kelly caught the look, decided to ignore it and not mention it. "Well, I am sure he is a big boy and can handle a few days on his own."

"Well, I'll get Sheldon," she said and added. "Which one of you is going to give us a lift to the house?"

"I will be happy to Kelly," Shel said as he headed into the house. He stopped at his father and started to say something, thought better of it and went inside.

Kelly came up to her father and watched Shel disappear inside. "What was that all about?"

Weldon smiled. "It's hard to explain," he laughed. You will meet Bryant soon. I am sure you'll understand then." He patted her hand. "Let's go get you and my grandson settled."

"Okay," she answered happily and followed him inside where Shel already had the still sleeping child in his arms. He was staring down at him then looked up at Kelly as they came in.

"His name?"

"Mom insisted," she answered back softly. He nodded and turned to the door to head for the car. He knew he would have to call Bryant shortly and tell him he may be alone for a few days longer than expected. But, he knew his friend wanted some alone time anyway so figured it would be okay with him that he was delayed in returning. Now, all Shel wanted was to spend time with his sister and nephew. He felt the last of the cold spot melt away. There were still lots of questions but the anger was fading. He knew he couldn't hold it against Kelly for what happened to him so many years before.

He drove them to their house and carried the boy inside. After he had him settled in bed he followed Kelly into the kitchen. She was checking cupboards, drawers and the fridge. It seemed everything was full.

"I guess my guardian angel made sure I had food," she laughed. "He must have anticipated I would be thinking of other things than buying foodstuffs."

"Guardian angel?"

"My solicitor," Kelly answered as she pulled out two beers and offered Shel one. He accepted and they went to sit on the patio for a while. They talked quietly for about an hour before he left. She patiently answered his questions. She felt he was accepting the situation better now. Kelly felt that they had a good start to a real relationship and hoped Shel felt the same way.

Chapter 18

The ground was aflame with burning vehicles. The stench of burning flesh and metal fouled the air. Screams filled the air with the explosions. Bryant screamed for his men as he crawled from one vehicle to another. The ground burned his hands. Hell had finally erupted on earth. The whistles of mortars sang through the air to crash to the earth and explode. One landed yards away and the percussion struck Bryant full force.

He could feel flying debris hitting his body as he hugged the ground. He felt pain in his leg as a piece of metal dug into his flesh. He clenched his teeth against the pain and preceded ahead, agonizing inch by agonizing inch. The eerie shadows of the burning trucks bounced and bobbled along the ground. He found each man, one by one, all dead. He stopped long enough to gather their dog tags and moved down the line. He finally made it to the final truck.

"Shepard," he screamed! "Shepard, where are you?" He raced to a pile of debris and franticly started pulling at it to get to the body underneath.

Another bomb exploded and Bryant woke up screaming. Dazed and confused he realized he was outside the cabin in the pouring rain. He was holding a log from the wood pile in his hands. The logs were scattered all around him where he had flung the wood. The explosion had been lightening striking nearby.

For a moment he could have swore he saw the outline of the cabin in a flash of lightening before darkness descended upon him. He stood in the freezing rain a moment longer before realization dawned on him. He was only in his jeans. Bare-chested, barefooted, and covered in scratches from wondering around the area unprotected. He had somehow gotten from his bed to the woodpile outside.

'What is going on?' he wondered as he stared sightlessly toward where he swore he had seen the cabin. Another strike of lightening hitting a tree not far in the woods followed immediately with thunder snapped Bryant out of his preoccupied thoughts. He ran in the direction he thought he had seen the cabin and stumbled on the first step of the front porch. Pain flared in his swollen ankle. The hair on his arms was standing straight from the static electricity of the nearby lightening strike. It had been close enough to feel the heat from it. He hurried inside.

Once inside Bryant striped his jeans off his shivering body, leaving them to lie in a wet heap by the door, he headed to the bathroom naked. Slipping into the shower he let the warm water wash the chill from his body. His head still reeled at the events leading up to this moment.

'How had he gotten outside?' he thought. 'Why had he felt like he was back in Afghanistan? What had caused him to sleep-walk like this?" That's what he had done. The spring storm had triggered a very vivid flashback. He also was positive he could see while he was in that dream-like state.

The lightening and thunder of the early morning rain had opened a door back to his experience in the final battle where he had lost all his men, except Shel. He had had flashbacks before, but he had never acted them out in his sleep. At least, he didn't think he had.

It still astounded him that for an instant, just a mere instant, he had been able to see when he was jolted back to his senses by the thunder. He'd been able to see! He had seen the cabin as plain as ever in the light of that lightening strike. Then fast as he had realized he could see it, it was gone. Blackness had engulfed him again. He now believed the Doctors that his sight was psychosomatic. The big question now was what was keeping him from seeing?

The chill of the water brought Bryant out of his trance. He must have been standing under that tap a long time for him to use all the hot water in the heater. He mused at the situation as he dried himself off.

He remembered the fear he felt that night. It was the first time he'd ever admitted to having fear for anything. The second time he would admit to having fear was when he had found out he was blind and that the people he thought he could depend on weren't there to help him.

Bryant dressed in dry jeans and a t-shirt and headed to the kitchenette to put water on for coffee. As the coffee began to filter Bryant let his thoughts continue.

His father had turned his back on him. He had a chosen path for his son and never forgave him for choosing otherwise. He couldn't forgive Bryant for wanting to be his own man and making his own mark in the world. His father couldn't understand why anybody wouldn't want the easy road. A ready made company that was making money was the easy road as far as he could see. It was the road he himself had chosen following Bryant's Grandfather into the business. It's what sons did. They followed their fathers.

Bryant was beginning to think there was more to it. Could his father actually be jealous of the fact Bryant had been able to stand up to him and follow his own destiny? His father hadn't questioned his own destiny but had let others choose it. Bryant realized he had never seen his father truly happy with his life. What dreams had he given up?

Now it seemed he couldn't stand that his son had had the nerve to defy him in a way he couldn't defy his own father. He had become a bitter hardened man who couldn't appreciate the good things he had.

If he couldn't follow his dreams than why should his son follow his? He wanted the same thing his father had wanted. He wanted his son to be like him. He wanted a little clone who thought like he did. He couldn't understand, didn't want to understand, that Bryant had more compassion for things, cared for others where the father couldn't see past his own wants. Of course he would have had to see past his wants to see a son who was nothing like him, mentally or physically.

Bryant's father was a smallish man. He was tall, about six feet, but he was slender boned, fragile actually, and never prone to athletic abilities. He was jealous of a son who could play any sport he wanted with talent. He didn't want a son who would rather be outdoors than in a room learning math, economics, or business.

It didn't matter that he had a daughter who had a head for the business and could do a lot more for it than Bryant ever could, even if he had wanted to. When Bryant had called home after the accident, his father expressed that he got what he deserved and to live with it. He then hung up. That had been the second time Bryant had called, the first time his father had refused to answer.

Bryant poured his coffee and went to sit on the sofa in front of the dying embers in the fireplace. He thought about building up the fire but decided against it. He leaned back and thought about the next person in his life he had thought he could depend on. He had thought about her a few times but with anger. Now, he was thinking with rational thought. He remembered just what she had been like and tried to see again what he had saw in her before.

Bryant's fiancée had also abandoned him when he needed her most. Not that he had ever really had any doubt that her love was more for his inheritance than for him. He knew where he had stood in that fact. 'Why hadn't it bothered him then?'

She had always been on him about going to his father to beg forgiveness and work for him instead of joining the service. At that time it didn't bother him. He thought he was in love with her and that was all that mattered. 'Okay, what did he think he loved about her?'

She was beautiful. There was no doubt there. It was an artificial beauty though. The best money could buy. Bryant had never seen her without her make-up. Even when he had stayed the night she wore it to bed and then got up to reapply before he awoke.

Her clothes were beyond tasteful. She bought from the most expensive and exclusive boutiques. She would never think of buying off the rack, the idea of somebody else wearing the same outfit would send her into spasms. Yes, hers was a cool beauty.

Emotionally she was as cold as her appearance. She wouldn't stand for any public show of emotions that was so 'common'. She held herself up above the masses and wouldn't bring herself down to act like them. She wasn't very respectful of those she thought lesser than her either. Bryant who was a big tipper and always had a smile for the service people had more than once been peeved at her treatment of a waitress or clerk.

He knew the true strain between them started when he joined the Military. He had thought he could win her over to the idea after seeing how happy he was in his own life. He realized now that that would have never happened. He had found out after the event that she had been cheating on him whenever he was deployed somewhere else.

She had told him herself when she had sent him a letter telling him she wouldn't come to see him. She had spilled her guts then about how she had felt slighted and had looked elsewhere. She had found somebody even before the attack.

Now in his blindness he could see her for what she was. He could see all he had turned a blinded eye to before. He just couldn't see why he was blind to her in the first place. Why had he chosen somebody so exactly like a female version of his father? He had always known that under that perfectly manicured appearance of hers was a heart of stone.

She had married a rich older banker from New York less than three months after he had been injured. He was the one she was seeing when he deployed to Afghanistan. She sent his ring back by mail. Her love for him was as third class as the postage she paid to send it to him. He wished her every bit of happiness that money could buy her.

Bryant realized his cup was empty and got up to refill it. He could hear the rain slacking off from a downpour to a dripping drizzle. The clock on the mantle struck 7AM. Bryant settled back on the sofa with his fresh coffee and continued to let his mind run through its litany.

Of all the people he had depended on only Shel had come to his rescue. That's exactly what it had been, a rescue. Bryant had let anger, shame, and pity reduce him to that diminutive state in which Shel had first found him at the hospital. Shel was the only one who came to help him.

He had offered no pity, just friendship. He offered a safe haven for Bryant to heal both inside and out. Shel, a man who had no ties to Bryant other than the bond they forged while in the service together, had dropped everything to help Bryant. It was a bond forged from both men feeling they owed their life to the other. They also shared the fact they both lost somebody they thought they loved. Neither talked about it, but they both knew the other understood. That was all they needed.

Bryant made his way back to the kitchen to make some breakfast. The chiming of the mantle clock told him it was now 7:30am. Shel and Weldon would have been up for a couple hours already, out in the barn doing the morning chores. Their wealth came from sweat and hard work.

Shel would inherit an established ranch, but it was something he would always have to work at to keep it prosperous. He excelled at the hard work. He lived for it, it was in his blood. At the same time Bryant wondered how much of that was to also keep the ghosts of his past at bay? If he thought he had problems with his family, Shel's problems would overwhelm him.

Bryant knew he was lucky in the fact that at least he had had both parents. But then again, having parents whose idea of love was to give their children everything but their time and love was not really all that great. Shel's father was as close to his son as Bryant's father was distant. Bryant had envied Shel for the close relationship he had with his father. He wished he and his father could have at least had some of that.

The ringing phone broke into his thoughts making him jump, nearly causing him to drop the fry pan in his hands. Okay, these retrospective thoughts were getting him down. He didn't like that at all. He had always

145

been a man who looked to the future rather than look back. Maybe it was time to let them go.

He reached for the phone, knowing who it was.

"Hey Shel," he answered without preamble. "How's Peachy?"

Shel noticed the strained lightness right away and wondered what was wrong. He nearly asked what was up but stopped. He figured that if it was serious Bryant would say something. He answered the question instead waiting for Bryant to say anything if he needed or wanted to.

"She'll be fine," he hedged. "She will need a few days rest to give the leg a chance to heal."

"How long we talking?"

"Maybe a week," Shel replied, "maybe two."

"It was that serious?"

"Not so serious," Shel continued, "as it just takes a while for the muscle to heal. That is a slow process." And he thought silently, he needed that long to get to know his sister.

He wondered what Bryant would think of this new development. He laughed to himself. Bryant was not the most trusting person and would have a hard time believing this scenario. He was nervously waiting for him to find out but now wasn't the time.

"Shel," Bryant's questioning voice brought Shel back to the present. He didn't realize he had paused long enough for Bryant to notice. "Everything ok at that end?"

"Oh Yah," Shel answered quickly. Maybe it was a little too quickly. This time Bryant had reason to wonder what was going on. Shel sounded rather funny. He wasn't sure if it was a good funny either. He sounded a bit distracted, but it was up to Shel to tell him if he thought Bryant had a right to know.

"We just got some new calves in and it's a good thing I was around to help." Shel hoped they would get some in before Bryant got back so as not to appear the liar he was at this moment.

146

"If you need the extra help," Bryant offered, "Bring up another horse and come get me."

"That's ok," Shel hastily replied. Bryant noted again how quick. "You think you can handle being up there for a week alone? I could come up with another horse, but then I'd have to lead you down." Peachy was specially trained for a blind rider. Trained to go the direction rider wanted to go but also use her own sense to find best way to go that way. She was one of the smartest horses Shel had ever seen.

"I am a big boy Shel," Bryant laughed. "I think I can manage here alone. You got the trail marked to the river, right?"

"Yes," Shel had gone up to the cabin earlier in the week to make it ready for their trip up there. He had brought in provisions and also taken a rope and strung it from tree to tree along the trail to the dock on the river for Bryant. All he had to do was follow the rope with his hand. "And there should be plenty of food."

"I plan on catching my dinners," Bryant laughed again, he liked the idea of time alone. He had to figure out what was going on with these flash backs. He knew if he told Shel, he would be up there faster than you can saddle a horse to bring him down. "You did leave some bait behind?"

"That's in the cooler in the back shed just outside the back door," Shel answered. He was relieved that Bryant was confidant in himself. It was a far cry from a few months ago. "All the tack and gear you need is stored there."

"Then I'm all set," Bryant replied. "You better get to those calves." Why did he have this strange feeling there weren't any calves? He and Shel traded good-byes and both hung up. Bryant went back to making his breakfast musing about what was going on with Shel. It almost seemed like he didn't want Bryant there for the moment.

Chapter 19

Shel turned and found his father behind him.

"I take it Bryant is alright," he asked as he went for the coffee pot.

"Yah," Shel answered as he followed suit. They sat at the kitchen table absorbing the smells of the breakfast their housekeeper/cook Rosa was making. The silence was comfortable between them. Shel had laid awake most the night thinking of that previous days events. He thought he should be angry with his father for not telling him about a possible sister. But the longer he thought about it the more he understood why. His father hadn't known for sure, because he was afraid of the answer. Shel could understand that.

Shel still had mixed feelings over his mother. He wanted to keep his hate for her so much, but the things Kelly had said the night before made him think. The fact she never forgot him helped tone down some his hate. He was very confused as to what he should be feeling.

Weldon watched his son as he silently drank his coffee. He could see the range of emotions play across Shel's face. He wanted to say something but knew Shel had to come to his resolutions on his own. He hoped getting to know Kelly and letting her talk about their mother would help Shel forgive the past if not forget it. He knew it would help him.

He had been so surprised at how fast he had felt comfortable with the girl. She had turned out good, strong and confident. He could see though that she was not without scars. Maybe living here with her real family would help lessen them.

He smiled when his thoughts turned to his grandson. That boy was going to wear him out trying to keep up. And he was going to keep up. They had a lot of time to make up for.

"What you thinking about." Shel's question broke into Weldon's thoughts.

"Huh?"

"You're smiling about something," Shel pointed out.

"Oh, that," Weldon laughed. "I was just thinking how hard it is going to be to keep up with that child."

"Oh yes," Shel laughed. "He is going to be a handful." Just then they both heard a car coming up the drive from Kelly's place. The both exchanged looks. Shel was happy to see the anticipation and joy on his fathers face. Weldon saw childish glee in his son's eyes. He was happy to see acceptance of his sister also in those eyes. Whatever had happened in the past, at least Shel wasn't holding it over Kelly's head.

"Grandpa," the boy burst into the backdoor! He launched himself into Weldon's lap and nearly strangled the man with a big hug around the neck.

"Let your Grandpa have some air," Kelly softly scolded the young man, a twinkle in her eyes none the less. "Hi, I hope we're not late."

Shel got up to get Kelly a cup of coffee. "Nope, you're just in time. Have a seat." They got settled in and Rosa served flapjacks, bacon, sausage, eggs, and toast.

"Oh, my," Kelly laughed looking at all the food on the table. "There goes my diet."

"Don't worry," Shel spoke up. "You will find plenty to do here to work it off."

"I am afraid to ask what," Kelly screwed her eyes upward as she speared a fat sausage link."

"Well there are always stalls to be mucked out," Weldon said in a false serious tone. He laughed at the look of horror on Kelly's face.

"I don't know if Bryant would want to give up his job Dad," Shel laughed

"You see," Kelly broke in, "I wouldn't want to take anybody's job."

"I don't think he would mind," Shel laughed.

150

"Who's Bryant?" Sheldon asked, tired of the adults not paying any attention to him.

Kelly noticed Weldon and Shel look at each other as if not sure what to say. It seems this Bryant was more than just an employee. They weren't sure what to tell about him. She wondered if maybe he was a trouble maker. That would maybe explain why he was the stall mucker. She figured she would meet him when she got more of a tour of the place and met some the men who worked there. She didn't say anything but waited for Shel or Weldon to answer Sheldon.

"Bryant is a friend of mine," Shel started out slowly. "The one I mentioned last night. He came here to work after he and I were in Afghanistan."

"What's an Afghanistan?" Sheldon asked.

"It's not a what," Weldon laughed. "It's a where."

"Afghanistan is a country on the other side of the planet dear," Kelly explained. She added softly to Shel. "Is that where you injured your leg?"

"Yes," he answered just as softly. "It was because of Bryant that my leg was all I lost." He attacked his pile of flapjacks with a false fervor.

Lost? So that limp was much more than a war wound. Kelly could see talking about it was still painful. She let that part of the subject drop.

"So," she asked, "This friend of yours came here to work after you both came home?"

"Not right away," Shel answered hesitantly. Kelly wondered what it was he wasn't saying. "He came here a few months ago. He needed a job, we needed help. It's as simple as that." Shel's voice had tightened some so Kelly dropped the subject all together. Now her curiosity about this man was rising as was her curiosity of what happened to Shel while he was serving in Afghanistan. She wasn't sure what to say now but was rescued once again by her son.

"When do I get to go riding?" he blurted out loudly. That broke the slight tension that had arisen between the adults. Kelly glanced at her new

151

father and he half winked at her, letting her know she hadn't said anything wrong.

To Sheldon he said, "As soon as you clean everything off your plate." The boy went straight to eating what was left of his flapjacks and sausages.

Kelly noticed a strange look in Shel's eyes as he watched Sheldon eat. It was a wistful longing look. It made her wonder why he wasn't married and had kids. She had a feeling he would make a great father.

The guys bolted down their food with gusto as Kelly ate at a more comfortable pace. They were done way before she was and sat there looking at her. Kelly looked up from her plate to see the three pairs of eyes on her and laughed. "I don't inhale my food so why don't you fellows go ahead and I'll catch up with you in the barn."

Sheldon gave a shout and jumped off his chair and headed for the door. Shel reached over and grabbed his collar effectively stopping him in his tracks. "Whoa there boy," he laughed. "We have manners here. You ask to leave the table."

Sheldon looked shocked for a moment then sat back down and sweetly asked, "May I please leave the table?"

"When everybody is done," Shel answered him. Kelly had to laugh at the boys crest fallen face. She liked the way Shel had easily handled her boisterous son. She took one more bite of bacon and announced, "I'm done."

"Yippee," Sheldon shouted and raced for the door leaving the adults laughing helplessly at the table.

"Well, you tried," Kelly patted Shel's hand, "but there is no way to harness the energy of a six year old."

"I am beginning to see that," Sheldon laughed. "You ready to go? I have the perfect mare picked out for you."

Kelly went ashen. "Me?" she squeaked from a suddenly tight throat. The two men looked at her strangely. "Sorry, I don't ride."

"That's ok," Shel said. "I figured you haven't ridden before. I will teach you how."

152

"It's not that," Kelly added uneasily. "I am afraid of horses."

"How can you be afraid of horses?" Shel asked flabbergasted. He suddenly wondered if Kelly actually belonged out here. He was just getting use to having a sister and she was turning out like the other women in his life.

"Calm down Shel," Weldon's quiet voice broke the stunned silence. He turned to Kelly, "I think the question should be; is there a reason you are afraid of horses?"

Kelly looked at Shel carefully and then rolled up her sleeve to show a long ragged scar running up her arm from elbow to shoulder. "It's a long story. Can we just say I fell off a very big one when I was very little?"

She saw the question in Weldon's eyes but he resisted asking it. Shel softened his stance measurably and looked contrite at his out burst. Just as he was about to say something Sheldon banged on the back door yelling in, "Hey, are we going or not?" The adults laughed and headed out the door. Kelly couldn't help from seeing another look in Weldon's eyes. She hung back letting Shel and Sheldon go ahead of them.

"I'll tell you the whole story at another time," she whispered. Weldon answered with a squeeze to her arm and they joined the other two at the barn.

Chapter 20

Bryant stood at the door of the cabin listening to the birds sing in the new morn. The rain had left a soft scent in the air. This would be a good time to go fishing and let his thoughts unscramble. First, he had to do one thing. He punched in the phone number and let it ring.

"Low," a sleepy female voice answered?

"You sleeping in this morning?"

"Bryant," exclaimed the voice, wide awake now! "Where are you?"

"I'm still on the face of the earth in case you were wondering," he answered his sister, Cynthia. It was nice to hear her voice. Despite the problems between him and their parents they had always been close. Maybe it was because of the lack of parental support that they bonded.

It had seemed at times it was just the two of them against the world. It made them both strong, but it also made them both yearn for the allusive love they were missing. He had given up and drew away from the family. She had, on the other hand, fought to be noticed by their parents by excelling at business and math and everything else she thought her Dad would notice.

This wasn't enough for her father who had his mind set on his son taking over the family business. At least at first it wasn't, but after Bryant was gone their father saw Cynthia in a whole new light. That was the one good thing about Bryant's absence.

"I was worried about you," she scolded. "After that fight you and Dad had I thought maybe we would never hear from you again."

"That was a possibility," Bryant admitted. He moved over to the railing and leaned against it breathing in the fresh air. The invigorating coolness stilled his nerves that were still stressed from the early morning events. "I needed time to consider my options."

"And have you found some?" she asked eagerly. She had always looked up to her brother. He had been the strength for her as they grew up.

155

She had understood why he needed to follow his own heart and had supported him. She herself had always loved the idea of being a business woman. Running operations and working figures came easy for her.

She felt bad that their father had cut Bryant out completely when he decided to join the Military. She hadn't felt bad that that bitch had dropped him. She had felt all along that she loved Bryant's money more than him.

"Yes," Bryant answered. "I found I had many more options than I thought."

"I am glad to hear that," Cynthia replied. She could hear the vibrancy in his voice. He may not be quite back to normal but she could tell he was on his way. "Are you still..." She paused not sure if she should ask.

"Blind?" Bryant finished the question for her. "Yes, but I have the feeling it won't be permanent."

"How can you tell?"

"I have been having flashes of vision," he answered. He felt no need to go into further details at this time. "They don't last but it's a positive sign, so I'm told."

"I'm glad to hear that," Cynthia was overjoyed in hearing this. "This means you'll be coming home soon?"

"I am home Cynci," he said using her knick he had always called her when growing up. "I am happy where I am now."

"I'm glad you found someplace to be happy," she replied, but still was sad he wouldn't return. She had always hoped he and their father could make up.

"I just need some answers Cynci,"

"About what?"

"About Julian," he simply said. There were some seconds of silence before Cynthia answered him. He could tell she was hesitant but knew she would also tell him the truth. She had never been silent about her dislike for the other woman.

"She's gone," she replied, "can't we leave it at that?"

"You always told me she was after my money," Bryant continued. "I agree with you now. But I need some answers."

"Okay," Cynthia answered, breathing out a sigh of relief. "I'll answer if I can." She made herself comfortable in her bed. Today she had planned on sleeping in. She glanced at the clock. Well that could be considered sleeping in she guessed seeing it was past 8AM.

"Basically, I have just one question."

"And that is?"

"When I left for the Military," he began, hesitated then finished, "was she faithful to me. The long pause answered his question before Cynthia answered.

"Well, I never actually followed her around," she began, "but then she never really hid it either."

"That's all I needed," Bryant stopped her before she could say more. His heart was totally free. Any remnants of doubt about his feelings for her were swept away. He knew he could move on now.

"You okay?"

"Never been better," he answered energetically.

"Bryant?"

Bryant knew that tone and knew the question before she asked it. "My door has never been closed to him, but he has to open his."

"I'm glad to hear that too," she answered. The beeping on her line let her know she had another call. She also knew who it was and gave another sigh. Her father didn't believe in personal days. "I got somebody on the other line, can you hold?"

"You go answer it," he replied happily. He knew he would always have his sister and could let her go do her thing now. "I got some fish to catch for dinner."

"Bye Bryant," she replied and added. "You better call me back soon. Don't be a stranger anymore."

"I will and I won't," he replied and shut off the phone. He leaned against the rail and let the sounds and smells of the forest fall over him. He felt at peace knowing the truth and being able to let go. He wasn't sad, nor was he angry. He was just glad he could let her go.

He turned and headed in to get his fishing supplies. There were fish with his name on them just waiting to be caught. Suddenly life didn't seem such a strain. He had a feeling things were going to change for the better. Now all he had to do was figure out what was going on with Shel. It didn't sound like a bad thing; there was no stress in his voice. It seemed more like relief and anticipation. Whatever it was he was sure Shel would tell him when he was ready.

Chapter 21

"Hey Mommy!" Sheldon yelled from his perch atop the little pony, "Look at me!" Kelly waved from her spot leaning on a paddock rail. Kelly could see he was having the time of his life.

In the last few days the boy had blossomed under the watchful eyes of his grandpa and uncle, not to mention all the cowhands who had adopted him into their circle.

There had been mild surprise when she was introduced to them that second day, but no hostilities. They seemed extremely happy to see how blissful Weldon was all of a sudden. These cowboys were a close knit group and Kelly had no idea how like family they were. She never experienced a real family in this positive way let alone seeing an extended family being there for somebody not even related to them.

Kelly had wondered what this move would do to Sheldon, but at the same time knew it couldn't be any worse than the atmosphere back in Chicago. Her two brothers never paid attention to the boy. They were too caught up in their lives to worry about a nephew. That wasn't the case here. No matter how busy Shel was he had time for his namesake. Her brothers hadn't bothered coming over after their mother died, so when she moved, she didn't bother telling them. Let them find out on their own she figured grimly.

"He's looking good," Weldon said as he came up beside her. He didn't tell Kelly that she also was looking good. The pale shy young lady who arrived a few days ago had vanished to be replaced by a smiling happy woman. She was already taking on color from being out in the sun and gained some weight from Rosa's good cooking. She had been way to skinny in his book.

Kelly smiled at her father. He couldn't know how it felt to be beside somebody and want to just hug the life out of them. He made her feel special without saying anything. He made her feel worthwhile. Most of all, he made her happy just being here.

She experienced a tang of anger at her mother for robbing her of this loving generous father. Kelly could understand why Shel had trouble letting go of his anger towards his mother's abandonment, but at the same time she knew she had to forgive her in order to slough off the past and have a good future to look forward to. She had to forgive her for her own peace of mind.

Kelly looked to her father and wondered how he had been able to forgive her mother. She knew he had, could see it in his eyes. She also knew he had forgiven himself for what he thought was his fault in her leaving in the first place. If nothing else, Kelly realized, her showing up with his grandson had given the older man a renewed thirst for life. She could feel the vibrancy of him whenever he was near. It was contagious and she gathered strength from him. Yes, she knew that for once life was worth looking forward to, not lamenting over.

"He loves that pony," Kelly agreed with her father, "He is learning so fast."

"How about you?" he asked. He didn't have to say about what. They had been trying to get Kelly on a horse since the first day. Kelly couldn't explain the fear she had. It felt so irrational but was so real, just looking at a horse from a distance made her stomach knot up.

To try and approach one sent spasms down her legs and froze her to the spot. She didn't know how to explain this fear to her father or brother. So, she just stayed outside and watched from a distance. She could see the disappointment in Shel's eyes but he didn't say anything.

"I'm not sure how to explain to you why horses scare me so," Kelly answered.

"Well dear," Weldon placed his hand on Kelly's arm, "Why don't you start at the beginning."

Kelly thought back to when she was just a little older than Sheldon is now. Her mother had taken her to a riding farm outside the city limits. There

160

Kelly saw her first horse and got to ride for the first time. She loved it, took to it like a duck takes to water. After that her mother took her nearly every weekend throughout the summer. She warned Kelly not to tell Morris though. Kelly already at that point in her life knew what her mother meant by not telling Morris. If he found out they were doing something fun, he would stop it.

Somehow he did find out. Kelly had no idea how. She had never told him, but near the end of that summer, Morris took Kelly for a ride in the car. She was surprised because he never took her anywhere. They drove into the country and he pulled into a riding stable she didn't know.

It was nothing like the nice one her mother took her too. This one was rundown and shabby. The horses were scruffy and looked half wild. They got out of the car and a man came up. He was quite rough looking. It was obvious he knew Morris. They talked a minute while Kelly stood by the car and looked around. This place scared her, she wasn't sure why till they led her to a corral. There was a very large rank looking horse inside saddled and waiting. His eyes were wild and he snorted and pawed his hoof as they approached. Kelly had always ridden smaller gentler horses at the other stables. She had never been near such a big beast. She stopped in her tracks. Morris turned around and laughed at her.

"What," he sneered, "you just a big baby or what?"

"No," Kelly whispered, shaking her head. She did not want to go anywhere near this beast. The horse lowered his head and stared right at her. Her stomach turned into mush and she thought she would throw up right there.

This was not a nice gentle mare like she was use to. She started to back up. Morris chuckled harshly as he grabbed her and lofted her up onto the saddle. The saddle was way too big as was the horse. She couldn't even reach the stirrups. Morris just plopped her down rather hard and let go and the men backed away. Kelly hadn't even gotten the reins in her hands yet when the horse reared up and took off. She hung on for dear life as the horse

161

bucked and plunged around the corral. Finally, it turned sharply and she went flying to the hard ground. Pain raced up her arm. She could hear the men laughing as she tried to get up. Morris sauntered over and dragged her to her feet.

"Try and sneak around on me again and you'll get worse," he hissed as he dragged her to the car, ignoring her cries of pain. When they arrived home her mother took one look at her and rushed her to the hospital. She had broken her arm in three places, having to spend months in casts. Kelly hadn't been near a horse since.

She relayed all this to Weldon and he listened to her story silently, only a tick in his left cheek gave away his growing anger as Kelly finished. They stood in silence after she finished watching the two Sheldon's on the horses in the middle of the corral. Shel had glanced over at them a few times and could tell Kelly was telling their father something. She had such a sad look on her face as she talked. He wondered what it could be. He saw her hand rubbing her right arm as she finished the story; it looked almost like it pained her.

Weldon reached out and put his arm around Kelly's slender shoulders and held her close. "Do you trust me?" he asked softly.

She nodded her head in silent answer.

"Then come with me and trust I'd never do anything to hurt you." He was thinking of all he would like to do with that ass Morris though as he spoke.

He never gave away his absolute hate for that man who had hurt the ones Weldon had loved. He cringed at the pain in Kelly's eyes. Morris had set out deliberately to hurt her and take away something she had obviously loved. He was now determined to give back to her what Morris had taken so cruelly away.

Weldon led Kelly into the barn and over to a stall. The horse inside was a gentle mare he knew would win Kelly's heart. "I'd like you to meet

Gracie. This old girl here loves to be brushed, so why don't we give her a good brushing."

Weldon handed Kelly a brush and taking one for himself, opened the gate and entered the stall. He turned and motioned Kelly to follow. She did, slowly. Her heart was in her throat. Her heartbeat threatened to burst her chest.

The mare turned her head and looked straight into Kelly's eyes. Kelly fully expected to see an evil glare emanating from her eyes, but instead she saw a big, soft, brown gentle expression. Gracie nickered softly to Kelly and reached out her long velvety nose to sniff at the new person who had just entered her stall. Weldon was already talking to the mare and scratching her behind the ears, her favorite place. Kelly stood still for a minute before slowly raising her hand to let Gracie sniff her hand. Gracie sniffed at the offered hand then pushed her nose into the palm and ran her tongue over it.

"Oh," Kelly giggled at the rough texture and stickiness of the tongue. Weldon dropped a sugar cube into Kelly's palm. She stood perfectly still while Gracie sniffed once again before carefully nipping the cube off her palm and happily crunching it. Kelly smiled at Weldon and with renewed confidence she stepped closer and placed a hand on Gracie's neck. The horse responded with a light bump of her head to Kelly's shoulder.

"She wants you to scratch," Weldon informed her. She started gently running her fingers up and down the mare's neck. Gracie responded with another soft whinny and bobbing of her head. "She likes you."

"She is precious," Kelly replied as she continued petting her. Weldon started brushing the mares back from his side and after watching him a moment Kelly followed suit. They worked in silence for a while till they finished brushing Gracie from front to back.

"You ready to try and sit on her back?"

"You mean ride her," Kelly asked as fear came flooding back suddenly.

"No, I mean just sit on her back right here in the stall." Weldon answered as he came around. "She won't move, I promise."

Kelly looked at the mare as she was happily munching her oats. As if knowing she was being stared at, Gracie turned her head to stare back at Kelly. The soft expressive brown eyes lay to rest Kelly's fears and she could have sworn the mare winked at her.

With renewed confidence she nodded once again. Weldon stepped in front of her and knelt to place his hands clasped in front of her. He directed her to step onto his hand with one foot so he could fling her leg over the mares back. Before she realized it, Kelly was perched on a horse for the first time since she was seven years old. She felt the warmth of the mare's back seeping through the material of her jeans. Gracie smelt of sun and air.

Kelly sat there amazed. How could she ever have been frightened of this gentle animal? She looked down at Weldon and smiled. He returned her smile.

"I told you to trust me," he said softly. "How's it feel?"

"It feels good," Kelly laughed softly. She found herself relaxing and actually remembered why she had so loved riding. The feeling of the powerful yet gentle animals beneath her was so pleasurable. "I think I am ready to try riding now."

"You sure?" he asked.

"Yes," she replied softly as she patted Gracie's neck. She leaned forward and laid her head on the animal's neck. It felt so right. "I am ready."

Weldon helped her down and led the mare out of the stall and over to the tack room. He tethered her and went inside to retrieve a saddle and reins. He had the horse ready for a rider in a few minutes. Kelly came up beside the mare and with his help swung into the saddle. Her body immediately remembered the long ago lessons and she settled into a comfortable position. Weldon adjusted the stirrups and backed away.

"Take her up and down here a few times." Kelly did as told and found herself guiding the mare in circles and up and down the barns length. She smiled widely at Weldon. "Thanks Dad."

They both looked startled at the word that just left Kelly's mouth. It had been totally unconscious and had felt so right for Kelly to say. It had come automatically. For Weldon to hear the word uttered by his daughter was pure music to his ears.

"You ready to show your brother and son what you can do?"

Kelly nodded and let the horse follow Weldon to the barn door.

"Hey you two," He called to the two guys in the corral, "You want company?"

The two guys turned as Kelly exited the barn and turned Gracie toward them. She let the horse trot over to them and reined in beside them. The grin on her face matched that on her brother's. She winked at him before turning to her son. "Let's go around the fence."

"Yah, Yah, Yah," shouted the boy as he turned his pony around and led the way. Kelly followed him, playfully sticking her tongue out at her brother as she passed him. He just stood there shaking his head. Seeing his father standing by the barn he headed that way to see how he had gotten Kelly on a horse.

Kelly and Sheldon road for another fifteen minutes and headed over to where Shel and Weldon were talking by the door. They had nearly reached them when a loud sound above caused all of them to look up. Kelly screamed as Shel pushed his mount into Weldon suddenly to knock him out of the way. They had just cleared the door when the bale of hay slammed onto the very spot they had been standing.

Kelly and Sheldon rushed over to where Shel was jumping off his horse to help Weldon up where he had fallen. Everything had happened so fast Kelly couldn't believe they hadn't been smashed by that huge thing.

"Dad," She called as she jumped off her horse and rushed over to him. "You okay?"

Weldon held up a hand as he leaned against a fence post to catch his breath. A moment later he nodded. "Just got the air knocked out of me," he said. "I'll be okay. Did anybody see what the hell happened? How did a bale fall out the loft door?"

"There's no way a bale can just fall from the loft door," Shel yelled as he jumped up and headed for the stairs leading to the loft. By this time the cowboys who had been working in the general area had made it to the barn and several followed him.

Kelly went over to where Sheldon was still sitting on his pony looking very scared. "Grandpa okay?"

"Yes dear," Kelly soothed him. "He'll be okay. You want to see?" He nodded.

She helped him down so he could go see that grandpa was okay. When she was certain the two were together and others were there to watch over them she followed Shel to the loft.

Shel was standing by the open loft door. That wasn't uncommon since they had dropped some bales out not so long ago that day. They usually dropped bales twice a day for feeding the horses. Far as Kelly could see, there weren't any other bales that close to the door. Shel was leaning over looking at something. Kelly went over to see what it was. The men parted to let her closer.

"What you got?"

"No way did that bale fall by itself," Shel said again. He pointed to a spot. "It was dragged from there to the door and pushed off. See the drag marks?"

"But who would do that?"

Shel looked at the men around him. The men all looked uncomfortable but not guilty. "Anybody see anything or anybody out of the ordinary?" The men all shook their head as they looked at each other.

"We had better get down there and let Dad know what's going on," Kelly said to Shel. They went down to see Weldon had scattered the other

166

hands and one look from him made the others run off to their various chores. He and Sheldon had unsaddled the pony and horses and were leading them into the stalls.

"Well?" He asked over his shoulder.

"It looks suspicious," Shel said. "That bale had been dragged to the door and pushed over."

"And you can tell that from the other bales that are dragged over and pushed off daily?"

Shel had the grace to blush at that. "There was a difference."

"Nonsense," Weldon scoffed. "It's obvious that the bale was left too close to the edge and finally slid off.

"Anybody who believes that raise your hand," Shel muttered as he lead his horse to the stall.

Kelly looked over to her Dad who was returning from settling his horse and the pony. "Has this sort of thing happened before?"

"No"

"Then why aren't you taking it serious?"

"It was an accident," Weldon insisted and turned for the main door. "Now, let's go for lunch before Rosa sends the Calvary."

167

Chapter 22

"Hey sis," Shel walked into the kitchen of her house a few days later. "Want to take a ride up the mountain?"

Kelly looked up from the veggies she was chopping at the man walking in and thought how much different things were here than when she lived in Chicago. You couldn't leave your doors unlocked and open let alone let people just walk in. She smiled up at her brother, something unheard of for her other two brothers in Chicago.

"Now?"

"Yes," he answered, "The horses are saddled, ready, and waiting for us."

"What about Sheldon?"

"Dad is waiting for him," Shel answered easily, obviously having an answer for any question she asked. "He thought they could go into town for lunch."

"Sheldon will love that," Kelly added absentmindedly as she put the veggies away and washed her hands. She couldn't help but smile at how close Sheldon has gotten to both his new grandpa and his new uncle. In fact she was surprised that they weren't taking the boy with them. It seemed the boy knew telepathically if a horse was being saddled and was ready to go along. "But why isn't he going with us?"

"I would but this trip may be too long for him," Shel answered. "Better take some extra clothes over also, he may need to spend the night."

"We won't make it back before night?" This surprised Kelly. She wasn't sure if she was ready for a camping trip up on a mountain slope.

"We should, but better to be safe than sorry," Shel answered. "We're going to go up the mountain to get my friend who's staying in our cabin up there."

169

"Oh," Kelly perked up as she realized this must be that Bryant guy Shel had mentioned before. Why just thinking of him caught her interest she had no idea. Perhaps it was because there was an air of mystery around him.

Bryant packed the last of his things in his backpack. Shel had called earlier saying he was on his way up with peachy. Bryant could swear there was something different about Shel. There was something exciting him. There was an upbeat tone to his voice. It was something Bryant hadn't heard in Shel's voice for a long time.

Bryant had felt a change in Shel from that first call telling him he would be at least a week. He knew something was going on down there while he was up here contemplating his life and it had nothing to do with new calves arriving.

He wondered if Shel's ex-wife had returned but would that be a good thing? Maybe it was a new woman in his life, somebody who would appreciate the wild isolation of the ranch and the man who lives there. Bryant shook his head. Man, why did those thoughts suddenly pop into his head?

Bryant stood at the window and stared sightlessly out of it. The cabin was surrounded by trees with just enough of a break in them one could see the mountain raising up in the distance through the branches. Shel had described it many times while they were camped out on maneuvers in Afghanistan. Shel would look around at the rugged rocky mostly barren mountains and point out the differences in his beloved wild Rockies.

Sometimes he talked about his wife. When he described her it was with the same love and reverent tone he used for his beloved mountains. Shel must have been devastated when she left. One lonely night he told Bryant about his mother and how she had abandoned him and his father. Bryant had heard the deep sadness in the other mans voice. He could see the hurt little boy in the story that Shel had told.

At the hospital when Shel had admitted his wife had left in much the same way Bryant had once again heard that sadness. This time it seemed to stay weighing down the man's all ready slow speech. Today there was this lightness to the man's tone Bryant had never heard. He was happy to hear it but couldn't help but wonder what had put it there.

Bryant shook his head; this was totally unlike him to be thinking so stoically. He had lived like a monk since his return from Afghanistan. With his injuries he figured no woman would ever be interested in him again. He couldn't see what he had to offer.

He stood tall and lean. His frame that had become so emaciated before his recovery had filled out. His dark blue eyes still emitted sparks when he looked at someone. His rugged facial features caused women to take second and third looks when he walked by. The light burn scars and the rugged shrapnel scar on his face only lent to add a roguish look. Of course he was 'blind' to this.

His confidence and strong will set him apart from any man around him. Unless told, most people didn't realize Bryant was blind; he didn't act like a blind man.

That was what led Shel to believe it had to be psychological blindness. It was like Bryant could see; just his brain didn't recognize it. He knew Bryant's other senses had greatly improved but that still didn't allow for how well he knew what was going on around him. It was like his brain knew he could see though his eyes didn't. Shel had decided to play the waiting game and hoped that soon something would happen to jog his brain back to normal.

Bryant heard the horses coming up the path. He finished dressing and made his way to the front door. He wondered what this surprise was Shel had. He heard three horses coming up the trail. Two had riders so that meant someone was with him. He was waiting on the front porch when the horses broke into the clearing.

171

Kelly was curious about Shel's friend. She took the long ride up as an opportunity to ask questions. He had been rather closed mouth, saying only they had served together in the military. When she gently pressed about his service in the Special Forces Shel had gone quiet. Kelly had figured she had gone too far and let him alone. After they had ridden silently for a while Shel stated talking. He described some of what they had gone through in Afghanistan. He carefully described the attack they had gone through and how Bryant had saved his life. This was the first time Shel had talked to Kelly about his injuries to his leg.

"I lost my leg during that incident," Shel explained. "But, if Bryant hadn't been there, I would have lost my whole life. I can live with one leg. I am just thankful to be alive."

Kelly asked if Bryant had been injured. Shel had simply answered yes but didn't elaborate. That left Kelly in the dark as to what to expect when they finally arrived at the cabin. Her thoughts ran wild.

Who was this man who got so much respect from her brother? Why was he now working for Shel rather than home with his family? And mostly, why was he hiding up here in the mountains all alone? What was he hiding? Kelly was very intrigued with this mystery man even before they arrived at the cabin.

When they broke from the woods into the clearing Kelly saw a Greek God standing on the cabin's front porch. A god who looked like he had gone a few rounds with mortality. This friend of Shel's body spoke of masculinity in every hard muscle that bulged through his tight shirt and jeans. Man what the sight of those narrow hips did to her pulse.

He turned their way and she felt lightening course through her as they got close enough to see dark sparkling eyes set in a chiseled face. As they reached the steps of the porch, Kelly saw the burn scars on one side and the long scar running down the other side of the cheeks. This man had been through the baptism of fire.

Bryant waited impatiently for the riders to approach the cabin. He was curious about who could be with Shel. He knew his imagination had been running away from him. The second rider had to be one of the cowhands from the ranch, though he had no idea why one would ride up there. Shel had made this trip alone many times and they both knew Bryant was capable of riding without aid.

The wind shifted and blew from the direction of the riders. Instantly, Bryant caught a light whiff of a flowery fragrance on the breeze. It was a fresh new scent that hadn't been there before. It wasn't his imagination. Shel had brought a woman with him. Who it could be, Bryant could not even guess. He wondered if it was the ex-wife.

Though it had crossed his mind the second rider could be a woman, it still surprised him that it actually was. He hadn't seen many women come out to the ranch in the last few months. There was Rosa of course. She wouldn't be caught dead on a horse. Mavis came to visit Weldon from time to time, but she wouldn't ride up here with Shel.

Chapter 23

He could only stand there waiting for them to dismount. Shel hadn't said a word to give away his secret friend until they dismounted and walked up to the porch. Bryant stepped down the steps to meet them.

"Bryant," Shel addressed him, "I would like you to meet Kelly. Kelly, this is my military buddy Bryant."

So she wasn't Shel's ex. She was somebody new. Shel had mentioned various attractive women in the nearby town of Bozeman but this lady's name was not one of them. He greeted her politely if not a little coolly. "Nice to meet you Ma'am."

"Please to meet you also," Kelly responded as she shook the hand that extended to her. There was an instant shock that raced through her body from the touch. His deep rough voice caressed up and down her senses roughly and erotically. Her knees felt suddenly weak and it wasn't from the long ride. She added rather weakly, "And please call me Kelly."

Kelly had also noticed that Shel had failed to mention that she was his sister. Of course anybody looking at them couldn't help but see the similarities between them.

"As you wish Ma'am," Bryant answered trying to ignore the electricity that had run straight to his groin. That soft voice filled his ears with glorious sound.

"I mean Kelly." He smiled ever so slightly at that little slip. It didn't quite reach his eyes she noticed. Kelly tried to imagine that stone sculptured face smiling in a full grin that went all the way to his eyes. She imagined it would transform those stark hard features dramatically. His eyes were so dark she wasn't sure what the color was. They could be brown, a dark chocolate brown that she could imagine melting with desire.

'Oh please,' Kelly thought with an inner groan and made a note to throw out all her cheesy romance novels. Shel couldn't help but notice the spark between them. It was either a good thing and they would like each other or, it could very well mean they repelled each other at first sight. Or in Bryant's case first touch. Shel knew that so far Bryant had no idea Kelly was his sister. He wondered how Bryant would react to that. He decided to wait before telling him.

He hid a secret smile at the results of this first meeting. The electricity in the air was not all due to the storm that was approaching. As if reading his thoughts, lightening streaked through the sky followed by the clash of thunder. Kelly and Bryant both jumped and that magical moment ended as they abruptly broke off the hand shake.

"I think we better get these horses under cover before that rain hits." Shel had no sooner said the last word and the first big drop plopped the ground next to his feet. He turned and led his horse toward the back of the cabin. As he walked past Kelly he winked at her and she instantly realized what he was up to. She threw him a dirty look and he just laughed.

Bryant, who had automatically gone over to his horse, felt instant jealousy toward his friend. He also felt instantly ashamed. Shel deserved to find a good woman and to be happy. He remembered the reaction he had at just Kelly's touch. He was sure that she also had felt something. Her voice had fractionally wavered for a moment when their hands had touched. If she was so affected by just a handshake of a stranger, then how strong were her feelings for Shel? Bryant knew he had to find that out. He also tried to tell himself it was for Shel's sake he had to do this.

Something deep inside of him that he had tried to bury had suddenly come to the surface. Bryant wasn't too pleased at this. He was just starting to get use to his new hermit surroundings. He wasn't sure he wanted those other feelings loose again.

Kelly followed Shel to a shed behind the cabin as Bryant followed her. She stole a few glances back at the man as he led his horse after her. He was stroking the mare and whispering to her. It was obvious the mare knew his voice and seemed happy to see him.

176

Suddenly Kelly felt hot flow over her skin as she imagined those strong hands stroking her body. Oh God, she groaned silently admonishing herself for letting those thoughts cross her mind. With the approaching storm it was obvious they would all three be staying the night in the cabin.

It was already late afternoon and Kelly was surprised they had left as late as they had. Shel would have known how long it takes to get to the cabin by horse. She glanced forward and caught Shel looking back at her with a smirk on his face. Damn that man. He had planned this. She gave him what she hoped was a very disapproving look but instead of being admonished for his actions, he burst out laughing.

Bryant heard the laughter and suddenly felt like the third man out and wished it wasn't too late to head down the mountain to the relative safety of his digs in the barn. He had moved from the house to an apartment at the back of the barn. It had once been used by the foreman of the crew but he had since left and the new foreman was married and lived just off ranch. Bryant had been more comfortable being on his own as much as possible. He knew he couldn't depend on the charity of Shel and his father indefinitely.

Now, he felt a pang of jealousy when he heard that soft sweet burst of laughter come from her lips. He could picture those lips full and luscious, ready to be kissed, but kissed by Shel and not him. Bryant shook his head to clear those lecherous thoughts.

How could he be jealous of Shel? He had been hoping the man could find somebody to make him happy again. Shel deserved as much. All he could think of now was how miserable he was going to be tonight listening to those two get all cuddly and warm in front of the fire.

Bryant felt the electricity raise the hair on his arms before the percussion of the nearby hit sent him flying. For a moment he swore he saw the scene before him, including the two in front of him. They turned as the bolt hit the tree next to him with looks of horror. That's the last thing he remembered as the jolt threw him across the clearing.

"Bryant," Shel shouted as his friend was tossed across the clearing! He and Kelly rushed to Bryant. Fortunately he was still alive. Shel couldn't find any burns on him and he was breathing. Kelly started checking for broken bones, but everything seemed to be okay except for the warmth that swept through her as she ran her hands up and down his legs and arms. A groan told them he was starting to come to.

Bryant opened his eyes and thought he must have died and gone to heaven for there was an angel leaning over him. With a face that was oval and slight in bone, a nose that tweaked up just so. The lips were full and very kissable. Her hair was soft and strawberry blond the same shade as Shel's. In the instant he realized he could see her, the world faded back into black. Then Bryant closed his eyes again and let out another moan. Nope, this was real life alright.

"Bryant," Shel shouted into Bryant's ear making him jump. "Hey buddy, can you hear me?"

Bryant tried to sit up. "I'm blind not deaf Shel," he replied sardonically. He managed to reach a sitting position but wasn't sure he could stay that way. "What happened?"

"You nearly got hit by lightening," Kelly answered him. She was still digesting the fact he said he was blind. He certainly didn't look like it, or act like it. She couldn't believe he was. When they first met she could have sworn he had looked right through her eyes straight into her soul.

"Lightening?" he laughed. "I guess it'll take more than that to take me out. Help me off the ground will you Shel?"

"Oh, no you don't," Shel placed a firm hand on Bryant's shoulder. "You went flying at least twenty feet. You could have injured something."

"You mean more than my pride?" Bryant joked, and then wished he hadn't tried laughing. He realized his head was buzzing. He tried a different approach, keeping his voice light, he asked, "Am I smoking?"

"Well, not that I can see," Shel answered. He gave Kelly a wink. He knew Bryant and he knew that from the way he was acting, he may be singed but not seriously hurt. "But, what I need to do is make sure there are no bones broken from your tumble."

"Christ, Shel," Bryant suddenly flared, "It would take more than flying twenty feet to hurt me and you know it! Stop babying me and help me up."

Kelly burst out laughing. She didn't mean to be rude, but she had never seen a man trying to be more macho. She wondered if this was an act for her benefit, or over compensation for his blindness, or was he actually always like this. She wasn't sure that was a good thing or not. She realized Shel and Bryant were looking her way. She had the curtsey to blush over her outburst.

"Don't you think we should be trying to get him and the horses inside, before this storm break loose?" she asked. Shel nodded while Bryant just sat there looking at her. How could he stare so frankly if he couldn't see, she wondered? A big raindrop hit her nose and she jumped. Shel was on his feet and helping Bryant up as more followed.

"Shel, you help Bryant inside and I'll gather the horses and take them to the shed," she ordered and ran toward the horses before either could answer. She glanced back and saw Bryant had made his feet and though unsteady seemed to be able to move.

Fortunately the horses knew where safety was and had already gathered near the shed. All Kelly had to do was open the door and they went right in. She followed them inside as the drops became a downpour. Kelly looked out the door and saw Shel leading Bryant up the stairs of the cabin. She was safe and fairly dry but the men were both drenched and she couldn't help but laugh to herself at the comical sight of them trying to reach the door.

Shel and Bryant raced for the cabin fast as Bryant could manage. It wasn't fast enough to beat the deluge as the skies opened up. Shel got the door open and pulled Bryant inside.

"You okay buddy?" he asked.

"I think I'll live," Bryant replied sardonically. He was embarrassed more than hurt. But he was starting to feel somewhat stiff. He was sure nothing was broken but a few muscles were starting to protest. He didn't bother telling Shel that though. "We should get out there and help your sister with those horses."

"I'll go once I am sure you are…" he stopped in mid sentence and stared at Bryant in surprise. Bryant turned towards his room to go and get dried off, but was also hiding a smile. He knew he got Shel's attention on that one. "How did you know she was my sister?"

"Either you changed a lot in the last week," he replied simply, "or that woman is your sister, though I don't ever recall you mentioning a sister in any of your stories about home." He didn't wait at his door for the barrage of questions but started stripping off his soaked clothing. He was about to drop his jeans when he heard Shel follow him into the room.

"You could see when you came to?"

"Just for a second," Bryant answered. "Then it faded, but I got a good enough look to see that she wears your looks better than you do."

Bryant went to the dresser and pulled out dry clothes. He silently pulled on a dry shirt and then dropped his pants and stepped into dry ones. He was waiting for Shel to continue. When he didn't he asked the question that had come to mind first. "You never mentioned having a sister?"

"That's because I didn't know," Shel replied. "Apparently my mother was pregnant with her when she left us."

"I am sorry," Bryant could imagine the shock to find out a sister existed. "How did you find out?"

"My grandmother left her an inheritance," Shel answered the questions simply without offering anything more. Bryant wondered if he should drop it.

"I guess it's really none of my business," he said as he finished dressing and turned back to Shel. "I am glad to see you both seem to get along."

Shel laughed at this. At Bryant's questioning look Shel finally told him what happened. "You see, I had a hard time believing it myself," he said, and then continued in a rush. "Then I saw her and her son. I couldn't deny how much we looked alike. If she had been the child of that other man, well, there was no way she could look so much like me."

"It must have been a shock," Bryant said as he picked up his wet things and deposited them in the bathroom hamper then headed for the front of the cabin. Shel followed.

"Shocked isn't the word," he added. "But it didn't take long to see she was…" he trailed off trying to think of the word he wanted to describe what he had thought after that first time they talked.

"Nice," Bryant supplied for him?

"Yah, nice for sure," Shel continued. "I didn't want her to be nice. I wanted her to be …I don't know anything but likable. Anyway, she is very nice considering how she was raised."

"I take it her upbringing wasn't as solid as yours?"

"That's for sure," Shel agreed. He stopped and looked at Bryant getting on a rain slicker. "What are you doing?"

"If you're not going out to help her, I will," was all he said as he turned toward the door.

"Oh, no you don't," Shel grabbed his arm to stop him. "You just about nearly got fried. You need to stay in here and rest."

"Do I look like I am having a problem?" Bryant asked a bit testily. "I am fine now."

That was true for the most part. He could feel a twinge in his shoulder where he had taken the brunt of the fall but other than that he felt quite well. He knew he had been very lucky. If that strike had hit the ground next to him instead of a tree he could have been fried as Shel had so succinctly put it.

Now, curiosity about this woman was turning his insides to mush. That was something that worried him more than the near lightening strike.

181

No woman had ever affected him the way that first touch and then sight of her had affected him. He wanted to see if it was just a one time thing or if her mere presence would cause his skin to feel like fire again. He issued an order to Shel as he went out the door.

"I got some fish in the fridge for our supper. You can get them cooking while we take care of the horses."

Shel stared out the door as it slammed shut. He shook his head as he automatically turned to do as he had been told. Bryant hadn't lost his take charge way about him that was for sure. Good thing Bryant hadn't been able to see the smirk on his face though. He had formulated his scheme the night before.

He had learned from Kelly the bare sketches of her life from Morris' abusive up bringing to her brief marriage to a much older man. Though he hadn't been obviously abusive he controlled all aspects of her life. He could see she was now just learning her independence and fighting all the way for it. She wouldn't let Weldon or Shel do things she thought she could do herself.

He could see where she would be gun shy about men, but that didn't stop him from thinking of matching her and Bryant up. He had seen how Bryant treated women and knew he would treat Kelly the way she deserved to be treated with respect.

When he had mentioned to his father about inviting Kelly to ride up to the cabin with him to retrieve Bryant the older man had just raised an eyebrow in the Shepard way they all had. Sheldon didn't mention his idea but Weldon got it and didn't seem to disapprove. All he said was tread lightly and went back to his paper.

182

Chapter 24

Kelly turned to the horses who had gathered around a feeding trough. She busied herself at finding the feed and filling the water trough. She wanted to keep busy to keep thoughts of Bryant out of her mind. It wasn't working.

Did his scars go down his body or just cover his face and neck? Had he had other injuries besides the superficial? 'Of course he was blind idiot,' she thought. So he had to have other injuries. Shel wouldn't go into details of that attack in Afghanistan except that Bryant had saved him. That meant he was a man whose loyalty superseded his own welfare. The fact that he was here on the ranch proved that the loyalty to each other went both ways. Shel wouldn't let a friend down when he needed help.

She wasn't sure why the idea of watching him shed his wet clothing had entered her mind or why it sent shivers of delight up her spine. She hadn't even thought of another man since her husband died. She had sworn she didn't need a man in her life anymore. Now she was going hot and cold from thoughts about a stranger shedding wet clothing. She told herself it was a chill from the cool breeze coming through the slightly open door that made her shiver now and not errant thoughts. She continued telling herself that as she started unsaddling the horses. She had nearly finished putting the saddles up when she realized she was being watched.

"How's your friend?" she asked without turning thinking it was Shel standing in the doorway. She could imagine that quick grin on her brother's face.

"I'm fine, thank-you," Bryant answered dryly. He managed to hide the laugh he felt from the look on her face he imagined as she twirled around to face him.

He had hoped she wouldn't notice him for a while. He had stopped in the doorway and listened to her murmuring to the horses as she fed and unsaddled them. She had a soft and gentle nature about her. He could picture her in his bed whispering sweet nothings in that same soft voice. He felt a certain part of his body respond immediately to those thoughts and thought maybe he should step back out in the cool rain. But, before he could move she had realized he was there and spoke. She had good senses he noted since she had known somebody was there before she turned around.

"I...I'm sorry," she stammered. "I figured Shel would come out to help me."

"He planned on it," Bryant answered as he stepped inside and grabbed a brush. He made sure to place himself on the opposite side of a horse from her. "But I put him on KP detail."

"Your still giving the orders," she laughed. Bryant let the soft sound wash over him. It was pure bliss. How could he have ever thought he liked the cynical stingy snorts Julian had?

"Actually, who is boss has switched since I came here," he answered with what he hoped a normal voice. "Since Shel is the boss now he usually issues the orders. I can't help but take advantage when the situation presents itself."

"So, you work for my Dad and brother?" she asked. She wanted to keep him talking. She hoped to find out all she could about him to strip away some of the mystery of this man.

"Your brother was the only one who gave a damn when things weren't going very well for me," Bryant answered slightly bitterly. Kelly could sense it in his voice. "He came to my rescue and when he was sure I could handle things around the ranch without walking under a horse, he gave me a job."

"From what I have learned about my brother in the short time I have been here," Kelly responded to that information, "I can believe that." She wondered how much Shel had told him about her but decided against asking. Things fell silent as they worked on the horses till they finished the last horse.

185

Kelly was putting away her brush when Bryant came up behind her. She felt his body heat through her clothes even though he didn't make contact as he reached around her and put his brush on the shelf next to hers. She breathed deeply his manly smell. He had a light musky scent. She was glad he didn't go for those flowery aftershaves she was use to smelling on Morris. The soft musk suited him perfectly. It accented his masculinity. Here was a man who didn't have to prove he was a man.

She waited for him to move back but he didn't. She could feel his body just inches from hers. She wanted to lean back against his hardness and feel his arms come around her and hold her close. His lips were hovering near her ear. She could feel his soft breath on her neck. He took a deep breath as if pulling in her scent.

Mark hadn't been one for displays of affection and he had never come up behind her to just hold her close. It was something she had always hungered for, the feel of a set of strong arms to hold her tight and let her know all was right. As if reading her mind he gently wrapped his arms around her and pulled her back against him. He folded his arms just below her breast and pressed his nose in her hair.

"I love the scent of natural hair," he said softly as he moved his lips to her neck and let them trail along the line just below her hair.

"How, do you know my hair is natural?" she asked breathlessly. His lips were leaving a trail of fire behind them on her neck.

"It's the same color of Shel's," he answered. "There is no way to get that shade from a bottle." Kelly suddenly stiffened in his arms and pulled away. She swiftly turned to face him. They were still very close in the cramped space. His arms were still resting lightly at her waist.

"I thought you were blind?"

"I am," he answered quietly. He breathed in her scent remembering what she looked like. That soft reddish color with blond highlights streaking through it accentuated her full cheekbones. He loved the way it had curled around her square features softening them. Those soft full red lips and eyes

186

that were so much like Shel's to be scary. He would never have described Shel's features as feminine but those same features on Kelly were as feminine as they got.

"Then how do you know my hair is the same as Shel's?"

"I saw you as I came to after being thrown by that bolt," he continued in the same firm but soft voice. "You see, they tell me my blindness is cause from mental problems not physical."

"You mean hysterical blindness?"

"Something like that," he answered, happy she didn't jump to the conclusion he was just plain crazy. "Apparently that jolt of electricity stimulated my sight for just a second. That's how I figured out you were Shel's sister."

"Oh," she answered quietly. She gazed deeply into those steal blue eyes and realized that's why he didn't seem blind, why he could seem to look right through you. "That means you should get your sight back someday?"

"There's always hope," he replied softly and started to move closer to her again. He couldn't believe his boldness. He usually moved slowly with women but he couldn't with Kelly. Something about her drew him ever closer. He wanted to taste those lips beneath his. He also knew instinctively that sexual desire weren't the only feelings running through him. If that had been the case he would never had made a move on his best friends sister nearly the instant he had met her. He didn't understand how he knew, but her lips weren't the only things he wanted.

Kelly didn't back away, she wanted him closer, wanted his lips to touch hers the same way they had touched her neck. She got her wish. He leaned down and found her lips instinctively and pulled her close in a deep kiss that went on and on. Kelly melted to him and opened her lips for the onslaught of his tongue. She had never been kissed like this. The fire raced through her body and formed a hot pool in her lower section. She wanted more. She wanted to feel his body naked against her skin. She wanted to feel

187

him pushing inside her. She wanted him like she had never realized she had wanted a man.

A small voice deep inside kept trying to tell her she shouldn't be kissing a man she had just met less than an hour before. It was wrong to want him to touch her in places even her husband had neglected. She sighed as she pushed that niggling voice even deeper and let his tongue taste her mouth.

Shel's voice yelling from the cabin door startled them both. Bryant reluctantly pushed away and stared down at her face wishing he could see her eyes. He hoped they were misty from the deep kiss they had just shared. He could imagine her lips swollen from that uninhibited kiss. His hands rested on either side of her face and his fingers slowly caressed her soft cheeks. Never had just kissing a woman heat up his body and mind as kissing Kelly had.

He sighed silently deep inside. His ex had never responded like this to one of his kisses. He had often wondered if perhaps he wasn't a good kisser, but Kelly's response told him otherwise. He had found himself wanting to remove her clothes right there and feel her soft skin against his. He knew it was a long time since he had been with a woman, but the feeling that overcame him took him totally by surprise. He stepped back another step.

"I guess we better get inside before he comes looking for us," he said softly.

"Ye...yes, "she stammered. "I guess we better." She quickly stepped around him and hurried to the door. She heard the soft masculine chuckle follow her as she stepped outside. It was still raining fairly hard so she had an excuse to rush to the cabin. At the door she looked back and saw Bryant following at a more leisurely pace.

Bryant let her go though he had wanted to pull her close once again. He knew if they didn't answer Shel he would come looking for them and he didn't want the man to find him kissing his sister so passionately. That might not help their friendship very much.

Then again, he thought, Shel had brought her with him to retrieve Bryant from the mountain. That could mean he was hoping they would connect. He shook his head. He couldn't picture Shel as a matchmaker. He picked up his speed and headed to the cabin before he could think anymore on the subject. This was best left to nature to see what happened next before he started thinking too deeply about it.

Shel was in the kitchen area when Kelly came in. He glanced around and saw her flushed look. He turned back to hide the smile on his face. Looks like he was right, there was something that connected between them. Was he good or what?

"You're done with the horses I take it?" he asked easily.

"Yes," she answered quietly. "They are fed and brushed. I need to change out of these wet clothes though. Damn, I left the saddle bags in the shed."

"You can use the bedroom down that hall and to the right," Shel replied as he went back to frying the fish he'd skinned while they were out in the shed. "We keep extra things here at the cabin you can use. There is no sense in going back out in the rain. Though, I am afraid they are men's clothing and may be rather big."

"I'll figure something out," Kelly said as she stared at Shel's back. He'd planned this, Kelly realized suddenly! He wanted her and Bryant to meet and click. Why else would he have brought her up here to pick up his friend?

Sure the alone time was nice for them to get to know each other. It had been hard to be alone on the ranch. There was always her son or their father hanging around, as well as the other men who worked there. That was what she thought was his reason for bringing her along.

Now, she was sure it was a more personal. She stared at his back for a moment before heading for the bedroom. One thing she knew, this was going to be an interesting evening.

Kelly reached the room Shel had indicated and realized right way it was occupied. The room had Bryant's mark all over it. His things were all about. Some of his clothes were hung over the back of a chair. A man who picked up after himself, now that was a unique find, she thought. A sighted man couldn't be any neater. Everything had a place and was in it.

Kelly stood in the doorway and noted each item, inventorying what the man owned. He did like things simple, but then again this was a hunting cabin and one usually didn't bring a whole lot with them here. What he brought though did tell her a lot about the man. She couldn't help but like what she saw in him. He was a man who was independent, simple in his possessions, and liked to keep clean. This was totally unlike Morris and Mark had been extremely fussy with his belongings. Everything had to be just so. Bryant had things where they belonged but she could see they weren't lined up like soldiers marching to war as Mark's had been.

She heard Shel greet Bryant as he came in the back door and quickly exited the room and went inside the other one. This one was clearly unoccupied. There were clothes in the dresser. Kelly figured they belonged to Shel. They were the size he usually wore. She found a pair of jeans that she was able to wear with the aid of her belt and a T-shirt that hung to her knees.

She would have just done with the t-shirt if there hadn't been men about, especially Bryant. Then again, if it had only been Bryant, she would have felt very comfortable with only the t-shirt on. If it were one of Bryant's would have made it all the better. The feel of it on her body, the scent of him in the soft fabric would have been erotic in the least. She could imagine his scent wrapping around her like his arms did out in the stable.

Kelly shook her head and admonished herself for the erotic thoughts that had crept into her head. She had never been given to fantasy and thinking of the love at first sight sort of thing. How could a blind arrogant cowboy bring those thoughts to her head? Because, she told herself, you just know he is more than that. Proof was Shel's loyalty for one thing.

She could see deep into his soul when she looked into those eyes. The eyes she had thought were brown the first time she saw them had turned out to be a dark deep blue, a blue that could turn nearly black with emotion. The one advantage of his being blind was he didn't hood his eyes when she looked into them. She had felt herself falling into the depths of those dark blue pools.

Here was a man unlike any she had ever met before. This much she knew. Kelly heard somebody coming down the hall and she hurriedly finished dressing. She opened her door as Bryant reached his.

He stopped and turned at the sound. Shel had said she was in the back room looking for some clothes to wear till hers dried.

"Did you find anything to fit?" he asked.

"Yes," Kelly answered in her soft voice. "Shel had some things left in the dresser. That is I think they are his."

Bryant wished he could see Kelly in her brother's jeans and shirt. He could imagine them just loose enough to be a problem keeping on right. "Yes, the clothes in that room are Shel's. I can bet they are a bit large."

"Actually we are not that far different in size," Kelly laughed, "maybe in shape, but not in size. We both have narrow hips."

Bryant knew she had narrow hips. His hands had rested on them and had itched to go further. Bryant suddenly threw back his head and laughed.

"Yes, you are definitely different in shape," he chuckled. "And that is a good thing." Kelly laughed with him. Suddenly she felt self-conscious in this tiny space and felt the urge to flee.

"I better let you change," She said softly as she inched past him toward the living room. "You got soaked twice in less than an hour; we don't want you catching a cold."

Bryant wasn't going to let her escape that easily and stepped in her way affectively barring her escape. "You really want to run away?"

"I wasn't running," Kelly whispered because his closeness caused her throat to suddenly constrict on her. "I think Shel will wonder what's keeping me."

Again Bryant laughed as he leaned closer to her, one hand resting on the wall on either side of her face. "I think Shel is well aware of what's keeping you." With that he leaned even closer and kissed her. It was a kiss that promised more to come in the future. He knew where her mouth was and latched easily onto it with a kiss that Kelly felt in her toes. She was grateful for the wall behind her. It was the only thing holding her up.

Neither one saw Shel come to the head of the hallway or his secretive smile. Yes, this was going just the way he had hoped. He knew they both needed somebody who was capable of great depths of feeling but he also knew that neither realized that they were each capable of those depths. From the looks of that kiss, he figured they were finding out. He made a hasty retreat to the kitchen area before yelling out for all to hear that supper was on.

A few moments later Kelly came out of the back rooms trying to look normal. Her flushed cheeks gave her away, but Shel ignored it. He was slightly disappointed to see she had found the spare room he used when he came up and not Bryant's. Then again he guessed seeing Bryant's things strewn around would be a dead giveaway. He was surprised she didn't chew him out for sending her to the wrong room.

"I see those fit better than I thought they would," he said as he watched her closely. She actually flushed a deeper shade of red and wondered why what he said made her do that.

"Bryant better hurry or these fish will be cold." Shel started putting the food on the table and Kelly hurried to help him, anything to keep busy and not have to try and make small talk right now. Again, she had a feeling this was going to be an interesting evening.

192

Chapter 25

Weldon was reading the evening paper when his phone rang. He thought it might be Shel since they hadn't returned from the cabin. That didn't surprise him since they had left fairly late. It was about a three hour trip, longer if you took your time.

Weldon also knew what was on Shel's mind. He had even thought of it a couple times this last week. He had watched Kelly and little Sheldon down with the horses and wondered what Bryant would think of her. As far as son-in-laws went he could do a lot worse. This was something to just sit back and watch though. He wasn't about to push anybody on anybody, but if they happened to spark when they met and headed towards each other, that was a different matter.

"Hello," He answered on the first ring. He listened for a few seconds before dropping the phone onto the table and running out the back door. There was trouble in the paddock. The ranch had wild horses as well as trained ones. The riding horses were kept in the barns at night. The wild ones were kept in a series of paddocks. He raced to the barn and found his men getting their horses out. The foreman was handing out flashlights and barking orders.

"Mike?" Weldon yelled over the general din. "What's going on?"

"Somebody opened the paddock gates and let the horses into the alfalfa field," Mike yelled back.

"All the horses?"

"All the breeding stock," he confirmed. "That's including both studs."

Weldon had been heading for his horse when he stopped dead and turned back to Mike. "Your telling me both studs are loose in the same field?"

"Fraid so sir," Mike answered contritely. "And, there are several mares ready. There will be a fight if we don't get them separated."

"You're telling me, "Weldon muttered as he ran for his horse. Somebody had already pulled him out of his stall and saddled him.

"Everybody here?" he yelled so all could hear him? The men all answered affirmative. "Go for the studs first. We have to stop them from getting together. If they meet they will fight to the death over them mares. Let's go."

As they rode into the field they could make out the forms of the wild horses. It looked like most had herded together at the western edge of the field. Weldon looked and listened for the larger studs. This was not a good time of year for the horses to be mixed. Some had foaled and those tiny ones could be trampled from panicky older horses.

Some were coming into fertility and their scent would bring the studs to them. This had to be stopped. They had two studs for a reason. Some of the mares were related to one stud or the other. They couldn't let them breed. Also two studs would fight for supremacy over the herd. These were wild range animals and the rules of the range worked here.

A shout brought Weldon's head around. He heard the fight before he saw it. 'Damn,' he thought we're too late. He spurred his horse in the direction of the fight.

"Tommy," He yelled. "You take three men and flank Ranger. Billy, you take men and flank Roamer. Try and separate them. Get men between them."

Weldon didn't sit and just give orders, he was rushing in with his lasso swinging over his head and went for the stud they called Ranger while several men tried to force their horses between the two studs. Billy was doing the same with his men trying to lasso Roamer.

The two studs were already wild with blood lust and kicked out at any horse that came near them. Ranger got too close to Tommy and reared up. Weldon saw the hoofs strike the man's horse before he heard the mares

194

cries of pain. The horse went down taking Tommy with it. Weldon saw another hand swing his horse into the foray and get between Tommy and Ranger waving his rope yelling at the top of his lungs to turn the horse away.

It distracted Ranger just enough another man got close enough to drop a lasso over his head. This gave two other men the opportunity to drop more ropes over his head and force him away. Weldon turned to see Tommy grab a hold of somebody's saddle and swing behind him to be pulled out of the raging horses.

Billy's men managed to get lassos around Roamers neck and also lead him a distance a ways. Weldon pulled up to where Tommy had been dropped off.

"You hurt?"

"Only my pride sir," the man coughed as he brushed himself down. "Where's my Belle?" Just then a hand rode up leading the injured mare.

"Take her back to the barn and call the vet," Weldon instructed. I have a feeling we'll need him for a whole lot more before this nights over."

He swung away and headed to where each stud was being held and gave instructions to put them in stalls in the barn, on opposite sides of course. Each group of three led their not very cooperative charges away. Weldon turned to the others.

"I want you to try and weed out the mares with foals first," He instructed his men. "Some of them are barely days old. Put them in paddocks and make sure they are all accounted for and if they need any care from the vet. The others will no doubt group down in the gorge. We'll be able to herd them back later once they've calmed down. Now get moving."

"Bernie?" Weldon called to a man a short distance away.

"Boss," the man answered as he rode over.

"Can you tell me what happened?"

"All was quiet just before dark sir," the man answered nervously. "I had personally ridden around the paddocks checking the gates. They were all secure."

"I am sure they were," Weldon assured the man. "Having one come loose maybe even two is one thing but all of them including the studs? No, this was no accident."

"Like that hay bale nearly hitting you and Shel was no accident?"

"I'm beginning to wonder if Shel had been right," The older man replied. He was suddenly feeling old. What the hell was going on? "Make sure you keep guards on all the paddocks tonight. I'll call the Sheriff in the morning. Don't worry about the mares. Get the ones with foals."

"Yes sir,"

Weldon turned towards the barn to go check the gate locks and also see how Tommy's horse was. This was going to be a long night.

Chapter 26

Kelly was right about it being an interesting evening. Both men set out to amuse her with stories of their service life. They had her laughing till her sides hurt. She didn't know where the time went when Shel indicated it was time they went to bed. She didn't even realize she had been yawning for the last half hour. Kelly said her good nights and made her way to the spare bedroom she had gotten her clothes from.

She could hear Shel and Bryant good naturedly arguing over who got the bed Bryant had been using. Kelly softly closed her door. She didn't want to know who won. Actually, she didn't want to think of Bryant being just across that narrow hallway. Just the thought of him being so close made her stomach quiver.

"I'll get some blankets from your closet and take the couch," Shel said as he started toward the hall. Bryant stopped him.

"I'll take the sofa, you can have the bed," he said. He hadn't had a chance to tell Shel about the dream of the sleep walking yet. He didn't want to be in the bedroom and end up stumbling into Kelly's room by accident or even into the living room if another storm hit and he knew there would be one. Even now he could hear distant rumbling. When Shel started to protest Bryant used the argument he knew would sway Shel to give in. "You really want me just across the hall from your sister?"

Shel looked at Bryant for a moment and burst out laughing, "I guess you're right about that. You win, I'll take the room."

The cabin soon settled into silence. Kelly was laying in her bed thinking about Bryant. How could a man get under her skin so fast? True, he seemed like nobody she had ever met before but then again she thought Mark had been different from what she was use to and he turned out to be the flip side of Morris. How would she know that Bryant wasn't just another abusive man? How would she know he wouldn't try to control her?

197

She closed her eyes and tried to stop thinking this way but that only brought his image before her. She could remember every feature on his face. That strong brow line, his bushy eyebrows, narrow deep blue eyes, and Adonis nose stood out in the darkness against her eyelids. She remembered the feel of the scarred skin beneath her finger tips. The skin had been soft and bumpy but not repulsive. She had traced the line of the scar on the other side and smiled now as she remembered the feel of it. Those scars were now just another part of Bryant's personality.

She remembered the feel of his firm lips on her softer ones. She could feel his tongue assaulting hers again. Her body shivered with desire. Even when making love with Mark, her body never reacted like this and all Bryant had done was kiss her. She rolled over and with shear willpower emptied all thoughts from her head and finally fell to sleep.

Bryant sat on the sofa in the dark for a long time after Shel had gone to bed. He knew that half of his statement about Shel not wanting him across the hall from his sister was true. The minute the statement was out of his mouth he knew that he would have wanted to steal across the hall to be with Kelly. The desire he felt for her went beyond sexual.

He remembered every detail of her face from the brief look he had before his sight had faded. Her light gray blue eyes, her small nose, and strawberry colored hair were just a couple of things he found pleasing. Her soft singsong voice played on his ears. He remembered her soft skin and the mild strawberry scent of her shampoo.

He felt a stirring in his groin and moaned at the thought of how long it has been since he had been with a woman. Even though his relationship with Julian was sketchy at best, he had never cheated on her. He had known she hadn't been so strict with herself while he was away, but he didn't use that as an excuse to do likewise. And it wasn't from lack of chances with the fairer sex. He had always considered himself a man of honor and didn't take that lightly.

The other reason he was afraid to go to sleep was he would once again walk in his sleep and hoped by being in the living room he wouldn't disturb the others if he did it again. A clap of distant thunder reminded him of the approaching storm. He hoped he could fall asleep before it got any closer. Maybe he would sleep through it this time. He wasn't too hopeful though as he laid down and closed his eyes.

Kelly opened her eyes to the dark room. Something had awakened her from a deep sleep. Lightening flashed through the window followed closely by a crash of thunder. She jumped from the intensity from it. She realized the rain was pounding the roof in a static rush. Another storm, that's what had awakened her. She started to lay back down when she heard another noise above sounds of the raging storm. It was a thumping of something blowing in the wind. A window shudder must have blown loose she thought. She listened a moment and realized it came from the front of the cabin.

She got up and pulled on an old bathrobe she had found hanging in the closet, and ventured out into the hallway. She could see in the flashing light of the lightening that the door to Shel's room was closed, funny he didn't hear this, Kelly thought as she started up the hall towards the front. She saw the origin of the noise. The front door was standing wide open and the wind was pounding it against the wall. The rain was being blown in torrents into the cabin. Kelly ran to the door wondering why Bryant hadn't heard this. As she was pulling it shut she turned her head to the sofa and another flash showed an empty sofa with very mussed up blankets where he should have been. Where could he be she wondered.

A noise different from the storm caused Kelly to look outside. She couldn't see anything at first. She was ready to give up and shut the door when more lightening showed that a large tree had blown down in the clearing in front of the cabin. It's a good thing that monster missed the cabin, Kelly thought. Another Flash showed movement at the edge of the branches.

As her eyes adjusted to the dimness of the night, punctuated by the lightening, she realized it was Bryant. He was bare from the waist up with only his jeans on. He appeared to be fighting the tree. He was lunging at the branches wrestling with them. She heard a garbled scream as he once again attacked the branches. It looked to her as if he was trying to tear them apart.

The sky was aflame with fires burning everywhere. Bombs were exploding all around. Bryant dived for cover and crawled along the ground. He came to an obstacle and jumped to his feet, clawing at the debris desperately yelling for Shel. He had to be here, this was the truck he had been in. Bodies lay all around but none were Shel. He had to be in this pile of burnt twisted metal. He screamed again for his friend. A hand landed on his arm and he turned attacking the intruder instantly like a loaded spring.

Kelly didn't think of her own safety or even to get Shel, she lunged off the porch calling to Bryant. She tried to yell above the roar of the wind, rain and thunder, but he didn't hear her. She reached him and put her hand on his shoulder to get his attention.

That was the wrong move. Bryant screamed out a blood curdling yell as he turned and lunged for her. The force of his body knocked them to the ground with him on top. Pain burst from Kelly shoulder as she hit the ground under Bryant. Her breath exploded out of her and darkness threatened to overcome her. She struggled to stay conscious.

"Bryant," she screamed!

Bryant was throwing a punch at his attacker when he froze at his name. That was no voice of an Afghan rebel. It was female and very frightened. He stopped dead and stared down as the rebel turned into a woman underneath him. He blinked once, then twice, and then let out an oath that would melt metal.

"Kelly?" he asked hesitantly, blinking once again. He saw her there but couldn't believe the picture before him wasn't fading. He actually wished it would fade, fade out of existence that was. What had he done?

"You were expecting somebody else?" Kelly weakly tried to laugh and winced at the pain. She was having trouble catching her breath and wasn't sure if it was because of the pain in her shoulder, or the fact Bryant was rather heavy and still on top of her, or just the fact that that very hard male body was still on top of her.

Bryant cursed again as he rolled off her and knelt beside her. "Are you injured?"

"I'll survive," Kelly tried to sound sincere but the moment she tried to sit up she gasped at the new surge of pain that rushed through her shoulder. Stars exploded in her head and she started to slide into darkness. Bryant caught her as she started to fall back.

"You're hurt," he said. It wasn't a question, just a statement of fact. "I am so sorry."

Kelly grabbed hold of his arm to steady herself. She stared at him through the still pouring rain. He was looking right at her. He could see! She was sure of it. But right now she concentrated on not passing out from the pain. "It's just my shoulder," she tried to sound as if it was minor though just the effort to speak caused red hot pain coursing through her body. "I'm sure I just pulled a muscle."

Bryant leaned forward and started to run his hands over her shoulder. He touched a spot and Kelly automatically winced. Bryant grimaced along with her. "You dislocated your shoulder," he said as he moved to place himself even with her shoulder. He gently took Kelly's arm and stretched it out. He looked at Kelly, searching her eyes. "You trust me?"

Kelly could only nod as she felt herself falling into those eyes. Bryant nodded back and kept his eyes locked with hers as he manipulated her arm with a sudden sharp jerk to pop the bone back into place. A quick burst of pain shocked her then just as fast it started to fade. She was surprised at how much of the pain subsided instantly. She continued to stare at Bryant as he finished and let her arm down gently to her side.

"We need to get you inside out of this rain," he said as he started to stand up. He leaned down putting his arms under her good side and pulled her to a stand. As Kelly came face to face with him he added, "I am so sorry."

The pain in his eyes melted Kelly's heart. It was clear he was horrified at what he had done, even though it had totally been out of his control.

"It's not your fault," Kelly whispered leaning against him for support. "You were sleep-walking, I think."

"Aw, yes, that," Bryant ran his hand through his soaked hair. "I think I was."

He looked so lost Kelly couldn't help placing her hand on his cheek and sliding her fingers over the scar there. "Your sight?"

"My sight?" Bryant looked confused for a moment? He was lost in the sensation of her fingers playing across his cheek.

"You can see," Kelly pointed out to him, still softly stroking his cheek.

Chapter 27

Bryant looked shocked for a moment as he realized that what he was seeing before him was real. He was seeing Kelly. She was exactly as that first glance had showed him. Even drenched she was beautiful, which reminded him they were standing in the middle of a clearing in the pouring rain with lightening around them. The wind was still whipping around them and one tree had already fallen. He could feel the chill on his bare skin and realized Kelly had only a t-shirt on under that grubby robe.

"We need to get inside," he said as he put his arm around her and led her toward the cabin. They got inside and Bryant closed the door behind them. "Go and get out of those wet things and take a hot shower, you need to warm up."

"I'm fine," Kelly protested, "you need that shower worse than me. You take one while I change and I'll get one later."

Bryant was chilled to the bone and couldn't argue with that logic, but he was to be damned if he took a shower before her. He took her arm and led her toward the bathroom. At the door he pushed her inside.

"I'll bring you some dry clothes and leave them on the sink.

"What about you?"

"I'd join you but," he glanced toward the room where they could hear Shel's snores emanating, "he might not understand very well about seeing me in the shower with his sister. He's not going to be very happy in first place at hearing what I did to you."

"I don't blame you for what happened," Kelly whispered softly. "I should have known better to confront a sleepwalker in the first place. Now, you better get some dry clothes for yourself."

"My clothes are in Shel's room," he whispered.

Kelly looked at the closed door across from hers. "There should be something in my room that fits you," she said not realizing how provocative her voice had become. "You and Shel look about the same size."

Bryant looked down at her in the dim light. The flashes of lightening illuminating her face in flashes making it seem very mysterious. He wanted so badly to kiss those lips but remembered her shoulder and knew he had to maintain control for the both of them.

"I have a feeling that if I entered your room at this moment I would find it hard to leave," he said softly as he brushed her lips softly with his. "Go and get your shower, I'll have your clothes ready." Bryant then reluctantly backed away and slipped quickly down the hall before he changed his mind about joining her in the shower.

Kelly stood shocked for a moment. She knew in her heart that if he had accepted her unspoken invitation, she would not have wanted him to leave either. Her body was crying out for him in a way she had never reacted to a man before. She wondered if it was just the sexual side of him she was attracted to or the man himself. The last thing she wanted or needed was more complications in her life. But, man, she could not forget that caress of a kiss as she slowly opened her door and went into the shower.

She knew one thing, complications or not, she was going to look forward to seeing Bryant around the ranch now. A sudden dismaying thought entered her mind. What if he decides to leave now that his sight has returned? She said a silent prayer that he was happy there and wouldn't want to leave.

As Kelly shut the door to the bathroom Bryant went back to the rooms. He decided to chance waking Shel and get some of his own clothes. Bryant tried to be quiet as he searched by lightening light for some dry clothes.

"I sure hope you know which room you are in Capt'n," Shel's lazy voice came out of the darkness, "Then again, I should be happy you're in this room and not the other one." He laughed as he turned on the light next to the bed. He stopped short when he saw Bryant's soaked muddy condition.

"What the hell happened to you?" he exclaimed!

"I had a little accident," Bryant explained. "I...A tree fell outside."

Shel sat up just a little bit curious. "And you had to go out in this storm to investigate it?"

"I didn't know I had gone out," Bryant replied. He knew he had to tell Shell the whole thing, including his accidentally attacking Kelly and injuring her. He wasn't very sure how Shel would take that, but he knew if it was reversed he wouldn't be too pleased.

Could this be the end of their friendship? He hoped not, because that would mean leaving the ranch and leaving Kelly and he knew that would be harder than anything he had ever done. He had finally met a wholesome woman who didn't see him for a bank account but seemed to see him as a man.

"You lost me," Shel started. "How could you be out there and not know it?"

"I was back in Afghanistan," Bryant answered. "I was sleepwalking. It seems the storms trigger flashbacks."

"This wasn't the first one?"

"The other day, early morning was my first one," Bryant continued his explanation. "I woke up outside. One thing I noticed then was I thought I could see for a moment when I woke up then it went black again."

"Why didn't you tell me," Shel asked? He remembered also that Bryant had thought he could see for an instant after the lightening nearly struck him. But now Bryant was continuing his explanation and Shel left this thought for a moment.

"Tell me when I had a chance," Bryant answered with a laugh. He walked over to the chair by the window and flopped into it and stared out the window at the eerie shapes of the trees in the lightening. This storm was still rather intense. He marveled at the raw beauty in the vision outside his window.

He realized how much he had taken for granted when he could see before. Before this it would have been just another storm. Now it was a wild living painting suitable for framing in his mind. "I was going to tell you when you arrived, but you had Kelly with you, the storm was threatening, then that lightening hit, and so on.

"That's true," Shel replied scratching his head. Why did Bryant seem different? Something was different but he wasn't sure what it was. "So what else happened?"

That was the question Bryant had been dreading. He hesitated a moment before answering. He wasn't relishing telling Shel what he had done to his sister. He was sitting there staring out the window trying to figure out how to word the account when the door opened.

Kelly had finished her shower, and realized there were no dry clothes waiting for her. Bryant had forgotten to leave her clothes it seemed. She wrapped a towel around her body and peeked out the door. She saw a light under Shel's door and figured he must have woken up. She went out into the hall heading for her room and heard the voices in the other room. So Bryant was trying to tell Shel what happened.

She rushed into her room and threw on some dry clothes. Fortunately hers were in there now as Shel had brought in the saddle bags before they went to bed. She went to the other door and listened to Bryant telling the story of what happened. When he hesitated she decided she needed to be in there to urge him to tell the truth.

She didn't blame him for what happened and hoped Shel would understand also, but Bryant also had to face the truth to see how much trust his friend had in him. So, hoping she had Shel pegged right, Kelly opened the door and peered into the room. "Tell him the simple truth Bryant," she said stepping into the room.

Shel and Bryant stared at the door for a long moment. "Why are you also all wet," he asked slowly?

"I just took a shower," she simply answered.

"It's just past 5AM," Shel voiced as he glanced at the clock. "Why are you up so early?"

"I heard…" Kelly started to say but Bryant stopped her.

"I can explain it all," he said. "Since we all seem to be awake, why don't I change my clothes and go get some coffee brewing. Then I will explain everything."

Shel looked dubiously from Bryant to Kelly. Something was going on here and it obviously wasn't what he had planned. He suddenly realized Kelly seemed to be favoring her right arm.

"I'll go start the coffee," Kelly said hastily and hurriedly left the room.

"What happened to Kelly's arm?"

"You're observant as usual I see," Bryant said dryly. He grabbed some clothes. "I'll go get cleaned up and meet you at the table."

Shel looked closer at Bryant. "You can see?"

"Good thing you're half asleep," Bryant said sarcastically. "Otherwise you would be really able to see what was going on." He left the room leaving Shel with a confused look on his face. A half hour later that confused look was still on his face.

"You jumped Kelly," Shel asked astonished? He was hoping he heard that wrong.

"Well, not on purpose," Bryant protested the way Shel had put that. "I said I came out of my trance and found I was on top of her."

"Where did you think you were?" Shel continued to question Bryant to make sure he understood completely what had happened. He knew his friend. He had a very high code of morality where it came to how you treated women. If he attacked Kelly, that meant he didn't know what he was doing. But, at the same time he wanted to slug the guy for hurting his sister.

"I was back at the attack in Afghanistan," Bryant said wretchedly. Just saying it brought back the sights, sounds and even smells of that night he lost all his men except Shel. He let his face drop into his hands for a moment as he tried to force the thoughts out of his head. Why had this started now after over two years since the attack? He had faced his demons over the incident while in the hospital, or so he had thought. He had dreamed about it but never left his bed before the other night, not that he knew of anyway.

Of course his idea of facing it was to tell the shrink to piss off and then bury the incident deep. Well, he thought, I guess this means it doesn't want to stay buried. He thought of Kelly's sweet smile and the way she had forgiven him instantly for what had happened outside. He had knocked her to the ground and she was concerned for him. He had never met anybody like her before.

He lifted up his head and stared at Shel who was sitting holding his cold untouched coffee patiently waiting for Bryant to pull himself together. Oh, yes he had met two people like Kelly before, her brother and father. A forgiving nature seemed to be a trait that ran in the family.

"I was looking for you in the debris but you weren't there. Actually, I guess I was struggling with a tree limb when Kelly came up behind me and put her hand on my shoulder. I automatically turned and attacked what I thought was the enemy." He paused a moment.

"Actually it was the root base," Kelly interjected. "I thought he was going to climb right through it."

"And," Shel pressed as he threw Kelly a look, "you naturally followed him?"

"It seemed like a good idea at the time," She barely suppressed a giggle. She couldn't help it, Shel was looking so serious.

"I knocked her down," Bryant continued slowly. "She screamed my name and that's when I realized I was on top of her. She had dislocated her shoulder and I put it back into place. I can say your sister is a real trooper. My sight stayed this time after I came to my senses. I can still see now." He looked up into Shel's eyes. He was surprised he could still see. As he had changed clothes he was expecting the darkness to return. It stayed at bay.

Shel sat quietly for a moment. It was obvious Kelly held no ill will for what happened, and he knew Bryant enough to believe this story. He couldn't see Kelly lying for him in the first place. He glanced at the clock and saw it was nearly 6am and stood up. "I'll go start breakfast."

"That's all?" Bryant asked in surprise

"No," Shel stopped on the way to the kitchenette, "I'd appreciate if you stopped jumping my sister in the rain." He walked away before Bryant could answer. The absurdity of the situation was finally sinking in. Kelly laid a hand on Bryant's for a second. They exchanged startled looks then she followed her brother over to the kitchenette.

"How's your arm," Shel asked as she approached and started taking the food from the fridge?

"Its sore," Kelly admitted, "but I have felt worse." She thought back to the time she had broken her arm. Thankfully, the worst of the pain had subsided as soon as Bryant had reduced the shoulder. "Good thing Bryant knew how to put it back into place."

"Yah, good thing," Shell answered dryly. They worked on making breakfast together as they talked.

"You can't blame Bryant," Kelly asserted, "I was the idiot who woke up a sleep walker."

"That's true," Shel replied and ducked as Kelly tossed a mushroom at him. They broke out laughing as he tossed chopped green peppers at her.

"Hey, you all having a food fight and I'm not invited?" Bryant asked from a few feet away. He had been watching them talk for a minute to gage the atmosphere. He was immensely relieved to see them laughing.

Kelly turned at Bryant's voice and couldn't help but stare at him. Shel looked from Bryant to Kelly and back. He suddenly felt like a fifth wheel, but he'd be damned if he would leave the room now. He turned back to the veggies and took up the chopping knife.

In his best military voice he said, "Grab a bowl and start cracking eggs man, there will be no laziness allowed in this company." That affectively broke the spell between them two and chuckling Bryant came and obeyed the order.

The sun was trying to peek thru the clouds as they finished the dishes. Bryant and Shel excused themselves to go and get the horses ready for the ride back down the mountain and Kelly went around picking up the dirty clothes and stuffing them into a duffle bag to be hauled down with them for washing.

She gingerly picked through Bryant's things blushing as stray thoughts filled her head as she hastily stuffed his things in the bag. She carried the bag into the front room and set it by the front door. As she was walking around straightening things up Shel came back in. He watched her from the doorway. Kelly turned and saw the frown. "What's wrong?"

"You think you're able to stand the ride down the mountain?" he asked worriedly.

"I'm not feeling much pain now," she stressed. "I took some aspirin and I am sure if we don't go down at breakneck speed, I'll be able to handle it."

Shel still looked rather preoccupied and acted like he was going to say something when Bryant came through the door. Shel shut his mouth and turned to Bryant.

"Everything ready?"

"As it'll ever be," Bryant answered. He turned to Kelly who was coming toward them carefully putting on her sweater, it was still chilly outside. Bryant frowned and Kelly knew just what he was going to say. She stopped him with a finger to her lips and briskly walked out past them pointing to the bag on her way. Shel shouldered the bag and they looked at each other with smiles. Each had their own thoughts about what kind of person Kelly was.

Chapter 28

The ride back to the ranch was okay at first, but as they slowly made their way down the mountain, Kelly could feel her shoulder stiffening up. When they stopped for a break at the stream at the foot of the mountains she swallowed a couple more aspirin and gingerly stretched her arms over her head trying to relieve the strain on her shoulder. Bryant came quietly up behind her and started to gently massage the shoulder. Kelly sighed as the warmth of his fingers seeped through her shirt to her skin. He leaned in close and whispered into her ear.

"When we get back," he asked softly, "I would like a chance to really get to know you, without throwing you to the ground."

"You mean more than we got to know each other in the shed?"

"Well, that would be nice too," Bryant replied with a grin. "But I was thinking more along the lines of you telling me more about yourself, us sharing time together, things like that."

"I think I would like that very much," Kelly answered back with a soft laugh. Then she remembered something very important. "You don't know I have a young son do you?"

Bryant stepped back abruptly and Kelly started to turn away thinking she had lost the guy before even having a chance to get him, but the look on his face stopped her from saying anything.

"Really?" he asked. "How old is he?"

Actually he remembered Shel saying something about a son but decided to play dumb. He wanted her to talk about it.

"He's six," she answered, trying to read his eyes. The look she saw was everything but unfriendly. Was he really interested in her son or was he just being polite. "His name is Sheldon. My mother named him and I didn't know the connection till I came here."

Kelly and Shel had filled Bryant in on how Kelly had no idea she had a father or brother till after her mother died last fall, so he knew the basic facts. It was just that the mention of her son never came up. Kelly had figured Shel would say something but when he didn't she decided to wait also. She didn't know he had already mentioned it to Bryant while she was in the shed with the horses. Then the subject had been turned to Shel's and Bryant's escapades together in the service. She waited on mentioning her son

Bryant looked deeply into Kelly's eyes. Normally his extra cautious nature would have questioned the fact her son was conveniently named after his unknown uncle, but the fact Kelly and Shel looked so much alike and hearing the story the night before, he had no reason to not believe what she told him. In fact from nearly the first moment he had realized she was Shel's sister only relief had filled him. He never questioned her intentions.

He stepped forward to her and put one arm on her shoulder and lifted her chin gently with his other hand. Just before laying a soft kiss on her lips he asked a question. "Do you think Sheldon would like a new Daddy?"

"Don't you think we should wait till we have known each other more than a day before talking about giving my son a Daddy?"

Bryant kissed her lightly then backed away far enough to look into her eyes again. They were serious and sincere.

"You didn't answer my question."

"He never knew his real Daddy. He died before he was born," she answered. Morris' words echoed in her head. 'How could she expect a man to love another man's child?' But looking into Bryant's eyes made her realize that not all men were as shallow as Morris and that if there was a man out there who would and could love her son as if he were his own, it would be Bryant.

She knew right then that she could fall in love with this man given the chance. Then it hit her, there was no could in this thought, she had fallen in love with him at first sight. Her inner self had recognized the man she had always dreamed of finding but had not really believed existed.

213

"I think if the right man came along and could love him as his own," she said quietly never taking her eyes off Bryant.

"I would like that chance to show you how much love I have to give," Bryant answered back just as quietly. He kissed her again, only this time it was for much longer.

They had both forgotten about Shel who had stayed down by the stream with the horses watching them from a distance. He smiled as he realized how serious the talk was and the kiss that followed. He had hoped something would bloom between them but had not in his wildest dreams thought that it would burst into a flower so fast.

He hoped his father would be as happy about this as he was. Especially now that Bryant could see, Shel knew good things could happen for them both. He was also happy that circumstances this week-end had worked to bring back Bryant's eyesight. Shel was no doctor or scientist but common sense told him that the combination of the flashbacks and then meeting Kelly had been what did it. Bryant's body and mind was telling him he was ready to move forward, and meeting Kelly was the reason to move forward. At least that's what he was hoping.

Shel led the horses up the bank back toward the two and broke into their study of each other.

"You two plan on spending all day here?" He asked jokingly. "Or are you going to follow me home?" With that he jumped into the saddle and rode off leaving Bryant and Kelly to stare after him.

"You think we should follow," Bryant asked softly while feathering kisses along side her lips.

"I think so or Dad will send a posse out for us when Shel arrives home alone," Kelly answered back breathless from the soft touches. She knew they had to go but was disappointed when Bryant backed slowly away and led her to her horse. He helped her into the saddle watching to make sure she didn't jam her shoulder getting on.

214

He was so solicitous. Kelly was amazed at the attention. She had never had anybody care about her comforts in this way till she came home to her real father and brother. She never dreamed that another man so good was also nearby. She looked skyward and silently thanked her mom for making sure she did find her real family after all this time.

She forgave her for taking so long. Kelly was beginning to understand why her mom couldn't let her go. She had needed Kelly. She had no hard feelings. There was still a lot of sadness for what she lost, but Kelly was ready to look forward to the future and let the past go.

She looked at the man who was mounting the horse in front of her and thanked all involved for finding the people, family and the man she now believed she needed to be happy.

It didn't take them long to catch up to Shel, he was just letting his horse lazily walk along the trail till they arrived. He didn't say a thing as he nudged his horse and they started back out at a nice brisk walk. Kelly knew they were just an hour away from home and couldn't wait to see Sheldon and her Dad. She hoped Sheldon liked Bryant.

An hour later Kelly was very happy to see the roof tops of the ranch appear. Her shoulder and head were competing with each other to see which caused the most discomfort. She was looking forward to her bed and some aspirin.

She saw Weldon and Sheldon standing by the barn entrance as they came into the Yard. The sight of her son and father brought a leap of joy to her heart. She wasn't use to being away from her son even overnight. The horses were also eager to reach the barn and their stalls.

Kelly waved to her guys as they got closer and suddenly realized they weren't alone. A finely dressed woman stepped forward. She was clearly out of her element in her expensive city clothes. She wasn't looking very pleased either, looking down before stepping anywhere in the dusty circle before the barns. Kelly didn't see the shielded look that came over Bryant's face as he realized who that woman was.

"Don't mention I got my sight back yet," Bryant whispered loud enough for both Kelly and Shel to hear him. Kelly stared in surprise but the stiff expression on his face stopped her question before it could leave her lips. She glanced back at the woman who was now waving to them. Something wasn't right here and it involved that woman.

She glanced at Shel and saw a very displeased look on his face. It seems he recognized the woman also and wasn't at all happy to see her either. He nodded at her that he understood Bryant's request so she nodded back acknowledging she would go along with it. It was funny, how they could already communicate so affectively but silently. It was one of things that Kelly loved about her new family. They connected on a level she had never thought possible. She realized that she and Bryant were beginning to connect on that same level. She instinctively didn't like this woman and she wasn't one who disliked people easily. They had to earn it.

"Who was this woman that caused such displeasure at the sight of her? "Kelly thought as they rode up to the barn and dismounted. The woman started over to Bryant. She gave Kelly a cursory glace at her dusty ragged appearance and dismissed her on sight. She then turned toward Bryant who was acting like he didn't realize she was there, as a normal blind man might not have, but Bryant was never a normal blind man and Kelly knew he would have known somebody was there by scent and sound. Kelly leaned toward Shel and whispered to him.

"Who is that?"

Shel shot a disgusted look at the woman. "That's Bryant's ex-fiancée," was all he said as he took both horses and headed for the barn. Sheldon ran up to her and launched himself into her arms. Weldon came up at a more leisurely rate to give her a hug. Kelly hugged them both trying to ignore the hard feeling at the pit of her stomach. She had no idea of the history between Bryant and that woman, and although the reunion didn't seem to please him, he had loved her once. What if he realized he still does? That would mean he would leave just as she let her heart out to him.

The woman sashayed over to Bryant and started to wrap her arms around his neck but stopped suddenly before she actually made contact. She wrinkled her nose at the strong horse smell. She backed away with the most disgusted look on her face. She didn't try to hide the look thinking that Bryant wouldn't know since he was blind.

Kelly, Weldon, and Sheldon all saw it though and were hard pressed not to burst out laughing. Kelly was afraid that in his youthful exuberance Sheldon wouldn't be able to keep quiet, but he took a cue from the adults and managed to stifle his giggle quite well.

"Bryant's eyesight came back," Kelly whispered to Weldon.

"You don't say?"

"He doesn't want her to know for some reason," Kelly continued explaining.

"They were once engaged," Weldon explained quietly. "She dumped him when she found out he was scarred. She never even bothered to see him in the hospital or call. She got married about three months later to some rich banker."

"She never even saw him?" Kelly couldn't believe the nerve of this woman.

"We better leave them alone," Weldon said as he turned her toward the barn. "Tell us how was your first long horse ride?"

"Mommy," Sheldon excitedly broke in. "The horses got loose and the big mean ones tried to kill each other."

"What?" Kelly looked at Sheldon in surprise then back to her Dad.

"I'll explain inside," He said as they stepped into the barn.

Chapter 29

The woman seemed oblivious to the other people there. She took a deep breath and stepped closer again trying to act sensual through her held breath.

"Bryant," she gushed, "I missed you so much."

"Oh, really?" Bryant asked without any display of emotion. He turned to loosen the strap of the saddle paying no attention to her. His overstated blind man act had the others struggling to maintain a straight face.

"Sweetheart," the woman stepped a little closer though careful not to touch Bryant's clothing. "I admit I acted impulsively. I got scared. I had no idea how to care for an invalid."

Bryant froze at those words. He had once thought of himself as an invalid but the hard love of Shel's friendship had showed him otherwise. He had known for a long time that even if he never got his sight back, one thing he wasn't was an invalid. Her words rankled on him. He wondered if her high pitched cultivated voice had ever evoked anything but the sensation of chalk scraping on a blackkboard. He watched her out of the corner of his eyes as he loosened the buckled on the saddle.

"Do I look like an invalid?"

"You look like you are trying to be macho," she answered. "I can't believe they leave a blind man alone to take care of a horse."

"You'd be surprised at what I am capable of," he said sarcastically. She was quiet for a few moments.

"Your face," she crooned as she started to reach out to touch the scar but couldn't bring herself to quite do it. She pulled back. "It had once been so handsome."

Bryant ignored this and startedtaking the horses lead into the barn. Julian had to follow. He thought of how Kelly hadn't hesitated to touch his scared face. She hadn't found it repulsive. He could still feel the light touch of her finger tips as they ran up and down his cheeks.

He had no trouble seeing the real Julian this time. She was perfectly dressed for making a statement. Her statement was look at me I'm all you should be looking at. But he now looked beneath the make-up and expensive clothes and didn't like what he saw.

The hard eyes, the thin tight lips all spoke of an inner hardness he hadn't noticed before or rather he had ignored. He couldn't have been blind before to her real self. He saw Kelly leave the barn with her father and son as they headed for the house. She glanced back at him momentarily.

He realized that what you saw with her was what you got. From her make-up free face to her scuffed cowboy boots to the soft way she spoke and her easy laugh. It said, look at me, don't look at me, I don't care, I am just me. He knew he was already in love with her for that very reason.

"Bryant," Julian gasped as she tried to keep up in her very inappropriate heels. "I know now that I made the wrong choice."

"You did?"

"I told you," she stopped. "Will you stop just for a second?" Bryant stopped and turned toward her. The anger in his eyes surprised her. How could he be angry at her for being human and knowing her limitations? She had done the right thing staying away. She had always abhorred hospitals and she wouldn't have been much comfort for him.

"I was scared," she continued. "I panicked and ran."

"If I recall," Bryant snapped back, "you ran right into marriage with the first man who came along. Or, did he just come along?" Julian had the grace to look guilty and since she still didn't realize Bryant could see, she didn't bother to hide it.

"You couldn't expect me to be alone while you were off fighting that dumb war?"

"I was your fiancée," Bryant choked on the words working hard to maintain his anger. "There are certain things one expects from the woman he

219

plans to marry." He turned and headed once again to the barn. He ignored Julian as she tried to follow along.

Shel was just putting his horse into its stall. Kelly's was already in hers munching away at its feed.

"Bryant," Shel said as he shut the stall door, "I'll take her for you."

"I can handle it," Bryant replied curtly.

He had stopped trying to act blind and just went about his business as he had done before. He wanted to see how long before she realized he could see, or if she even noticed.

"By the way," He asked casually, "What happened to that banker husband of yours?" He removed the saddle and swung it over the railing for later cleaning. He led Peaches to her stall and tethered her outside it to brush her down. He dipped his hand in her water bucket to see it was empty though he had known it would be. He had to keep up some appearance.

He noticed Julian had stopped a little ways away and was watching him closely. He ignored her as he got water and feed for Peaches before brushing her down.

"He died," she said without any sign of passion. "He had a heart attack a few months after we married."

"That must have left you well off."

"His damn kids contested the will and won," she spat, "I didn't get a thing."

"That's too bad," Bryant tried to sound sincere but had trouble hiding the amusement from his voice. She never noticed. Now, he knew why she was here.

Julian was getting rather impatient as he went through the motions of taking care of his horse. He wasn't going to rush for anything, especially her. He was rather enjoying her discomfort and refused to analyze the feeling. He noticed that Shel had finished up and headed to the tack room with his saddle, returned for Kelly's saddle and with just a glance at Bryant went back. Bryant winked at Shel and got a return wink. Bryant continued what he was

220

doing waiting for her to reach the end of her patience. He didn't have long to wait.

"Why didn't you let him do that for you," she asked peevishly. "I am sure he can do it better."

Bryant didn't even pause in his work as he answered her. "I know what I am doing."

"Oh, I am sure you do dear," she tried to placate her faux pas and rushed on. "But I am sure it is easier for him. You must have trouble knowing… what part of the horse you've already done." Bryant smiled at himself at how she was digging herself deeper into a hole. He let her dig.

"I assure you I know what I am doing," he dropped his brush and used exaggerated motions to find it, getting on his knees under Peaches belly. He heard the gasp as Julian watched, but she made no sign to come help him.

"Hey you," she called to Shel franticly, "He needs your help."

Shel sauntered over to the tack room door and watched Bryant down on his knees searching for the brush. He was hard put to keep a straight face but managed a slow drawl as he spoke. "It's to your left buddy."

Bryant found the brush and sat back on his heels. "Thanks buddy," he waved toward Shel. He was now basically sitting under Peaches' belly.

"That's all you're going to do?" Julian gasped. "He is under that beast and it could trample him to death."

Shel did laugh loudly this time. He walked over and slapped Peaches rump hard. All the horse did was shift her body a step over and continued munching her oats.

"Peaches don't care who's under her long as she has her feed ma'am," Shel touched his finger to his hat and went back to the tack room. Julian watched wordlessly as Shel sauntered away before turning to Bryant. When she let loose she didn't care how loud she was or if anybody heard her.

"Some friend he is," she stormed! "He wouldn't even help you and he could have made that thing stomp you with that slap." Bryant lazily rose to his feet, slapped at the dirt on his jeans and finally turned to his ex-fiancée.

221

He studied her very closely seeing in her the cynical demanding woman she had always been. He could see it now, had always seen it, but had been blind for reasons he now couldn't remember. He counted to ten before responding to her accusations.

"Shel was the only person who helped me when I was injured," he said slowly, his voice deep with anger. "He came and found me, brought me here, helped me find myself."

"Find yourself?" she asked incredulously. "I find you on your knees in dirty hay underneath a nasty beast. How can you call him a friend?"

Bryant couldn't help it. He tipped back his head and laughed. Shel heard the deep sound from the other room he was in and smiled. It relieved him to know that Bryant wasn't buying anything from her.

Bryant turned back to peaches and finished brushing her. He then led her into the stall dumped the rest of the grain from the bucket into her bin, picked up the saddle and headed to the tack room. He could tell Julian was losing her patience. That made him smile even more. He just wished she would hurry up and leave.

"Your father sent a message to you dear," she said from the doorway of the tack room. She wasn't about to enter this filthy room. She waited for Bryant to acknowledge what she said. When he didn't but continued to clean the saddle she went on. "He said if you apologized and came home he would accept and find a place for you somewhere in the business."

Bryant froze in his actions at this. He could remember the last meeting with his father. It was many years ago when he had decided to go into the Military rather than follow in the family business. Bryant had no desire to become a businessman. The thought of spending his days in a stuffy office dressed in a three-piece suit held no appeal for him.

His sister was the one with the business sense and wanted the position but their father had been adamant it would be Bryant. Bryant knew the only option was to leave and let his sister have the chance to prove herself. His father had followed him to the door with sour words. "If you walk out of that door now, you will never be welcomed here again!"

Bryant had looked at his mother and sister standing down the hall. He knew they didn't have the same sentiment but couldn't express their feelings. In all his growing up, his father's rule had been absolute and nobody else's feelings or opinions counted. Now, his father was offering him a way home, only if he admitted to him he was right. There was no way in hell he would do that. For one, Bryant didn't regret leaving. He definitely didn't regret the Military or the friends he made from it.

"Apologize?" he replied sardonically.

"Yes dear," she answered, the mocking going over her head. "Just admit you were wrong, that you made the wrong choice. Then you can go home and we can start your healing."

"We?" Bryant stiffened and stopped what he was doing. He had his back to her so she couldn't see the twisted look of distaste on his lips. Shel saw and ducked his head to hide his smirk.

"Yes dear," she said from the doorway. It struck him as very funny how at home he was here and she couldn't even enter the tack room. "We can return home. You can be where you are safe and people will help you. You won't be expected to do these demeaning things alone. There will be people around to lead you and do things for you."

Bryant knew she had no idea what she'd just said to him. She didn't realize she was telling him she had no faith that he could take care of himself, even though she saw him doing just that. She thought he should be led and protected from life, but she never said it would be her. She said they would have people do it.

Bryant glanced over at Shel. He saw the other man had his back to them and his shoulders were shaking. Yes, he was finding this very amusing.

"Where will you be?"

"Right at your side dear," she said, thinking his question meant he was actually considering it, "where I belong."

223

"You didn't think you belonged at my side when I was in a hospital room in pain and misery."

"I don't like hospitals dear," she answered self-assuredly. "You couldn't ask me to go to a place with all those sick people could you?"

"A person goes where they need to go when the one they love needs you," he said cynically. "I have a life here now. I am good with horses. I like them. They are not beasts to me. I like getting dirty, and I like working in the sun."

He turned and looked right at her. He had long since given up his blind man effort and was waiting for her to realize he could see. She seemed to be unconscious of that fact. "And I like it here with my friends who accept me for who I am. They let me find my own way. They are there to assist when I ask for it. They don't lead, order or demean me in any way."

"That's what you want me to tell your father?"

"You can tell him what you want," Bryant answered as he stepped up to her. He got close to her and placed a dirty hand on her chin. "Would you be willing to stay here with me?"

She stepped back in horror. "You've got to be kidding?"

"On the contrary," he replied gravely. "I am very serious. If you want back into my life, you must accept that my life is here now. I won't be returning to the city."

Julian stared at him in disbelief. She had really thought she was offering him everything he could want. How could he turn it down? "That's your final answer?"

"Like they say on TV," he laughed, "that's my final answer."

Julian stared at him for a minute. Their eyes met and she still didn't see that he could see her. He realized that Julian missed a lot of things in life. He actually felt sorry for her. She turned and walked away not even looking back once.

He knew then for sure that she hadn't been with him for any love she might have, if he'd had any doubt in the first place. She had been there in

224

hopes of getting him back for what she could get from it. He may not have his father's riches but he would never be alone. She would always be alone no matter what she got.

Bryant followed her to the door of the barn. He called to her from there as she reached her car. She looked up.

"In case you hadn't noticed," he said scathingly, "I can see. My sight came back. If you had bothered checking, it was never a matter of if but of when. But, I could see through your scheme without my eyes telling me. It's a matter of heart and I can see you don't have one. Good-bye Julian and tell my father he knows where to find me."

Bryant went back inside and to the doorway of the tack room. He found Shel lounging against the wall. He had a big shit ass grin on his face.

"Very good old boy," he laughed.

"You think?" Bryant grinned back.

"I couldn't have handled it so cool," Shel slapped the other guy on the back. "Let's go get something cold to drink. Tell me though? What if she had said yes?"

"You forget, I was trained to read people," Bryant laughed. "I knew she would never degrade herself to live in a place like this. She's a paper doll that needs the protection of the city."

"Not like my sister, huh?" Shel smirked.

"Your sister is the first real woman I had ever met," Bryant replied and walked outside. Shel followed.

They reached the door in time to see Julian racing her car away down the drive. Bryant wondered briefly what she and his father had thought they were doing, but if his father had thought for an instant he would come crawling back just because he thought he was crippled for life then he didn't know his son at all.

He wondered what his father thought would be suitable work for a blind man in the family business. He laughed at the thought of him behind a desk answering phones for a living. He looked up at the house and saw a lone figure standing on the back balcony. He didn't try to hide the smile that automatically grew on his lips.

Chapter 30

Now there was a woman of real substance, Bryant thought. A woman who had endured a life of suffering from what he could gleam from Shel, a woman who despite that could look at the world with hope and good will. There, standing on the back balcony, was the woman whose very presence had brought back his eyesight.

There was the woman he knew he wanted to spend the rest of his life with. He hoped she felt the same way. He knew he would have to win over not only her but also her son. The thought of having the boy as his own filled his heart.

"Hey, you going to stare at her or go let her know she's the love of your life?" he heard an exaggeratedly annoyed voice behind him. Bryant flashed Shel a big grin and they both headed to the house.

Bryant knew he had to call his sister though with the good news about his eyesight. He was sure at least she and his mother would be happy for him.

Kelly watched the car careening down the drive. She felt her muscles relax and realized how tense she had been the last hour. All sorts of thoughts had been going through her head about what Bryant's reaction would be as that woman tried to weave her web around him. He must have had feelings for her once, though Kelly couldn't see a man like Bryant falling for a mannequin like that. Then again she knew very little about Bryant's past. She was hoping for the chance to learn more and to get to know the man he was now.

While Shel and Bryant had been at the barn Kelly had explained to her father what happened the night before or rather in the early morning of today. She had gone into detail sparing nothing. She didn't want him angry with Bryant over the deal. She had used poor judgment and said so. This earned a look of approval from her father. He had remained quiet while she told the story.

Her father's reaction to what had happened at the cabin had surprised her. He was of course upset about her shoulder but totally understanding of how it had happened. He seemed to have strong feelings for Bryant and it was like he thought of the other man as another son. He had also recognized right away that feelings had already blossomed between Kelly and Bryant. This brought a secretive yet pleased smile to his face. Kelly felt that Weldon would have no problem accepting Bryant into the family, mainly cause he basically already had.

Kelly saw Shel and Bryant heading for the house. She went inside to help Rosa finish setting lunch out. Sheldon was also helping. He had asked a dozen questions about that strange guy they had showed up with. Weldon had tried to explain who Bryant was to him. Sheldon seemed enthusiastic about meeting him.

Kelly hoped he would like Bryant. That would mean the world to her if he accepted him. More over, she was waiting to see Bryant's reaction to her son. How they interacted would mean everything to whether she and Bryant even started a relationship.

She did know though she had to slow it down. She already knew the sexual pull was strong. She needed time to see what else was there. She remembered Dr. Stein's words, 'your heart will know when the right man comes along.' She knew her heart had already accepted him, now she needed her brain to.

She heard the guys outside the door now. Now, she would find out one of the answers to her questions. She glanced over to Sheldon who was setting the table.

Chapter 31

"There was no way that could have been an accident," Shel jumped up after Weldon told them what happened the night before.

"I know that," Weldon replied. "I called the sheriffs office and Doug was out this morning. He had a look around."

"What was the damage?" Bryant asked.

"We lost several mares," Weldon sadly recounted what the light of day showed. "Whoever opened those gates frighten them enough to cause a stampede. Several broke their legs had to be put down. He opened all the pens so young foals were caught up in the rush and trampled."

Shel cussed under his breathe as he paced the floor. "How many?"

"We lost at least eight foals right off," Weldon continued. "We have another dozen with injuries, some severe."

"Who would do such a thing?" Kelly asked.

"I have no idea," Weldon said as he shook his head. "I have never had anything like this happen before."

"The studs?" Shel suddenly thought of them.

"They also were let out."

"And?"

"They found each other," Weldon barely whispered. Kelly could see this was nearly killing him. He had been up all night and most of today chasing horses. He had to be exhausted. "We managed to separate them but not before doing damage to each other."

"How bad?" Bryant finally spoke.

"Fortunately they both will pull through," Weldon answered. "The vet was up here this morning. He was hard pressed but managed to pull them both through as well as work on the other horses. Remind me to thank him next time he's up."

230

"I'll beat you to it," Shel said as he grabbed his hat. "I'm going to check on them."

"Sit your ass down," Weldon raised his voice just enough to get his point across. "Lunch will be ready and Rosa wouldn't like it if you're missing. The horses are all settled and don't need you stirring them up." Shel sat back down in his chair.

"You got guards out?"

"At each paddock."

The next morning Kelly and Sheldon were walking down the road from their house. It was becoming the morning routine. The houses were about a mile from each other. Kelly loved these few minutes it took to walk between them. It woke her up, got her appetite ready for the big breakfast Rosa always had ready, and gave her time with Sheldon alone. She wasn't use to sharing him with others and now there were dozens of uncles all around.

Kelly heard a shout as they approached the house and turned in the direction of the barns. She waved at her brother and Bryant as they also headed to the house.

"Uncle Shel!" Sheldon ran ahead and jumped into his uncle's arms. Kelly kept walking knowing the route would intersect theirs. Bryant said something to Shel and the other man nodded. He put Sheldon on the ground, said something and Kelly watched as they sprinted to the house. Bryant caught up to her as the boys reached the house.

"I didn't have a chance to say anything last night," Bryant said. "I think you got a good boy there. He put up with our adult talk during supper quiet well."

"He likes being able to sit with the grown-ups and act like one," Kelly laughed. "And Dad and Shel encourage him."

"Can I encourage him?"

"What do you mean?"

"I would like it if he would run to me like that some day," Bryant said quietly. He moved closer and dropped a light kiss on her waiting lips.

"It's up to you," Kelly said as she returned the kiss with enthusiasm.

"Grandpa?"Sheldon had noticed Kelly and Bryant from his view at the house.

"Yes Sheldon?"

"What's that man doing to mommy?"

"He's saying good morning to her," Weldon laughed as he looked out the screen with his grandson.

"Nobody else but you and uncle Shel say good morning that way," The boy murmured. "And you don't kiss her right on the lips, yucky."

"Your mom likes him better."

"Better than you and uncle Shel?"

"Let's say in a different way," Weldon replied. "Let's get our food before they come and take it all."

Shel was at the table trying to hide his shaking shoulders behind his morning paper. The silent laughter was nearly choking him. At least the boy only seemed to think the kiss was yucky and not the man doing the kiss. He seemed awed by Bryant last night. He had asked him right out what happened to his face. Bryant had patiently explained he had been hurt in a battle. This seemed to impress the young boy.

Kelly and Bryant came through the door and they all settled down to their normal noisy breakfast. Sheldon folded his paper knowing it would be impossible to read it now. Besides, he wasn't going to let them beat him to the food.

"How are the mares and foals doing this morning Dad?" Kelly asked.

"They are settling down now," The older man answered. He looked more rested today. Shel had been adamant about him getting sleep and he and Bryant would take turns checking the men guarding the horses. "The foals all seem to be getting better. We won't be losing anymore of them."

"I'm glad to hear that," Kelly said with relief. She knew how much each animal on the ranch meant to him.

"Hey Sheldon," Bryant spoke to the boy sitting across from him.

"Hello sir," he answered politely. He wasn't sure what to think of this man who was kissing his mommy. The man had showed up so suddenly and even though Sheldon thought it was neat he had fought in a real war like Uncle Shel, why was he kissing mommy?

"Your Uncle Shel and I were thinking of going fishing this afternoon," He asked seriously like this was something important to consider. "We were wondering if maybe you would like to go with us."

Sheldon looked over at his mommy with the question in his eager eyes. She laughed as she bit into a sausage and nodded her consent.

"Yes sir, I would like to go," Sheldon answered back as seriously as he had been asked.

Chapter 32

Kelly stood on the front porch of her house. She waved at Sheldon in the car as his uncle drove him to the bus stop at the end of the drive. It was September already and it seemed that Kelly had just arrived here, but three months had now passed. Sheldon was starting school and the air was getting decisively cooler.

Kelly leaned on the railing and surveyed the surrounding scenery. The trees in the mountains had already begun to change colors. The hills were full of deep reds, golds, and browns. They reflected how Kelly had changed over the last 3 months. She had gone from fearing life, people and the future to looking forward to what life holds for her, loving the people around her, and waiting for the future to open up.

Bryant had played a big role in all three areas. His patience, kindness and love had opened up her mind to the possibilities that lay ahead. After the combustible start they had when they met, things had calmed down and Bryant set out to woo her the old fashioned way. He would meet her at the house in the morning and walk with her and Sheldon to the ranch house. Sometimes he had flowers he picked along the way. They were wild flowers that grew along the lane between the houses.

Once a week they went into town for dinner and sometimes a movie, sometimes just a walk along the square. They went riding together sometimes with Sheldon sometimes alone. That was the second thing.

Sheldon's reaction to Bryant was heartwarming. He has taken to the man as instantly as it seemed the man was taken to him. Bryant took the boy fishing, riding, and exploring. Uncle Shel was with them a lot and at times the three of them seemed inseparable. It warmed Kelly's heart to see them all together.

Kelly's relationship with her father was also growing. They had plenty of time to talk and learn about each other. He told her everything he knew about her mother, which were the times leading up to her mother's abandonment of her husband and son. He painted a picture of a woman who despaired for another life, one that seemed greener from a distance.

Kelly began to understand what her mother had given up and the price she paid when she realized it was the wrong choice. She still didn't understand why her mother never went back home once she realized Kelly was Weldon's and that she would never be happy with Morris? The only thing Kelly could think of was that her mother must have felt she deserved what she got. Whatever the answer was, it had gone to the grave when her mother had died.

She and Shel talked about her mother also. Slowly he was coming to accept what she did and to forgive her. Kelly could see the peace seeping through him more and more each time. She knew the day would come when he could totally put pain to rest and let the future come.

Kelly was pushed out of her reverie from the sound of the truck returning. She turned to the house and made sure the lights were off and the door shut before going down the drive to meet the truck. It stopped in front of her and she got in. Shel flashed his customary big eared grin. It had thrown her off at first, till she realized that's the way he always was. This perpetual good mood was catching and Kelly couldn't help but feel good when she was around her brother.

"Feel like a ride to the upper pasture?"

"Where you're gathering the cattle to herd down for the winter?" she asked. She knew the answer but couldn't ask the question she really wanted to ask. Where had Bryant been for the past week? Since Bryant's eyesight had returned his talent with the animals seemed to increase. He could tame or calm down anything with his firm yet soft deep voice. Kelly knew that from personal experience.

Shel had promoted him to head cowboy. A sort of informal promotion since he wasn't the foreman, but the men knew that Bryant answered now to nobody but Shel and Weldon and they answered to him. Kelly had wondered if there were any hard feelings from those who had been here for years, but she had never seen any sign of it. Things seemed to settle into a close comfortable work situation. The men didn't seem surprised at all by the change in status. It was like they had all expected it to happen if Bryant's sight ever returned.

"Yes," Shel answered with a laugh, "to where Bryant has been hiding for a week." Kelly gave him a sardonic look but refused to answer. That man could read minds. At the very least he was very observant and could come up with the right sum when presented with two and two.

"Sure," she answered sternly. "I think a ride would be nice, as long as we got back before school let out."

"I guarantee it," Shel winked. Kelly knew that wink. She knew that it would be grandpa picking up her son today. Oh well, the boy liked that and Kelly knew he would be totally spoiled by the time they got back.

"Ok," she laughed, "I'll go as long as Dad knows he's stuck with the kid for a few hours."

"Oh, I know he'll resist, but we should be able talk him into it," Shel laughed along with his sister. He loved the camaraderie they had now. Oh, how glad he was that she had found them! They pulled into the circle in front of the main barn. The horses were already saddled and waiting.

Kelly had graduated from the sweet mare she started on to a vibrant young gelding. Once her fear over horses was no longer an issue her skills quickly developed. She could now keep up with the best of them. Weldon was finishing up on Kelly's horse when they pulled near the stalls. He straightened up and waved as they pulled up.

"Hey sweetie," Weldon greeted her with a kiss on the cheek. "You ready to ride?"

"You do know you're stuck on kid detail this afternoon then," Kelly laughed as she kissed him back. It felt so natural to be showing affection for him when she had never felt any sort of feelings of affection for Morris. "Don't forget to pick him up at 4 O'clock now."

They took off and Kelly was able to forget about everything except the beautiful scenery as they rode. They rode in comfortable silence, not needing to keep up a conversation for talking sake. Shel would point something out once in a while to her but mostly they just rode on quietly, each in their own thoughts.

Weldon turned toward the truck and decided to leave it down by the barns since he knew he'd need it that afternoon. He didn't see the glint of light reflecting from the raise about a half mile away.

Chapter 33

The fat grubby man watching Weldon grinned through his cigar. He was going to love stealing this man's grandchild from him as much as he had loved stealing his wife. It wasn't that he loved either one. It was just for the sake of taking from somebody who had more than him.

It wasn't his fault he was always down on his luck. Other people had everything. They didn't deserve it any more than he did, so he took what he wanted. He should have gotten the money or property from Kate's inheritance, not Kelly. He was her husband, that made it his. He didn't care that the marriage was illegal and therefore void. He had supported that bitch and her bastard child. He deserved anything he could get from it.

He had found out about Kelly's inheritance after she had left. Bobby had gone to her house and found her gone. The neighbor told him all about Kelly moving to Montana. Morris knew exactly where she had gone. He decided to follow her.

He stood up and half hazardly brushed some the dirt off. He tossed the binoculars to his oldest son and went to the trailer parked a short ways away. He deserved that money and he was going to get it anyway he could.

"Hey dumbass," he yelled for his sons who were still standing at the top of the rise! "Get your ass' over here!" Morris went inside waiting for his sons. Mitch and Bobby stood a little ways apart and looked at each other. They had never disobeyed their father but what he was planning now just didn't feel right. Mitch clutched the binoculars and headed toward the trailer in answer to his father. Bobby grabbed his arm as he passed buy.

"We can't be doing this," he hissed to his older brother! "Sheldon is our blood if not his!"

"You want to go in there and tell him?" Mitch reluctantly replied. Bobby looked at the trailer and swallowed. He let go of his brother's arm and angrily stomped away. He went to the top of the rise where they got a clear yet hidden look at the spread below. He could see the men going about their chores. He picked out the old man who seemed to bring an unwarranted anger to his father. He had no idea what this man had done to make Morris hate him so much.

Bobby remembered the different things over the last few months they had done to mess things up. The first had been dropping a bale from the roof next to that old man and his son. The second had been to let the horses out of the paddocks. Morris had told them it wasn't natural to keep wild horses penned up like that. It wasn't till after that he realized the trouble they had caused.

Bobby had watched the men scramble to go after the horses. He could see the field they had all ran into in the fading light. He saw those two big studs go after each other. Even to a city boy like him he knew they would have killed each other. It was like watching two gang leaders fighting over turf.

The next morning when he was watching the paddock areas he realized that many of the horses were injured. He remembered the stampede they had caused the horses to leave. There was a pile over to the back of the area and when he realized what it was he got physically sick. He had never meant for any of the animals to get hurt.

Morris decided to tone the stunts down when he saw the sheriffs department come out. He wanted to cause problems but not alert the cops. So, they had punctured tires, drove nails into gas tanks, cut straps on saddles. He had thought it was so funny when a cowboy had fallen off his horse after a cut strap broke all the way through. The other cowboys had also thought it was funny till the man pointed out the strap. All the men then looked at their saddles. Darn, but they found all the cut straps. That had brought the cops out again. Morris lay off the stunts for a few weeks since then. Now, what he was planning had Bobby's blood running cold. He knew his brother agreed with him but neither of them knew how to get out of it. If they went down to the ranch they would be arrested for sure. Morris had warned them what happened to young guys in jail. They didn't want to end up there.

Bobby and Mitch both thought that Kelly had been the smart one to get away from Morris as soon as she had been able too. She called them little clones of Morris but she didn't understand. They didn't stay with him out of love. They stayed with Morris out of fear.

Morris had controlled their lives with fear and manipulation and now they felt they had no choice but to do as he demanded. He had gotten them to do things through the years and kept evidence that could put them away in prison for the rest of their lives. But, now he was demanding that they help kidnap their own nephew. Bobby wasn't sure he or Mitch could do it.

He turned and watched his brother enter the trailer. The look he threw Bobby told him he wasn't too happy about this situation either. Maybe there was a way they could thwart Morris in this stupid plan. There was no way they could succeed, of that he was sure.

Chapter 34

Kelly saw Bryant before he saw her. They came over a rise and could look down on the herd and the men surrounding it. Bryant was going back and forth yelling orders to the others. He was used to authority but also knew how to use it without being abusive. The men gave him the usual guff they gave Shel and Weldon, which was the sign that Bryant's authority was accepted.

She smiled as she watched his straight figure. She never tired of watching him work, especially with the horses. He had a way with them that was nothing short of spectacular. She had watched him work with a rogue mustang over the summer. He spent many hours with the horse and eventually had won him over enough to let him ride him. He was now Bryant's horse. Shel had given him to Bryant since Bryant no longer needed Peachy.

Shel said that it would be a waste not to since the horse wouldn't let anybody else near him. Bryant in turn had donated Peachy to a local riding program for disadvantaged children. He also donated his time. On Saturday afternoons he, Kelly, Sheldon, and Shel all went to the stables they used and helped with the children.

Kelly loved watching him working with a blind child, helping him or her to gain confidence. He would whisper something to them. Kelly would see a look of wonder come over the child's face and suddenly they would be sitting straighter and urging the horse forward with more authority in their voice. Kelly knew the secret he told them was about him being blind once and learning to ride.

Bryant named his mustang Boss. At the strange looks on Kelly's and Shel's face he explained. "He knows who is boss," he had laughed. "He is only letting me think I am."

Kelly also was surprised at how well he and Sheldon had bonded. The boy had wanted to come on this run so badly he at first refused to go to school. Bryant had taken him out to the porch and they had sat and talked for the longest time. Kelly had watched them through the window. Bryant let the boy talk, then he said something, and then he listened again. This routine went back and forth for nearly an hour. At the end of the conversation, they both stood and shook hands. Sheldon came in first, all smiles and announced he was going to school after all and had run upstairs to get his things together. Kelly had turned to the man who was now holding up the door frame with his shoulder. He looked so natural just leaning there with a big shit ass grin on his face.

"What did you say to him?" Kelly had asked. Bryant only grinned bigger. As he pushed off the frame and ambled over to her. He took her into his big strong arms and held her close.

"That is our little secret," was all he said. He then kissed her softly. At her eager response he increased the pressure, and they were soon deeply entwined in each others arms. Kelly wanted much more from this man than just kisses. She knew it wouldn't take much to stay a night with him, to ask him to stay with her, but he had decided that waiting was the best thing. Kelly was sure his respect for her father and brother had a lot to do with that decision.

How had he put it? "We already know there is a sexual spark there and I would love to explore it, but first let's just get to know each other." Kelly also knew that it was out of respect for her as well as his friend and Weldon that he was trying so hard to take things slowly, and since she had the same thoughts because of her son she agreed to it. That didn't stop the deep passionate kisses they would steal whenever they could.

She loved this courting process but now was wondering when he was going to be ready to actually propose? She knew Sheldon would accept him and was sure Weldon and Shel had already figured it would lead that way and had no problem with it. So, why was he now waiting?

Boss was the one who realized they were being watched first and nickered out his greeting. Bryant turned his head and waved when he realized who it was. He turned Boss in their direction and let the horse have his head. He arrived and after a short greeting to Shel turned his attention to Kelly. Shel knew when he wasn't wanted and headed down toward the herd.

Kelly was wishing there weren't two horses between them but Bryant managed to lean over and give her a quick kiss. Even these quick little greetings warmed her to her toes.

"Couldn't wait for me to get back?"

"Oh, I could wait," Kelly laughed. "I just figured you must be missing me so much and decided to put you out of your misery."

"You thought right," he laughed as he gave her another quick kiss. "That does taste so good. I didn't realize how hungry I was." Kelly could see that hunger in his eyes and knew hers matched his.

"Want to learn how to herd a bunch of rambunctious cows?"

"I already know how to herd a nearly seven year old boy," Kelly laughed. "This can't be much harder."

"You got a point there," Bryant agreed. "Let's go then."

They turned and rode down to the herd. The rest of the day went fast with Kelly learning the finer points of herding cattle. When it was time to make camp for the night she was glad they weren't staying. The men had got the cattle to within a days ride. There was a service road near the camp and Shel had called for a truck to meet them, but it wasn't a truck that met them.

Morris had staked out a spot near the bus stop. He had a perfect shot of the whole area no matter where Shepard parked. At nearly 4pm when Weldon arrived and parked at the side of the lane, he parked in perfect line of Morris' sight. 'That's my good man,' Morris snicker to himself and aimed.

Weldon didn't turn his truck to head back to the ranch since he had decided to take Sheldon into town for dinner. He knew the others wouldn't make it in till fairly late. He pulled up to the stop and waited. Weldon turned his head when he thought he heard the bus coming up the road. He never heard the bullet that slammed through the car window. Weldon slumped over the seat against his seat belt.

A large dingy white RV pulled up along side his truck as a man from the past stepped out from his hiding place several yards away. He went up to the shattered window and leaned in to see Weldon laid over with blood pooling in the passenger seat from a head wound. He smiled and tucked the gun into his belt. No need to waste another bullet.

"Move the RV down the roar out of sight before the bus arrives and wait for my yell to come back," Morris yelled to Mitch, pointing toward the small rise he was just hiding behind.

He went to the back of the truck and crouched down out of sight. Just as the RV passed over the little rise out of sight Morris heard the bus pull up and the sound of the door opening. He heard the kids calling goodbye to Sheldon and he yelling his byes back. What a dreadfully loud little pup he'd always been, Morris thought. Morris heard the bus door close and the bus engine rev as it moved on down the road. He peeked around the driver's side and saw the boy running toward the truck.

"Hey, grandpa," the boy yelled cheerfully as he reached the passenger side door. Before he could reach for the handle to open it Morris sprang from his hiding place to grab him. Sheldon screamed and struggled to get away. A big hand clamped over his mouth and he felt himself lifted against a soft fat body. He bared his teeth and bit as hard as he could into a fat finger drawing blood. Morris screamed and yelled toward the rise and a moment later the RV appeared and pulled up. The side door burst open and Bobby jumped out. Morris all but threw the small boy into his arms.

"Take this little shit and tie him up in the back," he ordered as he pulled a dirty handkerchief from his back pocket and wrapped it around his bleeding hand. He glared at the little boy who glared back just as menacingly.

245

"You'll pay for this you little bastard." Morris climbed into the RV and Bobby followed with the still struggling boy. He glanced over to the truck and the shattered window. Their Dad had never mentioned murder as part of the plan. Now, they were in for it.

Mitch had started moving as soon as Bobby had closed the door. Bobby took Sheldon to the back bedroom and sat him on the bed. The boy immediately jumped up and tried for the door. Bobby grabbed the child and set him back on the bed holding him tightly.

"Shhhhhhhhhhhhhhhhhh," he whispered with his finger to his mouth. "I can't help you if you make a fuss." The boy stopped his struggles and stared at his uncle silently.

"That's a good boy," Bobby continued. He looked over to the door still holding his finger to his mouth went and looked out to see where Morris was. He could see and hear the man cussing at the sink up front as he rinsed his finger under water.

He went back to the boy leaving the door open so he could hear what was happening out there or if Morris came this way. "You have to trust me Sheldon," he whispered. "Your grandpa has gone crazy and I'll do what I can to protect you, OK?"

The boy nodded but still didn't say a word. He stared at his uncle with wide frightened eyes. Bobby knew now he and Mitch would have to do everything to help the boy. It was obvious that Morris wouldn't think twice about harming him.

"I have to tie you up for now," he continued whispering to the boy calmly. "It is safer to let him think he has control. Do you understand me?"

The boy nodded. "Good," Bobby patted the child on his head gently. "I know this is a lot to ask, but please trust me. Have I ever done anything to hurt you before?"

The boy shook his head, and then finally spoke in a shaky whisper, "I want my mommy."

246

Bobby felt a knife in the pit of his stomach twist completely around. "I promise with all my heart I'll get you home to your mommy, Okay?"

Once again the boy nodded. Bobby carefully wrapped ropes loosely around his hands and legs. He laid the boy down in the bed and placed a blanket over him. "Try and sleep," he whispered as he laid his hand on the boys head again. He then turned and joined the other two.

Morris was still nursing his hand. He had wrapped gauze around it and Bobby could see blood seeping through. He felt a secret pleasure at seeing Morris getting hurt for once after all he has done to others.

"Got the brat settled," Morris hissed.

"Yes," Bobby responded as he took a seat behind them, "but do we have to tie him up?"

"Damn right we do," Morris erupted! "Good thing I don't go in and throttle that little bastard!"

"You're not going to lay a hand on that boy," Bobby shouted jumping to his feet. Mitch hit a bump in the road and the jerk sent Bobby falling back into his chair. Morris only laughed mercilessly at his hapless son.

Mitch glared at Bobby through the rearview mirror, silently warning him not to over step his boundaries. After glancing at Morris to make sure he wasn't paying attention, he glared back at his brother.

He then saw an extraordinary thing, Mitch winked at him. Some of the tightness went out of Bobby's stomach. He now knew his brother was on his side. They would have to bide their time and get the boy away from Morris and back to Kelly. He looked back at Morris who was still cussing under his breath over the bite.

Suddenly he figured something out that made a tremendous impact on him. He and Mitch weren't like Morris at all. They didn't have to be like him and he knew that if he got out of this he was going to do everything he could to prove he could change.

The one person he wanted to believe him was his sister Kelly. If she could forgive him and give him a chance, he knew he could show the world he was not like Morris. He also knew the only way for redemption was to save the boy in the back of the trailer. Then maybe they will know he and Mitch had nothing to do with the killing of that old man in the truck and let them off easier.

Chapter 35

Kelly was looking forward to seeing Sheldon and her Dad. She was tired and dirty. She was looking forward to a shower and a nice quiet dinner on the balcony of the ranch house. They were just waiting for the truck to arrive to pick them up.

Kelly, Bryant and Sheldon caught sight of the sheriff's car coming through the trees.

"Shel," Bryant saw the car approaching first and asked, "What would Doug be doing here?" Shel and Kelly turned toward the car. They both got a sick feeling in the pits of their stomachs. Doug had been called out to the ranch several times this summer for various pranks and malicious stunts. Somebody seemed to have it out for the Shepard's but they haven't found out whom yet. The car pulled up and Doug rolled down his window.

"Shel," he called out! "You and Kelly need to come back to the ranch with me."

"What's going on?" Shel asked. Doug only shook his head.

"I'll give you a report once we are headed back." He popped the door locks so they could get in the car.

"I'm coming too," Bryant said as he opened the front door for Kelly then got into the back with Shel. Doug just nodded and turned around. The route to the house wasn't that far by road. It would take about fifteen minutes to reach the ranch house.

"Okay Doug," Shel asked leaning forward in the seat. "What's going on?"

"There's been an incident at the ranch."

"What kind of incident?" Kelly asked from beside him. She remembered all the incidents that happened this summer. A couple of them had been life threatening but then they suddenly calmed down to become prank like.

"It's your father," Doug started to say but was interrupted by Shel.

"What's happened Doug?" He yelled. "Will you just spit it out?"

"Somebody took a shot at your father," Doug informed them tightly. He always hated this kind of thing, "while he was at the bus stop waiting for Sheldon."

Silence met his words. Kelly didn't how to react. She couldn't ask the question on her lips. Bryant came to her rescue. He laid a hand on her shoulder and gave her a quick squeeze before turning to the Sheriff.

"What about Sheldon?"

"The boy is nowhere to be found." They pulled into the circle between the house and the barns. The truck was there. The driver's window was shattered.

Shel was jumping out of the car before Doug had come to a complete stop. He was running for the truck at full speed with Kelly and Bryant on his heels. Doug came up behind them as the looked in side and saw the seat covered in blood.

"Dad?" both Shel and Kelly asked at the same time.

"Weldon is inside," Doug said. He shouted after the three as they turned as one and headed for the house. "He's okay. The bullet just grazed him."

Shel pushed through the men around the kitchen door with Kelly right behind him. Kelly had registered the Sheriff's words with relief from one part of her brain but the other part was screaming 'where is my son?'

"Dad," Shel yelled. He knelt next to his father who was seated at the kitchen table with an ice bag held to his head. A paramedic was just packing up his things.

"Dad, Dad" Kelly cried! Bryant took a hold of her arm to steady her.

Weldon lifted his head and tried to smile but grimaced instead. "I am ok," he said in his strong voice. "The police and an ambulance are here, but I'm not hurt that bad."

"And," he continued looking at the paramedic, "I am not going to the hospital."

Kelly about melted inside with relief at the strength in his voice.

"Where's Sheldon?" she asked looking from her Dad to the Sheriff.

"I have no idea," Shel shook his head carefully.

"Excuse me," the paramedic broke in. "I recommend that Mr. Shepard go to the hospital to be looked at by a Doctor, but he has refused."

"Is it serious?" Shel asked.

"It was just a flesh wound," The paramedic explained. "He may have a slight concussion, but as far as I can tell no damage done to the skull. I still think it should be checked by a Doctor in the hospital. An x-ray will rule out any damage to the skull."

"My children here will tell you I am as hard headed as a rock," Weldon roared. "I will call my doctor in the morning if, and I say if, I get dizzy or any of them other things you mentioned."

"Okay sir," the man said resigned. "I can't force you."

"Is there a list of instructions you can leave of what we can watch for?" Kelly asked. He dug out a printed sheet from his case and quietly left. The rest of the people in the kitchen turned toward Weldon.

"What happened?" Shel asked as he looked at the wound. There wasn't anything to see. The paramedic had cleaned up the wound and applied bandages.

"Get away boy," Weldon waved him away.

They all were thankful to hear it was just a flesh wound, but judging from the blood in the cab it had bled quite a bit. Kelly leaned around Shel to get a better look at her father.

"You must be tired but we need to hear what happened, Dad," Kelly whispered. "We need to find Sheldon." Bryant came behind her and led her to a chair across the table from Weldon. He turned to get a glass of water but found Rosa standing there with it already. He took it whispering his thanks.

"I am afraid I don't know," Weldon said sadly. "I am so sorry sweetie," he reached out to her and took her hand. "I will do what I can to piece together what happened so we can find him."

Kelly took his hand and went back around the table to give him a light hug. "I know Dad," she said softly through a tight throat. "I don't blame you. We'll find out what happened."

The Sheriff, Doug, who knew the Shepards very well, decided now, was the time to speak.

"I understand it's your son who is missing?"

"Yes," Kelly answered. "Dad was supposed to pick him up at the bus stop after school."

"You were with the rest of the crew at the cattle drive?"

"Kelly and I rode out to meet Bryant and the herd," Shel answered for Kelly. "We just got to the road when you drove up." The officer nodded. He looked over where the ranch hands who weren't on the drive were standing near the back door listening.

"Does anybody know anything else?"

One the men known as Cappy stepped forward. "All we know is just before 4o'clock, Mr. Weldon jumped in his pick-up to go pick the boy up at the bus stop. About an hour later he comes driving in here very fast and rather haphazardly. His window was shattered and he had blood running down his face. He stopped right there and called for help. We come running and somebody called 911. That's all we know sir," he finished and stepped back with the others.

"Hey Doug," called another officer who had been searching the passenger side of the truck, "you might want to take a look at this."

"I'll be right back Shel, Ma'am," he said as he turned to the door and let himself out to see what the man had found in the truck. Shel and Kelly had no intention of staying where they were and followed the Sheriff to the truck with Bryant staying close to Kelly. They stayed a discrete distance away but close enough to see and hear everything the second officer was showing and saying.

"See this Doug," the younger officer asked as he pointed to a hole in the farthest edge of the dashboard? "An inch further to the right or an inch higher and it would have been lost out of the window."

"Who would want to shoot your father and kidnap your son?" he asked as he looked first at Shel then at Kelly.

"I have no idea Doug," Shel shrugged. "Dad has no enemies far as I know?"

"But, we do know you've been having vandal trouble all summer," Doug pointed out.

"I know who," Kelly spoke up. She straightened to her full height and clutched her hands. All eyes went to her. Kelly looked at Weldon, who had followed slowly behind them with tears welling in her sad eyes. "I am so, so sorry Dad. I didn't think he would ever stoop this low."

Weldon made his way to Kelly and enfolded her in his arms. "There, there my sweet child," he whispered in her ear. "You are not to blame for this man's psychotic behavior."

"If I hadn't come," Kelly started as the tears fell on Weldon's shoulders. He hushed her quickly.

"If you hadn't come," he whispered hoarsely with deep emotion, "many of us would never have felt the sweet presence of your soul." He pulled away slightly and took Kelly face between his rough work worn hands. "I will never regret the day you came into our lives. I knew something was missing and knew it was you the moment I walked into that diner. Now, you know that Morris is responsible for his own actions. Don't ever regret coming home to us."

Weldon pulled her close again and held her tight. He looked up at those around him, his son, Bryant, the rest of his ranch hands, and the police, most all of them he had known for years. He saw wet eyes in some he had never thought had it in them. Others he saw loyalty and joy he was not seriously injured. In Shel and Bryant he saw anger for whoever was responsible. He knew they all deserved an explanation. Though he was weak from blood loss he knew he had to give it now.

"Weldon?" Doug came forward. "You know who has been doing all this?"

"Yes," Weldon said slowly, straightened up, looked Kelly in the eye for a long moment before tucking his arm around her and turning to the semicircle of men around him.

"His name is Morris," he started. "He came into town one day looking for an easy mark. He was one of these men who felt the world owed him for the suffering he had gone through in life.

"Rather than earn a living for himself, he spent his energies in cheating others out of theirs. He thought I was that easy mark, but when I proved otherwise he decided on revenge. I thought he had left town only to find out he had met Kate and found her weakness. He used her to get back at me. He decided if he couldn't get my money one way he would get it another.

"He thought he could get Kate to steal from me. I found out and was coming home to confront her when I guess Morris realized they been caught. He and Kate left. I had no heart to go after her so I let them go."

Weldon stopped his narrative for a moment to look at Kelly and then at Shel. "I did hire a private investigator to keep an eye on them. I knew a child was born just short of nine months after they had run. I figured it was Morris' that they must have had an affair long before I caught on to them.

"I was heart broken when I found out it was a girl for I had always wanted a daughter. I pulled the investigator out and tried to forget her, him and the child I felt robbed of.

"Kelly, if I had let him investigate further," Weldon choked up for a moment. "I would have known long ago you were mine, just by looking at you. You're so lovely like your mother, yet you look so much like your brother. There was no way you could resemble him so much unless you were mine. It was my fault you went through life with the abuse of that man. I am the one who needs your forgiveness." Weldon had reached the end of his strength and started to collapse.

"Dad," Shel cried out! He and Bryant got to him before he hit the ground and helped him into a sitting position. "I think we need to get you to the hospital."

"I'm not going to a damn hospital," Weldon argued, "but I wouldn't mind some help getting back to the house." After some argument Weldon won and convinced the others all he needed was rest.

With the help of a couple ranch hands, Shel and Bryant got Weldon back to the house and in his bed. Shel did call the doctor who said he would be out in the morning.

After they got Weldon comfortable and sent the hands back to finish their chores, Shel, Bryant, Kelly, and Doug gathered in the living room to sort things out. They each found a place to sit. Bryant never far from Kelly led her to the love seat and sat next to her. Kelly looked ready to faint herself, so he called for Rosa to get something for her to drink. Rosa came back with enough for everybody.

"Okay, now that we are all settled here," Doug spoke up. "Would somebody mind clarifying a few things? Like who is this Morris?"

"You really believe Morris is the one who shot Dad and kidnapped Sheldon?" Shel asked Kelly.

"I know he did," Kelly answered shakily. "Morris is the man my mother ran off with as Dad said earlier. He is a vile man who would do anything if he thought it would profit him and hurt others. I know for sure he would have been very angry when he found out Mom had hidden the main portion of the estate she inherited from Grandma. He'd have felt that he was cheated out of what should have been his."

"Why would he think he deserved grandma's money," Shel asked harshly. "He was never legally married to Mom. Dad never divorced her."

256

Kelly nodded in agreement. "He acknowledged the fact that he and Mom had married without seeking a divorce. His explanation was he couldn't wait. He knew a child was coming and he also felt it was his. I guess Mom had told him she and Dad hadn't had sex in a long time." Kelly looked down at her hands which were entwined in Bryant's. She looked at him and he smiled encouragement at her. His strength gave her strength to continue. She didn't know what she would do without him.

"He told me the day of Mom's funeral," Kelly continued, her voice getting firmer as she went, "that I wasn't his kid, and he deserved everything he could get from her as payment for raising her bastard child. He said that nobody should expect a man to love another man's child." Kelly felt Bryant's hand tighten in hers. She looked at him.

"He was wrong," he whispered to her. "I find it very easy to love your child as I would my own. He's as fantastic as his mother." Kelly felt a new wave of tears and struggled to maintain composure. She smiled at Bryant with love in her eyes and he understood. She now had the strength to go through this ordeal. She turned to Doug

"Now, what do we do to find Morris and get my boy back?"

Doug stood up. "First, I and my men will go to where Weldon was when he was shot and see what we can find."

The other three stood up as one with Shel speaking first. "We are coming with you." When Doug started to protest Shel stopped him. "I know this ranch like the back of my hand Doug. You know that. If Morris took off across it I am the one most likely to find him." To his credit the officer acknowledged the fact then turned to Kelly and Bryant with a questioning eye.

"You think I'll not be there when you find them," Kelly asked simply? Again Doug nodded then looked to Bryant. He simply pointed to Kelly.

"I go where she goes," he replied.

"You will want Bryant along," Shel added for emphasis. "He's the best tracker I have ever seen. He could find the enemy no matter where they hid in Afghanistan."

"Ok, I'll let you three come along, but you follow my directions." Doug looked at each one and asked, "Understood"? They all nodded. "I ordered some lights in from town. My men are setting them up on the perimeter of the shooting site."

Chapter 36

Bryant was bent over a set of tracks straining to see them in the artificial light. He followed them from the site where Weldon was shot, down the drive over a rise. He then followed where it turned around and back to the original site. The others stood off to the side and watched him.

"Well, that got us far," one of the officers joked. Doug gave him a dark look and the man shut up. They turned back to watch Bryant as he then followed the tracks to the main road and searched the ground to determine which way they went. He turned back to the group and motioned them to come to him. He pointed to where the tracks were curved off the dirt drive to the main road. "They came from the left and went back the same way. They came in, stopped and a heavy man jumped down. The vehicle is more than likely an RV."

"That would be Morris," Kelly supplied.

Using his own flashlight as a pointer to follow the actions he was talking about. Bryant continued, "The man walked to that small rise and hid on his belly. He shot Weldon from there. I found a spent shell casing."

"What did you do with it?"

"I marked it with a stick," Bryant answered. "I know better than to touch it."

"Thank-you," Doug acknowledged and motioned for Bryant to continue.

"He then walked over to the truck standing in front of the window then he went around the back to hide I presume. He was never in a hurry. He seems to have a lot of confidence in himself."

"That's an understatement," Kelly spat out. Bryant gave her a tight smile.

"We'll get them back," He said softly before continuing with his observations.

"I am sure he had at least one accomplice for the RV returned and went over the rise to hide while Morris stayed here."

"That would be two," Kelly answered the unasked question in the eyes that turned to her, "my two brothers, Mitch and Bobby. They are little clones of Morris."

"You can see where Morris grabbed Sheldon," Bryant returned to the marks and pointed to where there were signs of a struggle. "You can see the boy was half dragged half carried to the RV. Then it took off heading back where it came from. The boy is a scrapper. See that blood, I would say he bit Morris."

"You sure it's not Sheldon's blood?" Kelly looked queasy.

"See where the blood is scattered?" Bryant asked. "That is consistent with shaking a hand and from a higher distance from the ground than Sheldon stands." Kelly sighed with relief.

"Then they could be halfway to the border by now," Doug said with a deep sigh. "I will call the Highway patrol."

"I don't think so," Shel said

"You don't want the highway patrol?"

"Oh yes," Shel quickly amended. "I meant I don't think they are very far away."

"What makes you think that?" Kelly asked. She didn't dare hope Shel could be right but prayed he was.

"If Morris knew to be here at this time," Shel explained, "and if he knew it was going to be Weldon he had to be hiding nearby so they could keep watch on us."

"That's a lot of ifs," Doug added, "and even if he was close by then there's no reason to go back there."

"But they are logical ifs," Shel pressed. "Morris had to be prepared to shoot Dad the minute he pulled up. Dad said he turned his head at the sound

261

of a vehicle pulling up from the road. He thought it was the bus. That was the last he remembered. Anyway, Morris would have had to camp in a spot hidden from us but close enough to spy on us using binoculars. Also, he is going to want to keep an eye on us to see what was happening. He has no reason to think that we would find him if we hadn't found him before. He has been here the whole summer."

"That's right," Bryant broke in. "They had to be close enough to pull those sabotages."

"You mean Morris has been watching us all summer?" Kelly asked feeling sick to her stomach. She had thought she was rid of that fool and here he was in her own back yard the whole time.

"I am afraid so," Shel agreed. He looked at Bryant. "What would they need to watch us? How far away can they be and still see clearly?"

"A high range over the counter pair of binoculars could give him about a half mile range," Bryant thought out loud, "we would have to look for a spot that distance from the ranch house and barns."

Shel turned toward the direction of the ranch house. The moon was rising in the east of the spread. "I know exactly where they are," he shouted.

"Where?" They asked in unison.

"West of the spread are the hills right?" Shel asked of no one in particular. He continued on before anybody could answer. "There is one hill that rises behind the house. The top is about a half mile away and on the other side is a flat clearing surrounded by trees. A road comes off the main road about half a mile from here goes around to the side of the hill, and up to the clearing.

"On that part of the land the road goes through what use to belong to Grandma. She and Grandpa would go up to that clearing on Sundays for a picnic. It was their way of getting closer to God and nature. The woods go around that clearing except at a spot overlooking the cliff on the opposite side of the clearing. It has a sheer drop about fifty feet to the stream that runs through the hills to the river."

"Is the clearing big enough to park an RV and make a camp?" Doug asked.

"Oh, yes," Shel replied "there's more than enough room for that. It's the most logical place for them to be. They can see both houses from there as well as the drive to the bus stop and it's far enough away for us to not notice."

"Ok, you three back to the house," Doug ordered as he got out his radio and started to order more men out to the ranch. "We'll have your son back in your hands in no time ma'am."

"Doug, you need us," Shel stood firm. "If you go racing up there with a bunch of men in cars Morris will hear you and Lord knows what he is capable of doing to Sheldon."

"I know," Kelly spoke up, her voice unyielding in the meaning that she wasn't backing down. "I know very well what that man is capable of. I experienced it. If he feels threatened at all he'll use anything he can, including my son as a shield. If he thinks he's lost, he won't go out without revenge. That means hurting Sheldon. He nearly killed Dad, in fact he thought he had and I don't think he would hesitate to harm Sheldon. I am going with you."

"I understand Ma'am how you feel," Doug replied, "but this could get dicey. I can't do my job and watch the three of you at the same time."

"Forgive me Doug," Bryant stepped up to him, "but you don't have to worry about Shel or me, we are seasoned Special Forces. We can take care of ourselves and keep Kelly safe. We can also help you devise a plan of attack. That is what we do best."

The Officer looked from Shel to Bryant to Kelly and back to Shel again. He saw the set look of determination on each one's face. He knew that either he let them go with him or he would have to worry about them making their own plans. He also knew he could use Shel's and Bryant's expertise. "Okay," he agreed, "Just don't forget who the boss is."

Shel slapped the man on his shoulder. He and Doug were close in age and had known each other most their lives. He trusted Doug and hoped he also had the same faith in them. "Of course Doug," he replied, "we all know who is in charge." Now why did Doug suddenly feel it wasn't him?

"It will take a couple of hours to get everything set up," He said. "Where should we set up our base of operations?"

"You think he would be watching the ranch at night?' Shel asked Kelly.

"There is a good chance he has one of the boys watching for him," Kelly answered. "Then again, with his big ego he will think he's gotten clear away and not worry."

Shell turned to Doug. "We can get everything done inside the barn but need to keep the coming and going to a minimum."

"He will expect us to be looking so having the Sheriff's department there won't alarm him," Kelly offered.

"You're saying this man is so full of himself he won't even think we could be on to him?" Doug asked incredulously.

"That's Morris in a nut shell," Kelly answered tightly.

Two hours later the horses had been saddled for each person going on the mission. They were kept out of sight in the barn. Anybody arriving came directly into the barn under cover of the far side in shadow from the hill. Shel had drawn a rough map of the area showing routes up the hill. He was pointing them out to the others.

"We can figure that if Morris was watching us after the kidnapping," he was saying, "he will know that Dad isn't dead. He will be angry and may want to find a way to finish the job or may take it out on the boy. So we need to finish this as soon as possible."

"You expect us to go riding up that hill in the dark," one of the police officers asked incredulous? "We are not as knowledgeable of the terrain as you are and we aren't near as good of horsemen as you either."

"Don't worry," Shel hurried to put the men's fear aside. "The terrain isn't that rugged. The trails are wide enough for horses to take easily. You won't be expected to go alone. There are two routes we are taking," Shel pointed to the map. "My man Dobbs here will take a group up this trail that goes up the south side of the hill. I'll lead the second team on this trail that winds at the base of the hill to the road that goes up behind it. Any more questions?"

"Yes sir," a man asked from the back of the group, "I was wondering who goes with which group?"

"Good question," Shel answered him. "Who are the sharpshooters?"

Several men raised their hands including the man who had spoken up. "Good, we need you to split into two groups," Shel said as he pointed to two spots in the barn. Those going with Dobbs stand to the left and those going with me stand to the right. You men will take up the best points for looking for a clear shot of Morris if we need it." The men split up and formed the two groups. Shel noticed the man who had spoke up had chosen his group. He suddenly realized that the man wasn't a police officer from the nearby town or county officer either.

"Hey Bryant, we seem to have a party crasher," he called out and pointed towards the man. Bryant turned and followed the direction of Shel's finger till his eyes landed on the man in question.

"Max," Bryant yelled as he went to greet the man. "You son of a bitch. What rock did you come crawling out from under?" The two men gave each other brisk hugs and shook hands. Kelly walked over to Shel and whispered, "A friend of yours I presume?"

"Hell yes," Shel responded enthusiastically. "We were in Afghanistan together. His unit and ours had a friendly competition going on who would complete the hardest missions and capture the most insurgents."

"Who won?" Kelly asked.

"We did of course," Shel couldn't help but brag, and then he got serious. "I don't know where he came from, but I am glad he's here."

"Why?"

"Because he's the best damn sniper in the whole Military," Shel answered enthusiastically. "If anybody can pick off a man hiding behind a child Max can."

Shel caught the look on Kelly's face. "He's going to be okay. You got the best men here to save him."

"I know."

Shel glanced over to where Bryant and Max were engaged in an animated conversation. He wished he could be there catching up on old times.

"Go on over and meet Max," he said. "I'll join you soon as I get these guys ready." He then turned his attention back to the rest of the men standing in front of him.

Kelly joined Bryant and Max. Bryant turned as she approached and draped his arm lightly around her shoulder. You could not sneak up on this man, not even in a crowded noisy barn. "Kelly, I would like you to meet Max, the best damn sniper in the Special Forces." Kelly shook the man's hand. "Max, this is Shel's sister."

"Thank-you for coming to help get my son back," she simply said.

"Shucks ma'am, I had no idea old Shel had a kid sister" the man pumped her arm with enthusiasm. "I was just trucking through the area and heard the call go out for help on the police scanner. When I heard they needed help to rescue a young boy who had been kidnapped, I had to come. I don't believe in being merciful to those who would harm children. Bryant will tell you that."

"I'll give you the whole story later," Bryant promised. Kelly nodded and turned back to the animated man in front of her. He wasn't much to look at. He was short, squat and had the face of a bulldog. His eyes were a warm hazel though and sparkled when he talked. Kelly had no doubt they could get hard when tracking down an enemy."

"You just happened to be in this area?" Bryant asked.

266

"Shucks, yah," The man looked contrite a minute. "I truck through these parts nearly every week. I been always meaning to stop and see Shel but well…" He trailed off for a second.

"Damn it Bryant," He cursed. "I heard what happened to your unit and well wasn't sure what I'd find. I sure wasn't expecting you."

"That's another long story," Bryant laughed. "But, you were telling us how you happened to hear over the radio about this?"

"Oh, yah," He growled to himself, scratching his head to get his thoughts back. "I keep my scanner on the Sheriff's departments as I travel through an area. You never know when my sort of expertise can come in handy. Places out here can't afford to keep sharpshooters on their payroll so they welcome me. In fact most places know me by name and contact me. Anyway I digress."

"I pulled into the town right up to that police station. Unfortunately they don't know me here. I think I scared a few years off a couple of them cops. Anyway though, when I told them who I was, a friend of Shel's and that I was a Special Forces sniper, they welcomed me along. That was when I found out it was for Shel's nephew. Shucks, and here I thought the old boy had finally got himself a boy. You could have pushed me over with a stick." Kelly had an instant liking for this big vigorous man.

"I sure am glad they asked you along," Bryant added. "This guy we're tracking is a peculiar bird, unpredictable. We can't take anything from him on just a surface level."

"How should we take him then," the Max asked, instantly business.

"Primal," Kelly spit under her breath.

"I beg your pardon ma'am?"

Kelly took a deep breath and spoke up. "You treat him as a dangerous primal animal. That's how he thinks, on a primal level."

"So, he's a man after his own interests and look out anybody in his way," the man nodded to his own description he had given Morris.

"In a big way," Kelly continued. "He already tried to kill our father."

267

"Ma'am," Max looked at Kelly closely as he asked his question. "I take it you know this baboon on a personal level? This ain't a random kidnapping for money?"

"No, this isn't a random kidnapping," Kelly replied bitterly.

"This man Morris," Bryant supplied for Max, "was Kelly's stepfather. He's a very abusive man. As we said before, he only cares about himself."

"I know that kind of beast," Max replied. Kelly could see in his eyes it was a first hand experience he was talking about. "I'm here to help the best I can."

Chapter 37

Shel was finishing up the instructions to the gathered men, so Kelly, Bryant and Max turned to listen.

"The rest of you split in half and go to one of the teams. You will back up the snipers." The men broke up in orderly fashion and filed into one of the groups. When they were in the groups, Shel did a fast head count and found that they were indeed even. Each group had 23 or 24 men. He didn't even know that the city and county had that many men. He looked at the different uniforms and realized there were many other city and state departments in the group. Seems the alert had brought them from all over. This was no small state so Shel recognized the hustle they had put in to get here. His heart filled with pride that so many would answer the call for help. He turned to Doug who was standing just behind him.

"You want to take over now," he asked in a slightly teasing mood.

"That's ok," Doug gave a slight laugh, "the one thing I learned about being in control is to know when to let the more experienced man take over. Now is the time. I'll be at your back the whole time."

"I'm glad you chose not to come with me into the Military," Shel said as they turned toward the men once again.

"Why is that," Doug asked somewhat surprised at the remark. They had known each other in school, had been pals if not best buddies. When Shel had said he was going into the Military Special Forces, Doug had thought about joining with him under the buddy plan where you and a friend go to the same place. At the last minute Doug had met the girl who would later be his wife and had decided to become a police officer instead. It had less excitement in it but was closer to home.

Shel looked at him for a long moment. It was true nobody really knew what had happened to him over in Afghanistan except that he lost his

270

leg. "The incident where I lost my leg in Afghanistan was when all the men in my unit died in an ambush. Bryant and I were the only two who made it out alive. That was only because Bryant found a small cave and the entrance caved in and the enemy missed us. The rescuers nearly missed us; fortunately I heard them and called for help. That's why I'm glad you didn't join with me."

Shel turned to the two groups of men waiting for their instructions. Doug knew the topic was now closed. He often wondered what had happened over there. All he had known was that Shel and his friend Bryant had escaped with severe injuries.

"Okay men," Shel's strong voice quieted the chatter. "I don't have to tell you this is dangerous. The man who has my nephew is unpredictable and won't hesitate to shoot back."

"Don't fire the first shot," Doug broke in to add. "Let him make the first move. The safety of the boy is the biggest priority."

"There are suspected to be two more men with Morris," Shel took over again. "They are his son's, Mitch and Bobby Morris. So be on the alert for them as well. We have no idea of the danger they present. So, till we learn otherwise they are also considered to be armed and dangerous."

"Now, group one go with Dobbs and he'll start you on your way."

Doug took over with instructions. "You will reach the hill from this side. There you will take up a perimeter ringing the front side of the clearing. Stay in radio contact at all times with your leader. Don't shoot unless you got a clear shot and he is showing the first aggression." The men all voiced their agreements and followed the old ranch hand to the back of the barn where horses were waiting.

Shel turned to the group left and surveyed them. He knew most of these men, had grown up with some of them. Bryant, Max and Kelly were standing to one side. He smiled at them as he headed their way. Doug followed behind and shook Max's hand as Shel formally introduced him. He had heard about the man showing up at the station and gave permission for

271

him to come out with the rest of the men. He had a feeling they got lucky having him show up.

Chapter 38

The young man watched the activity going on below him. He had noticed as more and more people showed up and entered the barn. Morris had been sure nobody would figure out they had back tracked from the original get away route. The route back to their camp was a half mile from the place Morris killed that old man. They had left going in the opposite direction for an hour. Then they turned around and came back the same way. The truck was gone and there was one cop car at the site as they drove slowly past. The cop didn't pay them any attention. They turned onto the dirt track leading up to the camp. Nobody followed. Morris wasn't worried enough to have either of them keep guard watching the ranch.

In the RV, after they first arrived back at camp, Mitch and Bobby were in the back bedroom with Sheldon. When Morris tried to go back to the child, both young men stood in front of him. They knew first hand what harm he was capable of causing to a young child. He didn't care if it was male or female. Their mother hadn't been as careful keeping him away from them as she had been keeping him away from Kelly. They figured she never knew. Morris had learned his lesson with Kelly trying to do it in the house. He always took the boys somewhere else for his sordid pleasure.

"You're not going back there," Mitch spoke shakily but stood his ground. Bobby nodded.

"You think you two puny ass' could stop me?" Morris had fumed.

"We will give it our best shot if you don't back off," Mitch had said more strongly. He stood taller trying to make himself look as menacing as possible to Morris. Bobby followed suit trying to emulate his older brother. They were rewarded with their effort by a derisive laugh from Morris but he backed up and headed to his liquor cupboard. They were for once happy to see him get drunk. Finally, he passed out. The young men each took turns watching at the door to make sure Morris wouldn't change his mind. The one not with the boy went out to watch the ranch.

It was Mitch who was out there now on his belly watching as the men in the barn came out on horses. One group turned toward the hill as the other group went down the road. Mitch figured they were going to come up the other side effectively surrounding them.

Mitch grinned. So, Morris was wrong. They aren't so stupid after all. They know exactly where we are. He knew now what they could do to help the boy. They just needed to wait till the rescue groups arrived. He watched as the men drew closer. When he knew they were nearly there he went back inside to wake his brother.

It was nearing 3AM when Shel and his men all took up their places. They had the clearing totally surrounded except where it ended at the edge of the cliff. The dirty white run-down RV was on the back side of the clearing. Shel spied the scene with a pair of night binoculars. There was a grill and some camping chairs scattered to the side of it. There was a campfire to one side. They must have only burned it during the day when it was less likely to be noticed. Still they had taken a chance with the smoke being spotted.

It seemed all was quiet inside the RV. The lights were off and no movement could be spotted in the windows. Shel radioed all the men dictating where they should position themselves. He didn't want anybody near the edge of the clearing just yet. He had no idea if this man had the sense to set booby traps or at least noise makers. He wasn't going to take a chance. Bryant, Max and Doug crept up behind him.

"What we got here?" Max asked. Shel gave a brief detail of what he had seen.

"I suggest then we wait till morning," Bryant added. "Maybe we can get a hold of one or two as they come out to do their morning constitution."

"Yah, that is a good idea," Max agreed. "We all need to do that at some time or other." Shel spread the word for the others to hanker down for the rest of night but to keep an eye peeled for any movement and to let him know if anybody sees anything

Max and Bryant were whispering among themselves. Kelly watched the gestures between them as first one or the other would point to the cliff side. They had both packed up their own packs, but Kelly saw ropes and other climbing paraphernalia in Bryant's pack. This had puzzled her since she knew they weren't going to try to come up the cliff side. Shel had said it was too dangerous, especially in the dark. They finished their talk and headed back to the group.

"I am going to go over toward that cliff to check it out," Max said as he hefted his pack. Kelly knew what it contained. She had seen him checking out his high powered rifle. She had wondered how he could keep that gun in his truck. Bryant had filled her in later. Max had a special permit to carry the gun since he did help law enforcement at times.

"I'm going to do recon with him," Bryant said as he also grabbed up his pack. "I don't like to leave any section unknown." He pulled Kelly to the side for a moment first.

He gave her a tender kiss and pulled her into a hug. "I promise you," he whispered into her ear, "that we will do everything in our power to get Sheldon back safely. Between Shel, Max and I, you got the best of the Military elite."

"I know," Kelly held him tight to gather some of his strength to her. "I know you will bring my baby back to me." Bryant gave her one more hug and followed Max into the darkness. Kelly found a tree and tried to find a half comfortable spot to wait out the rest of the chilly night. This was going to be the longest night of her life.

"Bobby," Mitch whispered into his brother's ear. "Wake up."

"What?" Bobby mumbled groggily, "Dad awake?"

"No," Mitch assured him. "He's still passed out. He should be out for hours yet."

"We should leave now."

"No, not yet," Mitch calmed his younger brother. "The people at the ranch figured out where we are. They are now surrounding us."

"What should we do?" Bobby asked his brother as they sat huddled on the bed with the boy between them. "Can we take the boy out now?"

"Not yet," Mitch whispered back. "I'm trying to figure something out."

"He's passed out now, lets sneak out," Bobby suggested. "We can make it to the woods to hide or find one of the men."

"What then?" Mitch asked. "Let them shoot us? They don't know we are on their side. Besides, we could get lost too easily in the dark. I don't want to walk off that cliff by accident."

"If we wait till light, he'll wake up," Bobby pressed. "He will be in a very foul mood and I don't want to try and stop him again."

"He's an old man," Mitch tried to sound brave. "We can take him."

"I wouldn't want to put that to the test," Bobby wavered in his resolve some. "You've seen him fight. He's like a wild beast. You don't know what he'll do next. How do you defend against that?"

"You don't have to worry," Sheldon spoke up. He looked from one uncle to the other. "My mommy and Uncle Shel will come with Bryant to save us."

Mitch patted his little nephew's head. "I don't think your mom is going to worry about me and Bobby very much."

"I'll tell her," Sheldon spouted off getting a little louder only to be hushed quickly by his uncles. He whispered loudly, "I'll make sure she knows you were here taking care of me."

"Thank-you Sheldon," Bobby gave the boy a quick hug. "Now, you lie down and try to sleep while we try to figure out our next step till your mommy and other uncle gets here." The boy nodded and lay down. They had untied him as soon as Morris had settled down to drink himself into a stupor. Mitch covered him and motioned for Bobby to follow him to the window.

"I am sure that they will be watching the RV by now," he whispered to his younger brother. "We will wait till it just starts to lighten up and then break this window, grab Sheldon and escape through it to the woods. I am sure somebody will find us once we reach there. If we can get a good start on Morris, we should make it."

"What about his gun?" Bobby asked fearfully.

Mitch looked over to the door that they had left slightly a jar so they could hear if Morris started moving around. He could hear the man's harsh snoring from down the hall. This gave him more confidence for the moment knowing he was passed out. You know when he went to the pot earlier?" he asked Bobby. When his brother nodded he continued. "Well, he left his gun on the chair when he went. I removed the rest of the bullets from it and got them with me. I also hid the rifle under the RV when I came back just a little while ago. I got the bullets from it also." He patted his pocket. Bobby sighed deeply with relief. They then settled on the edge of the bed to wait out the rest of the night.

"Bobby," Mitch whispered in his sleeping brother's ear, "Bobby, wake up."

"Wha...?" The young man started from his restless sleep, "what?"

"Shhhhhhhhhhhhhhh...," Mitch hushed him quickly looking at the door behind him. All he heard was Morris' snoring still echoing down the hall. "It's time to get out of here. You wake up Sheldon while I get ready to bust this window. Keep him quiet.

The noise from the window could arouse Dad so we'll have to act fast once I smash it, understand?" Bobby nodded as he inched over to Sheldon and softly shook him awake. To the boy's credit he didn't make a peep. He followed Bobby back over to the window where Mitch had a chair in his hands.

"Sheldon, you trust us to get you out of here?" he asked the boy. Sheldon nodded. "Good boy, now listen to me closely. I am going to bust this window and Uncle Bobby is jumping out. I'll hand you over to him and you two will run for those woods." He pointed to the ones on the far side of the clearing instead of the ones closer.

"Why not to the closer ones?" Bobby asked?

"Because the closer ones are away from the ranch," Mitch explained. "I am sure there are people hiding in the woods waiting. They'll help us get the boy to safety."

"Yah," Bobby agreed, "They'll help all right. They'll shoot us."

"No," Mitch assured him. "They will see we are trying to help him get away."

"Okay," Bobby agreed, not sounding too sure but willing to take the chance for Sheldon.

"Okay, now get ready," Mitch took position with the chair over his head. "Jump as soon as I got it busted." He swung the chair and it crashed through the glass with a horrific sound of shattering of glass. Bobby had a towel wrapped around his right hand and used that to clear broken glass from the window sill. He then jumped through and held his hands up for the boy. Mitch grabbed the child and lifted him down to Bobby jumping after. Bobby set the boy down and they went racing through the clearing toward the very spot Kelly and Shel were hiding in the woods with Mitch close behind.

Chapter 39

Kelly heard a crashing sound of shattering glass and started from her uneasy sleep. She stumbled over to where Shel was near-by and crouched with him behind some shrubbery. "What's happening?"

Shel pointed to the back of the RV. Kelly squinted in the gray early pre-dawn and watched the action that was happening at the back of the trailer. Bobby came flying out the window landing on his feet and turning to the RV with his hands up. Then Kelly saw Sheldon being handed out into his arms. She watched as they started running towards them with Mitch hopping out the window and running behind. She jumped up and screamed. "Run Sheldon run!" The RV door crashed open and Morris stumbled out and spotted the boys running. He took off to intercept them before they reached the woods cover.

Shel was up and shouting on the radio for anybody in range to take aim on Morris. Pandemonium reigned for a moment as Kelly stood screaming for the boys to hurry. Then Morris launched toward Sheldon in an action unlikely for a man of his girth. He got a hold of the boy's arm and snatched him from Bobby's grip.

"No," Kelly screamed running out into the clearing with Shel at her heels! Morris gained control of the child and aimed his gun to the boy's head.

"Get back Bitch," he screamed at her! He was totally out of control, still half drunk. "You know I'll shoot him! You know I will! I had no trouble killing that bastard Shepard! He deserved it! He has everything, everything, and he had to deny me some of it. But, I got the best of him, yes I did! I took his wife. I took his kid. I took his life and now I'm going to take his grandchild!"

Police came spilling out of the clearing blocking Morris on three sides. He moved toward the cliffs edge still holding the gun to the boys head.

Mitch came to a stop yelling something about the guns not loaded but nobody paid any attention to him. Two officers grabbed him and Bobby and forced them face down on the ground. 'At least they didn't shoot us,' Mitch thought as he tried to watch the action on the cliff from his sublimed position.

Some of the officers started to move close when Morris held the gun up briefly to fire it into the air causing everybody to back up a few steps.

"You stupid, stupid imbecile," he laughed harshly at the boys! "How dumb do you think I am? I saw the thing was moved and checked it. You didn't see me reload it." He then caught everybody off guard as he raised the gun again and fired it at Mitch hitting him in the shoulder. Kelly screamed and several officers rushed to the bleeding man.

Shel made a step toward Morris but he quickly put the gun back to the boys head. By now he was just a few inches from the edge of the cliff. Gravel and small rocks slide from the side. The edge wasn't stable and could give away easily. He looked over the side it to the rocky stream below. Laughing insanely he grabbed the boy and started to fling him toward the edge. "Let's see if the little bastard can fly!" He let go and the child screamed as he tittered at the edge trying to catch his balance. He started to fall over and Kelly screamed. She wasn't sure what happened next, everything happened at once.

Just as Morris let go of the child a single shot rang out and the man lurched backwards with a very surprised look on his face. He stepped back a step too far and slipped on the loose shale on the edge. While Morris was struggling to keep his feet a hand came up from below the edge and caught the boy pulling him over the edge. He disappeared over the edge with a scream. Kelly screamed with him.

Morris lost his battle and fell backward over the edge screaming as he fell to the rocky river floor below. Kelly cringed at the abrupt end to the scream. Then she was instantly scrambling to the edge screaming for Sheldon, followed by Shel and the rest of the officers.

Shel tried to keep her from looking over the edge but couldn't stop her. She dropped to her knees and peered over the edge. As the rest of the people crowded around the edge, Kelly saw a sight too good to believe. There, anchored snuggly to the cliffs edge with climbing gear was Bryant with the frightened boy clinging to his neck.

"Hi there," he smiled up at them, "I could use a hand here."

"Oh, thank God," Kelly fell back away from the edge repeating the words, "Oh, thank God. My baby, my baby." Max appeared from the woods and joined the crowd to the cheers of the men around him. He ignored them and joined Shel who was kneeling at the edge talking to Bryant and Sheldon trying to calm the boy down. Max looked over the edge at the two hanging there.

"Hey there Bryant," he called cheerfully, "how's it hanging?"

"Shut up and get us out of here," Bryant croaked. It was obvious that the death grip on his neck was taking a toll. Bryant's cheeks were turning beet red.

"Hey sport," Shel cooed softly to the frightened boy. "You got to let me take you now. If you strangle Bryant your mommy may not be too pleased." The boy smiled slightly at that and reached up with one hand to Shel's hand reaching down for him. Shel grabbed him and with others pulling at him he hauled the boy up over the edge.

He handed the crying dirt stained boy over to Kelly's lap where they clung to each other. Kelly had never thought her heart would feel so close to being wrenched from her body. Max and Shel gave Bryant a hand and pulled him up over the edge.

"Jesus Bryant, how did you ever come up with that idea," Shel asked as he clapped the man roughly on the shoulder. "That was ingenious."

"Wish I could take the credit but it was actually Max's idea," Bryant brushed off the congratulations from the men around him. "He figured if Morris was as mentally off as we thought, he could possibly consider throwing Sheldon off the cliff. After all, he had chosen to come back here for at least one reason. We know he could watch us from here, but also he could have thought the cliff a good way to get rid of the boy. His last act of revenge so to speak."

Bryant got a shiver down his spine at how right Max's prediction was. He went over to where Kelly was still sitting on the ground and knelt down in front of them. He placed a hand on the boys head and roughed his hair up more than it already was.

"Hey there," he spoke softly to the boy. "You know I am so proud of you. You did just the right thing."

"All I wanted to do was make sure I didn't fall," Sheldon lifted his tear streaked face towards Bryant to answer.

Bryant pulled the collar of his t-shirt away from his throat and coughed. "You definitely got a good grip." They all laughed.

"Is Uncle Mitch dead?" the boy broke into the laughter with his somber question.

"Oh God," Kelly jumped to her feet as Bryant lift the boy into his own arms. "I forgot about Mitch."

"Jeeze, thanks sis," Mitch tried to act dismayed by her words but couldn't quite keep the smile from his face. That smile turned into a grimace as an officer wrapped a bandaged around his shoulder.

"Is he going to be ok?" Kelly asked the man. He nodded as he finished up.

"We have an ambulance on its way," he answered, "but the bullet was a through and through. Doesn't look like any major damage was done."

"Good thing Dad's a bad shot," Mitch grinned slightly again before becoming somber at a memory. "I wish he had missed your real Dad."

"He did," Kelly reassured him, "He just grazed Dad. He'll be ok." Mitch's look of relief was tangible. He looked up as an officer brought his handcuffed brother over to them.

"Sis, we didn't realize what all he was planning," Mitch blurted out before they could haul him away. "We did everything we could to protect Sheldon."

"They did Mom," Sheldon piped up from where Bryant was still holding him a short distance away. "They wouldn't let that mean man anywhere near me."

"Please take those cuffs off," Kelly requested of Doug. "They had nothing to do with Morris' plan. They saved my son."

"I know that ma'am," Doug said from behind her. "We'll do everything we can to help them with the judge, but for now we have to take them in."

"It's ok sis," Mitch said. "I just hope you can forgive us."

"I already have," she said as she leaned over and gave him a kiss on the cheek. "I'll do everything I can for you and Bobby."

The ambulance arrived and they put both young men in it and headed for the hospital. Bryant came up with Sheldon and set the boy down next to his mom. He put his arms around both of them. "They have a car coming up here and said I could take you both home."

"Home," Kelly sighed, "how I love that word."

"Me too," replied Bryant, "and I think you and I need to discus making it a home for all three of us."

"The three of us?"

"Yes," he said quietly looking from her to Sheldon. "I think its time to make it official."

Kelly looked flabbergasted for a full minute. "You're asking me to marry you? Now?"

Bryant shrugged, "Can you think of a better time?"

Kelly shook her head absently and let Bryant kiss her softly and then lead her and Sheldon to the car that had just arrived. The future suddenly got a whole lot brighter.

Epilogue

Kelly stepped out onto her back porch and looked over toward the meadow that stretched out behind the house. There were now three horses grazing near the tiny barn out in the middle of it. The seasons have gone full circle. It was late spring and Kelly could smell the fresh scents of new growth.

The immediate back yard had gone through a transformation. There were chairs spread out facing a flower covered white trellis. Plants and pitchers of flowers lined the rows of chairs. Everything was coming along for the wedding.

Kelly would have been happy to marry Bryant right away after that bad incident with Morris. It was Bryant though that suggested they wait till things got settled. He knew her first marriage had been in front of a justice of the peace. He wasn't about to cheat her out of a fancy wedding. Besides he told her, Weldon would kill him if they didn't let him make a big deal out of it.

So, a big deal it was. Weldon's friend Mavis has been exceptional. She had become Kelly's shadow making sure all the arrangements were perfect. Between her and Rosa there was going to be a spread of food unseen in the county before this. She heard people from all over were going to be there. Of course they had invited all the men and their families who had helped rescue Sheldon.

Speaking of Sheldon she was expecting him home from school any minute. It was the last day of school and he was so excited over this coming weekend. He had been happy when Bryant told him he was going to marry mommy and be his new Dad. Bryant had seriously asked him if that was okay by him. The boy had a grin that split his face from ear to ear. He started calling Bryant Dad from that day on. The words still sent tingles up Kelly's spine when ever she heard it.

Mitch and Bobby had stood trial for aiding Morris. They were of course found guilty but with extenuating circumstances. The Judge gave them time served and let them off in the custody of Weldon and Shel Shepard. They were on five years probation and were to spend them on the ranch learning a skill.

Kelly was eternally grateful to her Dad and brother for stepping forward to help her half brothers. She was sure it couldn't be easy having the constant reminder of Morris around.

To the boys credit they were trying very hard. They knew they were given a new lease on life and seemed determine to make something of it. Mitch seemed to be showing an affinity to horse riding. He loved working with the horses. He was good with animals in general. Bobby was more into working with the equipment. Shel had turned him over to the capable hands of their mechanic to train him.

"It's all coming along," Bryant said as he came up behind her to nibble at her ear. "Everything is looking lovely, including the bride."

"I wouldn't have minded something just a bit simpler," Kelly replied as she leaned back against him. His arms came around her and held her close.

"I know you would have," Bryant laughed. "I may have also, but your Dad is calling the shots. I am not about to call him on it."

"I knew I was marrying a smart man." Kelly laughed. "By the way, how are the plans going with Shel?"

Weldon had finally told Shel about the property Grandma had left for him. He turned them over to him. Shel had approached Bryant with an idea to use some of the property to start an enterprise of his own. He wanted Bryant to be his partner. They had been working on plans all winter.

"They are going good," Bryant replied. "Your brother has some grand ideas."

"Are they doable?"

"Oh, yes!"

"Speaking of Shel," Kelly hesitated. "I feel like he's feeling out of the loop some."

"He's not feeling out of the loop," Bryant explained "He's just remembering his own wedding."

"That, from what I heard, wasn't a good thing."

"He repeated his Dad's history," Bryant said. "I know there is somebody out there for him. I just hope he doesn't wait his whole life to go find her." Something in his voice made Kelly turn in his arms and look him in his dark blue eyes. He stared back at her for a moment before dropping his head for a quick kiss. As he kissed her, Kelly knew he had something up his sleeve.

THE END